DARK SIDE OF THE MOO

ELLEN RIGGS

BOUGHT-THE-FARM
MYSTERIES

FREE PREQUEL

Rescuing this pup could bring Ivy
a whole new life... if it doesn't kill
her first.

Discover how big city executive Ivy meets Keats, her crime-solving sheepdog, in A Dog with Two Tales. Ivy Galloway doesn't know how desperate she is to escape the big city and her soul-sucking corporate career until she meets a sheepdog in need of rescue, too. This short prequel to the laugh-out-loud Bought-the-Farm Mystery series is a page-turner for lovers of animals, humor and spunky amateur sleuths. Join Ellen Riggs' author newsletter at **ellenriggs.com** to get this FREE prequel.

Dark Side of the Moo

Copyright © 2020 Ellen Riggs

ISBN 978-1-989303-51-1 eBook
ISBN 978-1-990613-79-1 Book
ISBN 978-1-990613-16-6 AudioBook
ASIN B0859P83G9 Kindle
ASIN 1989303501 Paperback
ASIN B0C4LYG7HK AudioBook

Publisher: Ellen Riggs
www.ellenriggs.com
Cover designer: Lou Harper
Editor: Serena Clarke
2406040020

CHAPTER ONE

I got a little thrill every time I turned into the long, dusty lane that led to my hobby farm. The last curve would open up to reveal the beautiful property, the small but stunning inn, the big red barn, and pastures full of animals. I still couldn't believe my luck. Despite all that had happened since I took ownership, buying the farm was in the top five most amazing things that had ever happened to me. Top two, actually.

The truck kicked up a cloud as we passed under the iron arch that said, "Runaway Farm." At least, that's what it had said long ago, before the "m" rusted away.

"Are you going to fix that sign?" Jilly asked, from the passenger seat. "It sends the wrong message, Ivy."

I eased up on the gas so that I could glance at the sign over my shoulder. "I think it's perfect. 'Runaway Far' is what I've done in buying the place, right? I left Boston and the corporate grind behind me for good. Country life isn't always polished."

"You can say that again." She braced herself on the dash. "But you don't want guests at your new inn to 'runaway far,' do you? This is about optics. We need to create a welcoming, come-hither vibe. That'll be challenging enough given recent history."

"You've got a point," I said, sighing as I faced the twisty, gravel lane again.

Jilly Blackwood, my best friend, always had a point. She was smart, skilled and sensible—a natural at so many things that didn't come easily to me. Or at least, didn't come easily to me anymore, after a pretty serious concussion.

"Careful, Ivy," she said. "Don't slow down. Steady, now. You know what happens..."

The truck lurched and then stalled. Despite covering a lot of miles in this big pickup since I arrived, I hadn't fully mastered the standard transmission.

"Sorry, Jilly." I looked into the back seat at Keats, the black-and-white border collie whose dramatic rescue had led to my move here. "You, too, buddy. I've been doing so much better, right? That was my first stall in a week." He stared at me with his blue eye, the one that seemed to look right through me and expose the little lies I told myself. "Okay, four days. Yesterday's bunny hop didn't count."

"You're getting nervous about today's grand opening, and that's no surprise," Jilly said. "But we've worked our butts off and I think we're ready."

Jilly had taken a leave from her successful headhunting business in Boston to help me get set up to open the refurbished and expanded farmhouse to guests. In fact, she'd done the lion's share of the work inside, while I learned the ropes with the livestock outside. I had no experience with farming or animals, but I loved getting to know the unique needs of my sheep, goats, cows, llamas, donkeys, chickens and alpaca. There was a large and varied menagerie of rescue animals at Runaway Farm. Some were sweet, like Alvina the alpaca, and others less so, like Wilma the dangerously sly sow.

On top of hard labor in the barn, I'd had bigger worries. Specifically, solving a murder. And escaping being murdered myself. Not to mention staying on the right side of Kellan Harper, the chief of police, who also happened to be my former high school sweetheart.

All in all, it had been an eventful month in my old hometown of Clover Grove. Running the quaint, farm-themed inn would be a welcome reprieve.

Now, with the worst behind us, I could take time to smell the roses. Or more specifically, the ever-present stench of manure. When people rave about fresh country air, they never seem to mention that. I was getting used to the farm bouquet, although I wondered if it permanently clung to my hair and clothes.

Turning the key in the ignition, I said, "How about I get Clover Grove's most famous artist to design a new sign? We can put Teri Mason's version out at the highway to create a first impression and leave the old one for posterity. I want to respect what the previous owners did here. Keeping the sign pays homage to them."

The luckiest moment of my life had come after the unluckiest. Hannah Pemberton, the heiress who'd bought this hobby farm and converted it into an inn, saw media coverage of my rescue of Keats and called with an offer to sell it to me for "what I could afford." In the end, she'd practically given it to me because my savings would barely cover the cost of finishing the reno and getting the inn launched. It was an honor to take over and care for the animals she'd loved so well before being summoned to Europe to run her family's business.

"I like that idea," Jilly said. Her blonde hair was in a messy yet stylish knot and her makeup was low key. The fingers gripping the dashboard were unpolished for possibly the first time since we'd met in college. If someone had told me that Jilly would "go country" so fast, I'd have bet good money they were wrong. I thought she looked all the better for the change in priorities. She thought I took things too far with my bibbed overalls and steel-toed work boots. Turning, she raised her eyebrows. "Any word from Chief Hottie?"

"No, it's been blissfully quiet on the police front," I said, keeping my eyes on the road.

"I meant the romantic front and you know it."

I shook my head. "Who has time for romance anyway? This place is ten jobs in one."

"That I know, too," she said. "Our time will come."

My brother, Asher, was carrying an obvious torch for Jilly but we really had been too busy to socialize with anyone but service people and Charlie, my farm manager.

Keats stuck his head through the seats and gave a sharp bark I had come to recognize as a warning. "Ow. Must you, Keats?"

He directed his long muzzle at the side of the dusty lane and his white front paw came up in a point. Like most border collies, he was smart enough to pilot a space shuttle. Unlike most border collies, he'd also mastered the inbred talents of many other breeds, from scent work, to retrieving and even protection. The only thing he didn't do was swim and he was unwavering about that.

My eyes followed his gaze and I gasped.

"Is that a little cow?" Jilly asked.

Keats barked again, a little higher, as if confirming.

Pulling over, I parked and flicked on the hazard lights. "Stay here, Keats," I said, opening the door. The dog was great with livestock, but he was still young and exuberant, and I didn't want to scare the baby.

When I got close to the black-and-white Holstein calf, I took a quick step backward in shock.

"What's wrong?" Jilly called. Her head was out the window and Keats was battling for real estate.

"He's missing an eye," I called back. "And one ear is just a little nub. Birth defects, I think."

Jilly elbowed Keats back as she slipped out of the truck. "Aw, poor baby. Where's your mama?"

The calf's tail twitched and a slip of brown paper fluttered. It was like a gift tag, tied there with twine. Reaching for it, I read aloud, "Take good care of me." Looking up at Jilly, I sighed. "He's been abandoned here. Hannah said it happened all the time. Alvina was a dump-and-run, too."

"Who'd dump an alpaca?" she asked.

"It's a disposable world nowadays, I guess. But Hannah said Alvina brought her good luck, so maybe the same will hold true for this little guy."

Jilly's eyebrows rose. "You're keeping him? Don't you have enough animals?"

"Yes and yes." I stared down at the calf. "I mean, he was dumped because there was probably nowhere else for a defective calf. Runaway Farm was welcoming rescues long before my time."

"But what about Heidi and Clara? Don't they get a vote?"

"For sure. I don't want to upset the heifers." Pulling the phone out of my front pocket, I texted the vet. "Heidi miscarried just before I got here. Maybe she'll welcome little Archie."

"Archie?" Jilly shook her head and smiled. "Well, how are we going to get Archie down to the barn? I'm not holding him in my lap, if that's what you're thinking."

"I'd never risk injuring you now, Jilly," I said, grinning. "Not with guests arriving in six hours. Those folks need to be fed. A good chef leads to good reviews."

She laughed. "I see my value has risen dramatically. But I bet these people are less interested in my culinary feats than my head-hunting skills."

Our first official guests were my former colleagues from the human resources department at Flordale Corporation, where I'd worked for a decade. My career had ended on a sour note, however, and I'd been glad to put the place behind me. Particularly my boss, Wilf Darby. But when my successor asked to hold their annual team breakaway at Runaway Inn, I couldn't say no. Any guests were better than none, I figured, especially when the Clover Grove gossip mill was still churning out stories about the death of the county dogcatcher, Lloyd Boyce, on my property.

I let Keats out of the truck and his brown eye, the compassionate one, pleaded with me. "You can take him to the barn, buddy, but you've got to be super gentle, okay? He's just a wobbly baby."

The dog's ears flicked forward and back in what I took to be agreement. Keats and I had developed a good understanding of each other in our few months together. I should have trusted him, now, too, because he simply walked down the lane slowly and the calf followed. Jilly pulled out her phone and took pictures of the two black-and-white creatures for the farm's social media page.

Watching them made my heart swell. I nearly lost my life when I saved Keats from a neglectful owner who also happened to be a criminal. But Keats had saved me, too. And a few months later, he saved me again. I hoped that wasn't going to become a regular thing. Fate probably hadn't allocated me nine lives, like a cat.

"It's exciting, Jilly," I said as we trailed after the dog and calf to the big red barn. "Our first rescue here at the farm."

"You always remember your first," Jilly said. "I'll even make an exception to my rule of never stepping into the barn while you go back for the truck."

Keats was torn. He was my constant shadow, but Archie had clearly become his new mission. He ran back and forth between us, until I said, "Stay, Keats. I'll be back in a few minutes. Jilly needs you more than I do right now and the vet's coming."

The dog gave me another pleading look with his warm brown eye and mumbled something deep in his throat. I nodded and smiled. "Yes, you can keep him. If he's healthy."

"Ivy?" Jilly said. "Can I suggest you avoid talking to the dog like that in front of the Flordale vipers?"

I rolled my eyes. "Like what?"

"Like he understands you, even when you're sharing complex ideas."

"He does," I said. "I don't know how, but he does. I think he's just smarter than most humans. Smarter than most of the Flordale vipers, anyway."

She laughed. "No argument there. Just don't give them anything more to gossip about, okay?"

"Let them bond over my eccentricities. They'll probably be scared they'll crack under pressure like they think I did." I gave an evil cackle. "Maybe I'll scare them a little more."

"It's not your corporate reputation you need to worry about now, my friend. It's five-star ratings online. My cooking isn't enough to float this ark."

"Fine," I said, starting to walk back to the truck. "I'll keep my weird under wraps until the vipers have slithered off to their big-city lairs."

"Eggs-actly," she called after me. "Do you see what I did there?"

"When I told you to work on your egg game, I meant in the kitchen," I called back.

The veterinarian had pulled up behind my truck to wait for me. Sticking her mop of short brown curls out the window, she said, "I was in the neighborhood delivering quintuplets."

"Sheep?" I asked.

"Goats. Cutest little things."

Senna York had recently taken over the local agrarian vet practice and I'd already called her out half a dozen times for what turned out to be non-issues. She was kind enough to charge me a lower rate for "coaching" while I got on my feet. Charlie was amazing and knowledgeable, but still on part-time hours after getting injured on the job.

It was unnerving to be a novice hobby farmer, a novice innkeeper and even a novice dog owner, all at the same time. I went from being at the top of my game as an HR executive to the bottom here. Although I was constantly racked with uncertainty, I had no regrets... other than wishing I'd held onto my automatic transmission sedan.

Senna followed me down the lane, parked in front of the barn and hopped out. Keats immediately circled to herd her inside. "Thanks Keats, but I do know the way," she said, laughing as he nipped her pant leg to get her to hurry.

"He's adopted Archie," I said, snapping my fingers to get the dog to fall back.

Senna examined the calf, murmuring kind words to the spindly creature. "Poor thing," she said. "He's just a day or two old. Abandoned because he's not perfect. But at least they didn't—"

"Don't say it." I held up my hand. "I know people think I'm too soft, but Runaway Farm is an escape from practicalities."

"Well, here's a practicality you need to consider, Ivy," Senna said. "Can you handle the work of bottle feeding with the inn opening?"

"No," Jilly said. "She can't."

"What about Heidi?" I asked, looking toward the pasture with the two cows, and finding them looking back. "Her milk hasn't dried up. Wouldn't she welcome a wee one?"

Senna tipped her head thoughtfully. "Grafting a calf sometimes works with easygoing cows. Heidi's a bit feisty."

"She's just young and spirited," I said. "A baby will calm her down."

Senna laughed. "Probably the opposite. But let's give it a try. I'll need some molasses."

"I'll run up to the house," Jilly said, looking happy for an excuse to get out of the barn.

Still kneeling beside the calf, Senna said, "I'll give Archie his shots, and then he'll need to lose his manhood."

I was aghast. "Already? He's a newborn."

"The sooner the better," Senna said. "You don't want a two thousand pound bull around here. There are few more dangerous animals on a farm."

Archie looked up with one big brown eye as if pleading to keep his parts, and Keats circled us all anxiously.

"So you need to knock him out?" I asked.

"It'll be fast and he'll get a painkiller. You don't want to know how most farmers handle castration." She got up and walked out to her Land Rover. "Maybe you should go up to the house while I take care of Archie."

"I don't like this," I called after her, and Keats whined in agreement.

She came back in with her big silver kit. "Do you trust me, Ivy?" Her voice was calming, like a sedative slipping into my own bloodstream. "It's just neutering, like you did to Keats, I'm sure."

Keats tucked his tail between his legs and we both laughed. He was a master of reading tone and body language.

When Jilly got back with the molasses, Senna pulled on a latex glove, poured the sticky black fluid into her hand and smeared it on the calf's back. She led him out to the cow pasture, and then hopped over the fence to apply molasses to Heidi's udder. Finally, after letting Heidi sniff the calf through the fence for a few minutes, she opened the gate and Keats escorted Archie inside. Heidi gave a few gusty snorts as she examined the calf. I held my breath, worried she'd hurt the sweet baby. The molasses was sweeter, however, and she started licking the calf so hard he almost fell over. He still managed to squirm toward the business end and find his molasses incentive. His tail began twitching happily and Heidi didn't seem fazed at all when he latched on.

"It worked," I said. "He's grafted!"

"It's good start," Senna said. "If you see any distress in Heidi or the calf, separate them and repeat the molasses."

"Can we leave the castration for another day, Senna? Please?"

"Go on up to the house," she said. "Keats can supervise."

My dog directed his honey-brown eye my way. The rumble in his throat said, "I got this."

Jilly tugged on my arm and I followed.

"Thank goodness we still have a few hours to ourselves," I said, when we reached the front stairs.

Jilly squeezed my arm harder as plaintive bawling drifted up from the barn. "Focus, Ivy. What we have is a long list of chores before the Flordale people get here."

"I notice you've dropped the term 'vipers,'" I said.

"I'll be professional until they leave. How much you want to bet we both get bitten at some point?"

Down the lane there was the crunch of tires on gravel and we both turned. "Grab your anti-venom," I said. "Because they're here early."

CHAPTER TWO

I'd expected Wilf Darby, the vice president of human resources, to pilot the extra-long white van. He wasn't the type to leave such an important task in the hands of his staff. But when the driver's door opened, Ben Miller stepped out. He was six foot six and heavy set, a veritable giant of a man. I'd been his manager for nearly three years and he was a sweetheart—one of my more successful hires as an HR director. I'd feared he wouldn't last long in the pool with the Flordale sharks, but perhaps his size and good looks helped keep him afloat.

He swept me into a bear hug. I didn't resist, although I wasn't a fan of public displays of affection and being squished into a colleague's midriff just felt wrong.

"Good to see you, Ben," I said, extricating myself. "Welcome to Runaway Farm and Inn. I'm excited to have all of you here."

The others were hopping out of the van one by one like baby ducks plopping off a log into a pond. A few noses wrinkled as they took in the fine farm bouquet.

"Wow, it really is a farm," said Nellie Cassios, dark brows furrowing. "I thought that was just a marketing thing."

She was wearing stretchy leather-look pants, a tank top with a fair bit of sparkle and black suede stiletto boots. Jilly and I exchanged a quick glance about Nellie's outfit. She looked ready for clubbing and Clover Grove didn't have any nightlife to offer. It wasn't the first time I'd wondered about Nellie's judgement. We'd had a memorable closed-door discussion about whether casual Friday attire encompassed tube tops and yoga pants.

"It's not a full working farm," I said. "Just a hobby farm with a few rescue animals." Jilly cleared her throat and I added, "Quite a few, if you count the chickens."

"They're all rescues?" The question came from the department's administrative assistant, Paulette Woodcrest, a silver-haired woman in her early 60s who'd mothered me through many a professional crisis, and covered my butt a few times, too. Seeing her friendly face reminded me that I didn't hate absolutely everything about Flordale. Those I'd personally hired were good people, and they'd managed to hold onto their souls despite a "survival of the fittest" corporate culture.

"Most, yes," I said, moving on to offer my hand to Keri Browning, my former second in command and now successor. Her normally rosy cheeks were pale and her hair hadn't been highlighted for some time—telltale signs of wear and tear. "People abandon animals here all the time," I continued. "The vet is down at the barn now caring for a calf someone dumped this morning."

"That's terrible," Keri said, pushing my hand away and going in for a hug. She smelled like the big city: perfume and hair product, with a vague hint of pollution. I wondered how I smelled to her. I'd been planning a shower before they arrived and mucking out stalls wouldn't have added to *my* bouquet.

"You look wonderful," she said, shoving me back to arm's length to scan me from my ponytail, past my overalls, and down to my heavy boots. "Country life's been good to you."

I laughed. "It has its moments. Sometimes it kicks my butt hard."

The last two women were standing beside the van virtually motionless. They were both tall and thin with perfectly highlighted blonde bobs. One had blue eyes and one brown but otherwise, they were so similar that people mistook them for each other all the time. Their precise movements and sharp expressions reminded me of birds of prey. Jilly and I called them "the Raptors," and though I'd never caught them in anything underhanded, I figured it was just a matter of time.

"Macy and Kate," I said, shaking each delicate hand in turn. "Welcome."

"Thank you," they said as one. It was uncanny how they did that, really.

Nellie shook back her shiny, dark, flat-ironed hair. Her features were too uneven to be pretty, but she was very striking. "I've never seen you without makeup before, Ivy."

"True. And you wouldn't have today, either, but you're five hours earlier than expected." I turned to Ben. "Traffic was that good?"

He laughed. "Keri was excited. She wanted to surprise you."

"Well, it worked," I said. "Come on inside and get settled. We'll meet back here in twenty minutes for the grand tour while Jilly rustles up something for lunch." My best friend was circulating and distributing hugs like they cost nothing. She had referred several of them from her headhunting agency, including Ben and Keri. Her flush told me she was embarrassed to be caught unprepared, whereas I was actually glad they'd found the new me before I could change back into the old me.

Just then the van disgorged a slight man with fine brown hair and an arty beard that screamed "trying too hard" to me. It was Neal Fife, the department's technology expert.

He didn't bother to offer his hand. "Hey Ivy. Where's this famous dog of yours?"

I hadn't been impressed enough by Neal, Nellie or the Raptors to hire them myself but Wilf Darby had overruled my decisions and brought them on board. None had the special spark of kindness that had always sealed the deal for me.

"Keats is at the barn overseeing the vet's work," I said. "He's promoted himself to farm manager. Nothing happens without his approval."

"Funny," Nellie said. "You didn't used to be so witty."

I caught the fleeting glance between Nellie, Neal and the Raptors and realized that what I'd said was being taken as proof I was still "off." The concussion I'd suffered while rescuing Keats had rattled my brain hard, and I'd made some ill-advised comments to the press. Flordale management had amputated me swiftly with a pittance of a payout despite a decade of excellent service. I wanted to leave anyway, but it still hurt, and it left me with only a small nest egg. In fact, if I'd gotten the payout I deserved, these people wouldn't be guests in my home.

"Right again, Nellie," I said. "When I was your boss, my nickname was the grim reaper. You don't fire as many people as I did and joke around." I walked around the van to help Ben pull out the luggage. "Where's Wilf? I expected him to be driving."

"He wanted his own wheels. Probably got a later start." Ben gave me a significant look I didn't have enough context to understand. "We'll have time to catch up before he gets here."

It didn't work out that way. A cloud of dust in the lane dispersed to reveal a red Corvette as it roared toward us. The sports car cut directly in front of the parked van and sent us scattering. The window rolled down and Wilf Darby blew out a hearty laugh. "Just cutting the flock," he said. "Gotta keep you sheep on your toes."

"Hooves," I said, with what I hoped was a civil smile to the man who'd exploited and bullied me back in my "suit" days. "We sheep have cloven hooves."

Wilf's big entrance would have been more impressive had he

leapt out of the car in a single bound. But the Corvette was low slung and at 54 he wasn't the athletic high school heartthrob he probably once was. Maybe he'd stiffened up after the long drive, too, because his flashy exit became an awkward scrabble. Ben hurried around the car to offer his hand, which Wilf slapped away.

Finally my former boss was on his feet, red-faced, either from exertion or embarrassment. Either way, I knew someone would have to pay. Hopefully it wouldn't be me.

"Get my bags, Stretch," he said. Everyone had a nickname. It was Wilf's way of keeping people in their place. Coming toward me with outstretched arms, he said, "Killer! You look... Well, less like the shark we know and love."

"I left my fins in Boston," I said, dodging his hug and shaking his hand instead. It was bone-crushing, but I didn't wince. "Welcome to Runaway Farm and Inn."

Regardless of the circumstances, I enjoyed saying that and would never tire of it.

Wilf scanned the house and property with small eyes that reminded me of Wilma's, the resident pig. She was one sly sow, always on the lookout for an escape or free food. Keats stayed on high alert with Wilma, and that's how I felt about Wilf.

"You did well for yourself," he said, sounding almost sincere.

He studied the beautifully renovated century-old red farm-house and wide, white front porch, and the vast property. The fields were turning brown now, but the leaves on the trees already had flares of color. October in Clover Grove crept in softly and began blazing later in the month. It had been my favorite time of year when I was growing up, although on principle I'd hated almost everything about the town. Most small-town teens probably felt the same way.

"She did do well, didn't she?" Jilly said, stepping up to run inter-ference. She hated Wilf with the passion of a best friend. He'd pres-sured me until I'd basically cracked from the strain and then burned me. Jilly's headhunting firm had severed ties with Flordale as a result.

"Why, Jilly Blackwood, I'm surprised to see you," he said. "You're recruiting farmworkers now?"

"My company's thriving in Boston while I pursue my dream here," she said, turning up the wattage of her dazzling smile. "I'm an aspiring chef and I'll be cooking for you over the next few days."

Wilf ran a hand through his sparse fair hair, looking as if he might just melt under the force of her smile. Then he shook it off. "Anyone can grill steak," he said.

There was a shout from the barn. "Ivy! Can you come down here?" Senna called.

"I'll take everyone inside," Jilly said, turning.

"I'm coming to the barn," Wilf said, marching down the path ahead of me. "I want to milk a cow."

Ben and Neal joined us, and soon I was sandwiched, feeling suddenly small. I wished Charlie had been working today, because he'd have put the men in their place. I still had a long way to go in learning how to channel my authoritative alpha handler.

Wilf strode into the barn like it was a boardroom and demanded, "What's going on?"

I winced as he stood on the exact spot where I'd been nearly strangled not long ago. Most of the time I passed in and out of the barn without thinking about it, because there was always something else to think about. The trauma ambushed me now, possibly because Wilf brought back terrible memories, too.

"Calf castration," Senna said, kicking her medical instruments aside so no one would trip. "I just put Heidi and Archie back outside."

"Every farm needs a bull," Wilf said, wincing himself. "Sounds shortsighted to me."

"No farm needs a bull anymore," Senna said. "They're dangerous. We use artificial insemination for breeding."

Wilf rolled his eyes at the other men. "Women rule the world, even in farm country."

"You got that right," Senna said, bending to collect her things.

Heading toward the back door of the barn, Wilf asked, "Where are these cows?"

I rushed to catch up and he stuck out an elbow at precisely the right moment to shove me into a fresh cow flap still steaming in the cool air. My brother used to prank me like that and I should have been more alert. Instead, I planted a boot squarely in the manure, skidded and fell backward in a tailbone-crunching pratfall. My butt landed squarely on the pile with a squelching sound. Although I had smelled far worse, the strange warmth under my butt was revolting.

Wilf turned, his shoulders shaking with laughter. "Oops. Sorry about that, Killer. You still haven't learned how to watch your step."

"Oh, Wilf," I said, letting Ben grab my hands and hoist me to my feet. "You should see what I can do with a baseball bat when I'm upset."

"Was that story really true?" Ben asked. "About how you rescued the dog from a criminal? I thought the press exaggerated that."

"Some of it was true." I shook my butt to loosen the manure. "Not all of it."

"You look like a duck waggling its backside," Wilf said, laughing harder as he headed for the cow pasture. "Watch it, Killer. You're becoming your setting."

Keats was sitting beside the gate to the cow pasture, tilting his head this way and that to observe the Flordale men with his blue eye. I got his attention and signaled for him to monitor Wilf. The dog immediately got up and started herding my former boss away from the cows—so subtly that Wilf didn't seem to notice he'd been redirected to the goat pasture.

Meanwhile I had more pressing matters to deal with because Neal had circled the barn to head for Wilma's enclosure.

"Neal, don't!" I called as he took a running leap at the fence and hopped over. He was nimbler than I'd expected for an IT guy who looked like he didn't see much daylight. "Wilma's unpredictable. She almost drowned me in a swamp a few weeks ago."

"It's just bacon," he called back. "Here, piggy-piggy."

"She's a rescue and this isn't a petting zoo," I said, grabbing a long wooden pole with an iron hook on the end. I never entered Wilma's pen without it because she was smart and slick, and quite happy to plow people down if they stood between her and freedom. Opening the gate, I said, "Out. Now, Neal. She'll crush you in the mud without a second thought. Is that how you want to go?"

He sauntered out ahead of me as I alternately brandished the pig poker at him and at Wilma. "I hope you have insurance," he said.

"You bet I do, and it's a good thing since you boys are into playground antics." I had barely got the gate latched when Keats summoned me with a sharp bark. Turning, I saw my former boss with his loafer on the bottom rung of the fence holding the alpaca and llamas. "Wilf, no! Get away from there."

I should have known better. Wilf hated being told what to do and it always caused the opposite reaction. Now he hastened to clamber over the fence before I could get there. Neal filmed the awkward ascent, laughing so hard the phone shook visibly. Without treads on his loafers, Wilf slipped on the top rung, straddling the fence. I gasped, thinking we were about to have our second castration of the day. But something of his old athleticism surfaced in his moment of desperation and he managed to push up and over. He landed inside and fell over with a thump that made the rest of us cringe. I dropped the pig poker, scaled the fence and jumped in after him. Then I snapped my fingers at Ben, who handed me the poker over the fence.

Wilf's eyes were open but he stayed down long enough that I started to worry. Finally he sat up, took stock, and then struggled to his feet. "I thought you said this alpaca danced," he said. "I'm ready to tango."

Alvina had retreated to the far corner with the two llamas. Their protectors, a pair of cranky donkeys, were now advancing on us. Holding the long poker horizontally, I reached into my pocket for the cookies that usually kept everyone sweet-tempered. I tossed them in a wide arc and the donkeys fell for the decoy.

"Wilf, please stay out of the livestock pens," I said, herding him toward the gate with the poker. "At least until you come up to the house and sign the waivers."

Ben laughed. "Smart lady. Sounds like your concussion has healed."

Closing the gate behind Wilf, I let Keats take over from there, bringing the men together and closing in to herd them up to the house. When Wilf tried to dodge away, Keats lightly nipped his pant cuff.

"Hey!" Wilf lashed out with his loafer and would have connected if Keats weren't so agile. "I'll kick you, dog."

Keats evaded him easily, but fury rose from my belly. I pressed my lips together and drew in a long breath with my nose. My temper controls had short-circuited during Keats' rescue and hadn't come fully back online. When I finally opened my mouth, my tone was surprisingly calm.

"Wilf," I said. "Sir. If you try to kick my dog again, I'll ask you to leave Runaway Farm."

His already ruddy face turned florid and his mouth worked. "You wouldn't dare. You can't turn away paying guests from this pile of crap. We're doing you a favor. I bet you go under in six months and come crawling back to Flordale."

I pulled in another long breath, counting to seven like Jilly told me. Not more, not less. It helped that I could see Wilf was upset about more than getting evicted from the alpaca pen. Maybe he was enraged I'd left Flordale, or possibly even hurt. There was a reason he was being an even bigger jerk than usual, and I'd be wise to de-escalate the situation by soothing his wounded pride.

"Wilf, I want you to know that I truly regret how we parted," I said. "As you always said, I was practically married to Flordale, and leaving was like a terrible breakup. But what's done is done, and I'll either sink or swim here at Runaway Farm. All I'm asking, sir, is that you avoid injuring yourself or kicking my dog. What do you say?"

It didn't hurt as much as I thought it would to be conciliatory, and Wilf's eyes seemed to lose a little of their feral gleam. I was willing to suck up if it meant getting through this ordeal without serious injury to man or beast.

He didn't answer, but he did let Keats press him forward to the house. Finally he called back, "Where can a boss get a drink around here? It's noon somewhere."

CHAPTER THREE

By dinnertime, Wilf's color had deepened to maroon as he worked his way through my best scotch. His mood had kept the rest of the team on edge during the grand tour, Jilly's lovely lunch, and then their breakaway session in the big, bright family room at the back of the house. Jilly and I stayed out of their way as much as possible, other than offering snacks and libations. Eventually I moved the scotch to the kitchen, but it magically reappeared in the family room on the coffee table. Wilf shared not only Wilma's eyes, but her capacity for stealth. All I could do was hope he'd pass out early.

When people started to file into the dining room, I ran upstairs to change again quickly. I'd assumed it would be casual attire, but the men had put on suits, and the women dresses. My only option was the charcoal pantsuit I'd kept from my Flordale days, last worn to the dogcatcher's funeral.

"Now *that* looks like the Ivy we know," Wilf said, nodding. "I figured if we scratched the surface, she'd still be under those overalls."

In a matter of moments, I started to *feel* like the Ivy they knew—stressed, subdued and suffocating slowly.

"Have a drink," Jilly whispered as she pulled me aside. "You're seizing up."

"I have to stay alert," I whispered back. "Even plastered he can outmaneuver me."

"Once they start eating, they'll chill out," she said. "Just hang in there."

Jilly served a fabulous appetizer salad with local pears and goat cheese. At least it *looked* fabulous. I felt too queasy to do more than push it around with my fork. The bread was freshly baked on site. Even the wine was from a regional vineyard that managed to coax grapes to grow in our short summer season.

Wilf subsided as he dug in but the look in his piggy eyes became even more wary. I knew from long experience that he was a mean drunk. His lips were too loose at the best of times, but when he was full of whiskey, his words sprayed out like bullets from a machine gun. Flordale got more internal complaints about Wilf than anyone else in the company, which was ironic considering he headed HR. I watched each and every complaint get swept under the carpet while others were fired for far less. Wilf obviously had friends in high places.

Jilly circled the table frequently, collecting plates and adding a scant inch or two of wine to waving glasses in hopes of slowing the pace of consumption. She reminded me of Keats, gently herding the guests. My left hand dropped to my side repeatedly, expecting to find the dog's warm, comforting ears. Each time I was disappointed. Keats had opted to stay down at the barn with his new bovine baby. Senna had recommended leaving him there all night because new mothers, even adoptive ones, could be broody and moody. I missed him and realized anew how dependent I'd become on my sharp-witted canine companion. When faced with my toxic Flordale past, I truly needed my unofficial therapy dog.

With Wilf silently shoving salad into his mouth, the others began to chatter nervously. At least, Ben, Keri and Paulette did.

They raved about the food, the inn's décor and finally the scenery. Nellie and Neal both looked supremely bored. Meanwhile, Macy Tavares and Kate Sussex, in their nearly identical little black dresses, kept their usual stone-faced silence. Three years ago, my team had been thriving and cohesive, but one by one, some of my best hires quit because of Wilf. The others had been brought on board while I crisscrossed the country firing people as the company downsized other departments.

I was slightly lightheaded by the time Jilly brought out the main course. She was beaming with pride over her two signature dishes: a Moroccan chickpea stew, and her classic, chicken with creamy tomato basil sauce.

Wilf lifted the lid on the tureen of stew and scowled. He was sitting in my seat at the head of the table, which was no accident. Jilly had decorated beautifully with seasonal gourds and harvest-themed place cards. He'd moved my card to mid-table and assigned himself to one end and Ben to the other.

"Excuse me," he said. "I ordered a steak. Rare. Running, in fact."

"I'm afraid steak's not on the menu tonight," I said. "Jilly's laid out the menu very carefully for the next few days. I'm sure you'll find the stew delicious."

He poked at it with disgust. "Are these chickpeas? You don't seriously expect real men to eat this. You know me, Killer."

"I don't go by that nickname anymore," I said, with a smile. "It doesn't feel right on a rescue farm."

Jilly had materialized beside him, placing a calming hand on his shoulder. "I'll make you something else, Wilf. We want our guests to be fully satisfied with the cuisine at Runaway Inn."

He thumped his fist on the table, making the china rattle. "Steak. Rare. Now."

"Done," she said, simply. "Well, give me fifteen minutes."

"Ten," he said. "And bring me more bread in the meantime."

Several mouths hung open as if we were all competing for what little oxygen Wilf had left us. My heart was racing with the old Flordale tension. I hadn't realized until I'd quit that I'd been suffering from panic attacks. Now I remembered exactly why.

Keri made another conversational volley. "Tell us about your best and worst moments since you moved here, Ivy."

"Hmmm... there are plenty of each," I said, pondering. "One of the best happened today, when that poor little calf found a new mother here. It was beautiful."

"A calf you immediately tortured," Wilf said, tipping more scotch into his mouth.

Keri's brow furrowed. "Tortured how?"

"Routine castration," I said. "He's fine."

"Let's ask the calf how he feels about that," Wilf said. "It's inhumane."

There was a sudden shift in the atmosphere, like a storm system had rolled in. You didn't need to be in the country long to start sensing changes like that on a primal level.

A voice behind me said, "Some beasts are just better castrated. We learn that early out here in the country."

"Oh no!" I jumped up from my seat and turned. "Mom! You're back."

"Oh yes," she said, her eyes on Wilf. "And just in time, it seems."

When I moved home to Clover Grove, three of my four sisters had fulfilled Mom's lifelong dream by taking her to Disneyland in California and then up the coast to Monterey. I'd contributed generously to the trip just to get Mom out of the way while I was settling in. It turned out to be fortuitous, given the dogcatcher's murder and the subsequent investigation. I hadn't expected her home for another week, by which point the Flordale contingent would be gone and she could be my top priority, as she'd no doubt expect. But here she was in the doorway, as full of herself as I'd ever seen her.

"It's fine, Mom. We're all good here."

Ignoring that, she swept across the room and stood on tiptoe to kiss my cheek. She was barely over five feet and slim, despite delivering six children. Her hair was back-combed into a blonde bouffant and her makeup was on point, if a trifle heavy. Even on a low budget, she managed to find plenty of pretty dresses that made her look bigger and more imposing.

"I'm Dahlia Galloway," she announced to the room. "Ivy's mother." Ben jumped up to offer his seat, but she waved it away. "I'm not staying. I'm not welcome, apparently. My daughter didn't invite me to her grand opening, I'm afraid."

"Mom. These are my former colleagues from Flordale. They're here for a team breakaway meeting. It's not a housewarming party."

I looked over her head at my sisters. Iris and Poppy weren't much taller than Mom. Despite being the youngest, I ended up taller than anyone except Asher. Iris' angular face looked thinner than I remembered. No doubt weeks on the road had taken years off her life. I would owe them forever.

As Iris mouthed, "I'm sorry," Poppy smirked at me. She was the wild card of the sisterhood. Daisy, our eldest sister, still had to work hard to keep her in line. I gave Poppy a glare now. Mom was a force of nature, but she couldn't have gotten to Runaway Farm without investing in cab fare, which she wouldn't likely do. Two years ago, the County had sent Asher, in his police uniform, to take away Mom's driver's license after she'd hit one too many stop signs. Witnesses had reported her knocking a variety of things over and her old, battle-scarred sedan proved it. Since her vision was good and she never overindulged, the issue was distraction. Her mind was on 500 things at once and then—oops!—another sign bit the dust. We were all grateful that Asher had taken that particular hit for the family. As the only son, and the golden boy, he'd gotten off easy in every other way.

Mom turned to stare at Wilf again. That worried me. While I hadn't shared many details about my departure from Flordale, it was distinctly possible my siblings, specifically Poppy, had looser lips.

"I assume you're Wilfred Darby?" Mom said. "Ivy's former boss?" She took a few steps toward him, slowed only slightly by Iris' grip on her belt.

Wilf leaned back in his seat, his smile showing more teeth than usual. "Yes, ma'am. Boss, mentor and all-around cheerleader."

Mom tipped her head like a harmless canary, watching him with bright eyes that missed absolutely nothing unless she was behind the wheel. "So you're the one who gave Ivy the titles 'grim reaper' and 'killer'?" she asked.

He cackled, clutching his belly like a bad Santa. "Guilty! It's all done in fun... Dahlia, you said? The flower-themed names are adorable, by the way."

"Mrs. Galloway will do." Mom drew herself up till she towered over Wilf. "My daughter had a wonderful career before you came along and crushed her spirit."

"Mom, stop." I grabbed her belt, too, and Iris and I pulled together. Mom slid backward but it didn't slow her tongue.

"I understand there's a long list of grievances against you, Wilfred," she said, looking around the table. "I bet every one of your staff here has complained about your bullying. But for some reason senior management turns a blind eye to your professional missteps." She shook her head. "How exactly do you pull that off? I've never been so lucky."

It was true. Mom had been "let go" from countless jobs, usually for the same reason her license was suspended. She was easily distractible and that meant cash didn't always balance, special orders got forgotten or mixed up, and food got spilled or spoiled. As result, she was frequently unemployed and we all kicked in to pay the rent on her small apartment over a knitting store on a side street in Clover Grove.

Wilf tipped more whisky down his throat and squirmed in his seat. "Dahlia, you know nothing about corporate life, I'm afraid."

"True," she said. "But I know about being a decent person, Wilfred. I don't push people to the breaking point."

Poppy cleared her throat. "Except her own kids."

That lightened the mood instantly and everyone chuckled gratefully.

Mom raised the back of her hand to Poppy, which miraculously silenced my cheeky sister. "Wilfred," she continued. "I called your office a few times and never heard back."

"Oh no," I said. "You didn't."

"I'm a busy man, Dahlia," Wilf said. "If all the moms called me I'd never get a thing done."

Mom's gaze followed the beefy hand lifting the scotch glass. "Well, I just wanted you to understand that your actions almost got my daughter murdered."

"Murdered?" Wilf's glass paused in mid-air.

"Mom, stop!" Moving directly in front of her, I started backing up, in my signature dump truck maneuver.

"Ivy, this man needs to understand the impact of his actions," Mom mumbled into my shoulder. "If he hadn't exploited and persecuted you, you wouldn't have been nearly murdered. Twice."

Wilf's piggy eyes had widened. "What is she talking about?"

"Nothing," I said. "She's exaggerating and being overprotective. That's what moms do, Wilf."

"It's true," she said, peeking around me. "Moms always protect their children. By whatever means necessary. No matter how drastic."

"Are we safe here?" Wilf asked me. "I can't put my staff in harm's way."

"Of course," I said, continuing to push Mom backward. "Unless you're worried about slipping on a cow flap like I did earlier." I gave a forced laugh. "Oh wait, you engineered that."

"Harmless prank," he said. "What's happened to your sense of humor?"

"Nellie said I'm wittier." I glanced at her and saw she was frozen in her seat, her dark eyes wide and stunned. All her carefully cultivated indifference had vanished.

Wilf glared at Nellie. "You and I will talk later. Stop worrying about your looks and remember that everyone's dispensable. We have a new grim reaper now." He turned to Keri. "I didn't think you had it in you, honestly. You never had Ivy's natural abilities."

Nellie and Keri both sank in their seats. Wilf was letting the manure Mom slung at him roll downhill.

"As for you two," he continued, looking at the Raptors. "I never know which one of you is which. Even your work is completely indistinguishable. You'll never progress in the company if you operate like conjoined twins. There's only room for one at the top."

I was quite sure he'd work his way through the rest of the team, sparing only Paulette, perhaps, if I didn't intervene. "Jilly," I called. "I could really use your help out here."

"Coming! Just taking the steak off the grill."

She pushed open the door from the kitchen, steak steaming on a platter. Her green eyes took in everything at once. She hadn't met my mom, Iris or Poppy, but she'd seen enough photos.

"Finally," Wilf said, as she set the steak in front of him with a flourish. "It had better be bleeding."

"Blood guaranteed," Jilly said, turning to me as I backed Mom toward the kitchen with smoother moves than I'd ever managed to deploy in my actual truck. "Dahlia, I'm Jilly Blackwood, Ivy's best friend. I've been so excited to meet you. I understand you're a marvellous cook and I could use your advice in the kitchen."

Mom gave me a little shove. "Jilly, you're a good friend and I know you've helped that mutt save her in the nick of time twice. But I won't be decoyed by your bogus ploys. I have five daughters, remember."

Two of them stepped forward now, and pretty much carried Mom through the kitchen door.

I summoned a bright smile from my corporate collection and took my seat again. Wilf was sawing into his steak and shaking his head.

"All this talk of murder makes a man hungry," he said. "Your mom's a firecracker, Ivy. No wonder you snapped that day." Popping a big piece of meat into his mouth, he continued speaking as he chewed. "I admit I had a few doubts about letting you go, but now I see I did the right thing in pulling the plug on your career."

There was a collective gasp around the table, but I raised my hand. "It's okay, folks. I'm fine."

"A nice, calm little farm is the best place for people like you," he said, meat juices trickling down his chin.

Don't ask, don't ask, I told myself. The words came anyway. "People like me?"

"Delicate flowers. You were never cut out for business." He sliced another piece of steak and shoved it in his mouth. "The rest of my team is tougher stock."

I raised my glass and said, "A toast to survivors."

CHAPTER FOUR

I was awake long before Aladdin, the resident rooster, crowed the next morning. Although I'd initially fallen into a deep, stress-induced sleep, I woke before four and that was it. My mind started racing and Keats wasn't there to calm me. I was proud of him for electing to camp out with his bovine charges, but we hadn't spent a single night apart since I rescued him. With Keats curled up on his bed beside mine, I felt safe from the past, the present and the future. Without him, I was fair game for frightening memories, some involving the guests sharing a roof with me. I'd expected to hear footsteps and flushing overnight, but Jilly and I had taken rooms upstairs in the back of the new wing. I would have preferred being in earshot of the barn but with potentially rowdy guests, sleep had to take precedence.

I doubted anyone had slept well except Wilf, who'd been half-carried to bed by Ben, still slurring dark threats about "downsizing all of you." His threats were often idle, but I was living proof that he could and would follow through. Although I was happy with my change in circumstances, none of my former colleagues aspired to be mucking out stalls or catering to fools like Wilf.

As for my mother, I'd expected her to be a drama queen when

she got back. I just didn't expect her to be a drama queen right then, in front of my guests. Her eccentricities were well known throughout Clover Grove, which made it even harder for her to hold down a job. The local economy was challenging enough, and of course, she couldn't drive. Conservatively, she'd cycled through around 50 jobs in my memory and been fired from most. Maybe that's how I ended up in human resources, come to think of it. My creative work to support her resume and interviewing skills started early. That meant people kept hiring her, but I couldn't control what happened after she got in the door.

With her track record, Mom shouldn't have been laying into any employer. She'd clearly forgotten that I'd been content at Flordale until it got so big it needed a vice president of HR, and Wilf got the nod instead of me. Jilly had always predicted I'd be the youngest VP in the company but it hadn't worked out that way.

Finally I heard a woof under my window. Keats had finished his shift in the barn and probably wanted to come in and relax. Despite his go-go-go attitude, he appreciated his creature comforts.

Opening the window, I whispered, "Give me a second, buddy. I don't want my guests seeing me in my pajamas. They've already seen me with my pants down, metaphorically speaking."

The heavy blanket of darkness that dropped over the countryside had lifted just enough for me to see Keats' blue eye shining up at me. In that moment, it felt like he was warning me to be careful.

"Gotcha," I whispered. I hadn't expected this experience to be a cakewalk, but the Flordale crew were like toddlers high on sugar.

Pulling on a clean T-shirt and overalls, I opened my bedroom door quietly and tiptoed past Jilly's room and downstairs to the kitchen. She'd set up the coffee the night before so that all I had to do was press start. Then I checked the back door for Keats. There was no sign of him, so I went to the front door and found him standing on the porch.

"What's up?" I asked.

Instead of coming in, he circled my legs to herd me down the stairs. The mumble deep in his throat that passed for conversation began. He wanted me to come to the barn. Pronto.

"No way," I said. "Coffee first. Plus I hear people moving. I invited everyone to join me for egg collection and it sounds like I have takers."

He resigned himself to wait and sat down at the top of the stairs with his white-tipped tail wrapped neatly around him. The blue eye was still fixed on me, however. Whatever he wanted to communicate was important, but perhaps not urgent. He mumbled at me again and it sounded like, "Fine, you'll see."

I went back to the kitchen and poured coffee into travel mugs for the early risers. Keri was first to stagger into the kitchen, yawning, arms outstretched like a zombie. I put a mug in her hands and she said, "You okay? That was quite a show, last night."

"Totally fine," I said. "Sorry about my mom. She's a piece of work."

She laughed quietly. "Sorry about Wilf. He's a piece of work, too. I don't need to tell you that."

"You don't," I said. "But we'd better be discreet. He'll need coffee badly this morning."

"He'll be out cold for ages." She took a long sip of coffee. "I doubt he'll regret missing the egg hunt."

Paulette and Nellie soon joined us. I hadn't expected the hen coop to be a major attraction. In fact, I'd counted on a quiet hour to gear up for the rigors of the day. Perhaps they wanted to debrief about what had transpired at dinner, or even about how things were going in the corporate office. I'd have to be quick on my feet to dodge the political minefields. Flordale wasn't my problem anymore —something Jilly had drilled into me before they arrived. "You cannot save them," she'd said. "Boundaries. Make them and keep them."

After everyone had doctored their coffee and taken a few fortifying sips, I led them out to the porch, where Keats continued to sit like a statue. Indeed, he was so still that Nellie gave a little scream when he moved.

"That dog is so creepy," she said, with a shiver. "It's like he's looking right through me."

I wondered what my perceptive dog saw inside Nellie. At Flordale, she was always on the hustle, trying to get promoted before doing her time in the trenches, and shamelessly using her looks to get ahead. Or at least trying to. Flordale's culture had come a long way and sexism wasn't typically an issue. It was a shame because Nellie was bright enough and could have honed her skills to climb the right way. I'd even hired an executive coach for her and the Raptors, but people needed to be ready to hear the message.

She gave Keats a wide berth as she went down the stairs and he swivelled to watch her, ears back. As I expected, he'd given her a failing grade in the character department. In fact, he blocked me from catching up to her and gave a little whine.

"Don't listen to her," I whispered. "You're not creepy, buddy, you're perfect."

Nellie turned. "Are you becoming a weird dog lady?"

"Always was, I guess, but it only had an outlet after I met Keats."

Our footsteps were nearly silent in the damp grass and all heads turned to stare at the slip of sun peeking over the meadow. It always started slow like that, before taking a sudden leap over the horizon. I held my breath waiting and then enjoyed their collective gasp.

"Beautiful," Keri said. "Now I see why you're way out here. It's so peaceful."

I held up one hand and folded my fingers one by one. "Five, four, three, two..."

Aladdin let out a crow that would have annoyed the neighbors, if they hadn't had a rooster, too. While I had the only proper hobby farm in the area, people had been migrating here—or back here—to keep chickens, grow gardens and make jam. They called themselves homesteaders. Mom called them hippies.

Keats subtly, and then more obviously, tried herding me around the front of the barn. He knew full well I was aiming for the coop out back, just as I did every morning. After dodging him a couple of times, I said, "Okay. You win."

"Who's that, dear?" Paulette asked.

"Keats," I said. "He wants his weird dog lady owner to check on his cow baby."

"You know all that *how*?" Nellie asked.

"Body language, mostly. Our first job of the day is the hens but he's relentlessly pressing me to the front of the barn." I looked down at him. "Just let me get the ladies set up and I'll come right back and check everything out, okay?"

He sat again, but this time his mouth opened in a wide pant. Since it was a cool morning, I had to assume he was stressed. That did give me pause, since he wasn't anxious by nature.

Round the back, I picked up three baskets and gave each woman her own. Letting them into the coop, I said, "Just poke around under the hens for the eggs."

"Just... poke around?" Nellie asked. "Won't they attack us?"

"Nope. They're used to it. Gently push the feathers aside and feel for an egg."

"It's a good thing I brought these," Nellie said, pulling a pair of lightweight white gloves out of the pocket of her leather pants. "Spa gloves. I don't want birds pecking my manicure. Keri, I have more in my room if you want."

"But we might not feel be able to feel the eggs," Keri said. "Or we could crush them."

"I'll take my chances," Nellie said. "I spend good money on these nails."

When Nellie subsided, I continued. "Some hens lay every day, some don't. It's like an Easter egg hunt each morning."

Keri and Paulette laughed. "So this is what you do for excitement now?"

"You're going to love it, you'll see," I said. "On top of the suspense of whether you'll find anything, you'll see that not all eggs are created equal. There are big ones, small ones, white ones, brown ones, gray ones, speckled ones and more."

"Do they all taste the same?" Keri asked.

"You tell *me* after breakfast," I said. "Eggs are always on the menu and I know Jilly would love to walk you through a nice scramble."

"It seems mean," Paulette said. "Taking away all their babies."

I shrugged. "It's a renewable resource. Every day there's a potential new egg baby. And trust me, I have plenty of chickens here without hatching any new ones. People are always getting bored with their backyard coops and dropping birds off here."

Keri walked into the coop, calling, "Get ready to surrender your eggs, ladies."

Paulette grabbed my arm before I left. "Thank you for having us, Ivy. I know it couldn't be easy."

"It's good to have you, Paulette," I said. "You were always so kind to me and I'm glad you can see for yourself that everything ended up just fine."

She gazed around at the sunrise and back to the serene hen coop. Aladdin had stopped crowing when we arrived, satisfied that he summoned the day. "It most certainly has," she said. "The property is gorgeous, the inn is warm and welcoming, and that dog is very special."

My eyes filled with tears and I sighed. I never used to be a crier, but rescuing Keats had unplugged my tear ducts and the mere mention of him could get me started. It was annoying at any time, but more so with a colleague who knew me as composed, possibly even tough.

"He sure is," I said. "Luckiest day of my life when I found him."

"But you almost lost your life, and then you lost your job." Her eyes filled too, and she squeezed my arm harder. "I could have strung Wilf up for firing you, especially after all you'd done for the company. It was inexcusable."

"Paulette, it's okay. Really." I scanned the horizon to collect myself. "The writing was on the wall when I told him I didn't want to travel anymore to downsize staff. He dismissed that and I can hardly blame him, when it was part of my job. Then when I banged my head and rambled to the press, I became a liability to Flordale."

"But he totally ripped you off with that insulting package. You must have wanted to kill him."

I swallowed hard over that. Wilf's unfair treatment had put me in a financial bind. By withholding the payout I deserved, Wilf left me in a position of taking guests sooner than I wanted. Not to mention taking guests I didn't want, like him.

"Wilf actually did me a favor by making it easy to go," I said, as Keats came around the corner and whined again. "Now, go hunt for eggs while I do my rounds. Duty calls."

Once I latched the coop door behind them, I followed Keats around the barn. "Thanks, buddy. I was dying to escape that conversation."

He didn't stop to chat. Panting hard, he trotted ahead of me and turned again and again to shoot a blue-eyed glance.

"What's the big rush?" I asked. "Now I'm starting to worry. Is Archie okay?"

He mumbled something urgently. The message sounded familiar but I couldn't quite place it.

Heidi and Clara bellowed before I got to the door. Then there was a bleating cry that sounded like a perfectly healthy calf to me.

In fact, he put more power behind that noise than the day before. Heidi must have donated generously at the milk bar.

It was dark inside and the first thing I did was walk across the barn to the bank of switches. When the lights came on, Heidi and Clara hung their heads over the side of the large stall, as usual, but Archie couldn't reach that high.

Florence the old blind mare gave a whinny that made me stop on the way over and stroke her nose. She grabbed my sleeve in her teeth and held on. That wasn't typical at all. She often surprised strangers like that, but my clothing got a free pass.

"What's up, girl?" I stopped to avoid a tear in my jacket. "You okay?"

She didn't let go, so I had to tap her under the chin to get her to release me. "Sorry, sweetheart, but I have to check out the new kid."

The goats and the sheep started up a chorus of bleating that seemed louder than usual. The cows and the horse were moving restlessly.

"What's with you guys?" I said, walking over to the cow stall. I stopped and rubbed Heidi's nose and she reared back, unleashing a deafening bellow. "Ow, ow, ow. I need these ears. Are your hormones making you cranky, mama?"

I stepped backward and then something shocking happened: Keats nipped me. More specifically, he nipped the back of my pant leg hard enough to feel a hint of teeth and drive me forward again.

"Hey, none of that, sir. You do not treat me like livestock. Hear me?"

Instead of looking sheepish, as he normally did when he overstepped, he dove in for another nip.

I stepped lightly around him. "Keats! What gives? I can see Archie and he looks totally fine. I don't have time to rock your calf like a baby. I've got guests now. Important guests."

Once more he dove in and I jumped right between the heads of

Heidi and Clara to get away. The girls were unpredictable and I didn't appreciate having my head in a cow sandwich.

"Easy now, ladies," I said. "It was his fault, not mine."

That's when I finally noticed what Keats had become so desperate for me to see, and it wasn't Archie, the one-eyed calf.

It was a pair of maroon velvet slippers and legs in blue striped pajamas.

CHAPTER FIVE

I crept into the bushes outside so that I could watch the house and the barn, but not be seen myself. Then I pulled out my phone. "Jilly. It's me."

"I know who it is." Her voice was pre-caffeinated and groggy. "What I don't know is why you're calling me. Couldn't you just knock on my bedroom door?"

"I'm at the barn. You need to come down here. Stat."

"Why are you whispering? Have the cows gone to the dark side?"

"Maybe," I said, kneeling on the damp earth. "Actually, yes, I think they have."

"Ivy, what's going on? You sound all freaky. Did something happen to Archie?"

All the grogginess had left her voice now. Adrenaline had done the job better than caffeine ever could.

"Archie's fine. It looks like the graft worked. But I think Heidi might have gone crazy from hormones."

"Did she attack you or something?" Now I could hear rustling as she got up. "Are you hurt?"

"Not me, no."

There was a long pause and stillness at the other end. "Who—or what—was hurt, Ivy? Tell me."

"Just come down here. Please, Jilly. The Flordale women are in the hen coop. They don't know what happened."

"Well, I don't know what happened, either." Her bedroom door clicked open. "I'm on my way but tell me now. The secrets you spring on me are bad for my heart."

"As soon as you get here, I promise. I don't want you to wake anyone. We need to think about the guests." I knelt down, slung an arm around Keats and pulled him to me. "At least the guests we have left."

"We lost a guest? Already?" The front door opened and she appeared on the porch. "Who's missing?"

Covering my mouth, I whispered, "Wilf. He's gone."

"Gone? He can't be gone. His Corvette's sitting right there." She pointed as she walked down the front stairs. "Although that's not where he left it yesterday." Suddenly she gasped. "Oh my god, Ivy, he ran his car into your truck and just left it there. He must have come out drunk after we all went to bed."

"I didn't notice that. But we have bigger problems than a dent in my truck."

Her pace picked up till she was almost running. She was still in her pink floral pajama bottoms with a light jacket zipped over the top. Her long blonde hair flew around in a Medusa-style halo. "Can we go back to Wilf being missing? Did he wander off in the bush?"

"I didn't say missing. I said gone. As in, gone the way of Lloyd Boyce, the dogcatcher."

She stopped abruptly in the middle of the gravel driveway. "You mean he's...?"

"Don't say it." I came out of the bushes and walked toward her. "But yes. Wilf is with Lloyd now. Wherever the bad people go."

She made a choking sound halfway between a laugh and a scream. "Oh no. He's actually..."

"Pushing up daisies. He bought the farm. Wilf is no longer."

Jilly started moving toward me again, slowly now. "What happened?"

"I don't know. He was in with the girls. In his pajamas."

"What girls? Nellie and Keri? The Raptors?"

A laugh slipped out and I cut it off with my free hand. It wouldn't take much to tip me into hysteria. "No, in the barn."

"He was in the barn with Nellie and Keri?" I could see her shoulders shift in a shrug. "I guess that kind of thing happened a lot in the old days. A roll in the hay and all that. And team breakaways are notorious for debauchery."

"No, Jilly, listen. I found Wilf with Heidi and Clara. And I'm afraid it looks like they... Well, it looks like they trampled him."

"He probably passed out in there after all that whiskey. Or had a heart attack. I'm sure it was an accident. Heidi and Clara wouldn't deliberately..."

Now I shrugged. "They're testy heifers. Charlie said Heidi's been extra moody since her miscarriage. Maybe the new calf fired up her maternal protective instincts when Wilf went into the cow stall."

She ran her free hand through her hair. "Why on earth would he do that? You warned him."

"Exactly. He did it *because* I warned him. Wilf doesn't like to be told what to do. I suppose he wanted to defy me, and in his drunken state he couldn't dodge the cows."

We were standing a few yards apart now, phones still to our ears. She took a deep breath and let it out. I could see that as well as hear it.

"Okay," she said, closing the small distance between us. "Well, this is unfortunate. Very unfortunate. You'll have to let Kellan and Asher figure everything out. You have guests to worry about."

"Right. Yes. I'll call Kellan now."

"You haven't called him already?" Her voice spiked. "Have you learned nothing, Ivy?"

"I was psyching up for it. This is terrible, Jilly. Another person has died at Runaway Farm."

"I know. It is terrible. And crazy. But we'll get through this, just like we got through it the last time."

"Okay. Okay." I turned and took a few steps toward the barn. "Where's Keats?"

"Ivy? *Ivy.*"

I turned back, and she reached out to squeeze my arm. "Let's not panic."

"I'm not panicking."

"No? Then why are we still talking on the phone?"

"Good point." I clicked the phone off and she did the same. "It's upsetting, for sure, but it's not the first time I've seen something like this. Or even the second."

"Then you know the drill. You go into that barn and call the police." She turned me around and started frogmarching me forward. "I'm going to leave you here and go to the chicken coop. I'll collect the ladies, take them up to the house and ply them with mimosas. No one will notice Wilf is missing for ages if I do my job right. They'll expect him to be hungover."

"Sounds like a good plan." I nodded at Keats as he came to the door of the barn to meet me. "Keep people at the back of the house. I don't want them getting in the way of the investigation."

She sighed. "They're going to notice the police eventually. Call me back in twenty minutes and we'll brainstorm some key messages."

I spun around at the door. "Right. Like, 'your boss died and my inn died with him.' No way will I ever get another guest when it leaks that my cows killed someone."

She sank her nails into my shoulder and shook me. "Stop that.

There are a dozen witnesses to say Wilf was plastered. What were you supposed to do? Chain him to his bed?"

The Flordale women came around the side of the barn carrying their baskets. Keri and Paulette looked blissfully happy. In fact, their expressions were exactly what I'd hoped to see on marketing material for Runaway Farm. The big city stress—and even the stress from the corporate politics at dinner—had washed away. Even Nellie looked less cynical. If one visit to the henhouse could do that, what could we accomplish in several days?

Without the murder, of course.

A murder would definitely steal the bliss from those smiles.

"Everything okay?" Keri asked. "You look worried, Ivy."

"Cow trouble," I said, forcing a smile. "It's always something on a farm."

Jilly slipped in front of me. "Let's leave Ivy to sort out the cows and go up to the house. We're going to sit out on the back deck and have mimosas with drunken pineapple spears. How does that sound?"

"Sounds like the perfect vacation to me," Paulette said. "This place is so lovely. I am going to remember this vacation forever."

"You are, Paulette," I said, heading into the barn. "You really are."

CHAPTER SIX

Kellan Harper's serious expression probably struck fear in everyone's heart, not just mine. Clover Grove's police chief could melt the bones in your body with one glance—not in a good way, although he could do that, too. I knew about the good way from our relationship in senior year, which ended with as much class as Wilf's red Corvette crashing into my truck. Watching Kellan direct a team of eight cops around like a crime scene conductor, I briefly wondered how many other women in town knew about his magical bone-melting powers. It certainly wasn't the right time for such thoughts, but the human brain works in mysterious ways.

One of the men he was ordering around was my brother, Asher, who had dirty blond hair, bright blue eyes and an almost-permanent smile. Growing up as Mom's literal and figurative golden boy had left him with a sunny outlook that police work hadn't managed to shake. Even a small town like Clover Grove had its share of unsavory stories. I groaned inwardly, knowing that my homecoming had already contributed two of them. The town grapevine had practically short-circuited when Lloyd Boyce died on my property, implicating not only me but my sister, Daisy, and a good selection of locals. Now here I was again offering up gossip on a silver platter.

Asher loped over and gave me a quick hug. The Galloways weren't a hugging family but I guess he could sense my defences were down. "You okay, sis?"

"As okay as I can be when my old boss is dead in my cow stall," I mumbled into his shoulder.

"He sounded like a jerk, anyway. If the cows took him out, maybe it's karma." He stepped back and gave me his impish grin. "Just kidding."

"Wilf was a jerk, no lie, but he didn't deserve to go like this." I twisted my hair into a ponytail and sighed when I realized I didn't have a tie. "I half-expected someone to toss him out the window of his corner office in Boston. Instead he's face down in manure here."

Asher closed his eyes for a second and I knew he wanted to laugh. He always wanted to laugh, which was one of his best qualities, if not always job-appropriate. Probably *never* job appropriate, which must have been tough for him. I hadn't always understood that. As an HR executive, I had such complete emotional mastery that Asher called me Sister Robot to distinguish me from the rest. But after my concussion, however, I was sometimes as tactless and impulsive as my older brother. Giving up my sense of superiority over him was hard, especially when the more I blurted things out, the happier he got.

"Kellan's going to want to talk to you about office politics," he said.

"Oh, I know. I already had PTSD and now I get to relive it again. It feels like I'll never escape Flordale."

"I'm sure this will be cut and dry. Drunk guy treats livestock like pet hamsters and gets rude awakening."

"Or permanent sleep," I said.

His lips twitched again. "Stop it. You're trying to make me laugh and get me in trouble. Just like you did when we were kids."

"Like it ever worked. Mom wouldn't hear a bad word about you."

The trace of a smile faded. "And now she's back in town." He rubbed one hand after another through his hair. "That was the most peaceful three weeks of my life."

Now I did laugh. "You're the favorite. You must have missed her."

"It's always something with Mom," he said. "First she was hitting stop signs and I had to take her license away, which you know was total drama. Plus I've had to collect her off the premises of half a dozen jobs because she refused to leave after getting fired."

I flinched. "Oh no. I didn't know about that, Ash. I'm sorry. It must be embarrassing for you with your colleagues."

He nodded. "The guys are pretty good about it. She drops by the precinct whenever she feels like it. Charms half the staff and alienates the other half, including the chief."

I closed my eyes briefly. "She paid one of those visits here last night during dinner. Total embarrassment in front of my first guests."

This time he rubbed his eyes—the only blue eyes in the family. "How'd we turn out so normal?" he asked.

"Normal? Scratch the surface and we're all eccentric, brother. Daisy did her best to shield us but it's in our genes waiting to be activated. For me it happened when I rescued Keats."

"You have been, uh, different since you came home."

I nodded. "The weird unleashed."

He gave me a blazing grin. "I like it. Flaunt it, sis." His eyes wandered to the house yet again. "Where's Jilly?"

"Entertaining my guests," I said. "And don't even think about distracting her. The Flordale crew doesn't know what happened to Wilf yet."

"Ivy." The voice came from inside the barn. Commanding. Bone-melting. "Can you get your dog out of here? He's annoying me."

"Annoying you how?" I called.

Kellan appeared in the doorway and stared at me with eyes several shades darker than my brother's. "I think you'd call it herding. He's circling me and taking little lunges. He nipped my pant leg."

Asher gave me a last grin and ran off to join his colleagues in the barn.

"Keats," I called. "Come." The dog walked toward me. Ambled, really. He liked to be in the middle of things. Like all border collies, he was curious and persistent.

"Tell him I'm not hiring," Kellan said, following the dog across the gravel drive.

"Tell him yourself." I summoned something that would pass for a grin. Kellan and I had been awkward together during my first weeks back. That was partly old history and partly from my interfering with his investigation of Lloyd's demise. In the end, the killer's attack on me seemed to blow much of the tension away. We weren't quite friends yet, but we were on the way. At least we had been, until someone else died on my land. Now, who knew?

Kellan had already started the day by getting annoyed with me for releasing the livestock, including the cows. I knew better than to disturb the crime scene, but all of the animals were stirred up and that could lead to injury in closed spaces. On top of that, Heidi was getting increasingly agitated trapped in her relatively small stall with a body. I wanted to keep her calm for both the calf's sake and Wilf's remains. I may not have been fond of my former boss, but there was no need for further desecration.

Kellan was even less knowledgeable about livestock than I was, and he wanted to keep it that way. He'd made no bones about disliking farm life, which was a definite strike against him in my books.

Now he rolled his eyes at me and said, "The day I start making conversation with your dog—or anyone's dog—is the day I surrender my badge. No one would trust a cop who chatted to dogs, let alone deputized one."

I rolled my eyes back at him. "There are tons of dogs in police work. It's discrimination that border collies never get the job."

"Normally I'd say Keats doesn't meet the size requirements," Kellan said. "But I saw him in action and I know he's quite capable of taking out bad guys. That ear maneuver is something else."

He finally smiled and my heart frisked a little, like the twin baby goats frolicking now in their pasture.

"Right? It's his signature move." Keats had twice latched onto someone's ear during a violent attack on me and disabled the villain. "But I hope he never has to use it again."

"Let's make sure he doesn't," Kellan said. "You need to promise me you'll stay well away from this investigation."

"What's to investigate? Wilf got drunk and locked himself in with the cows. I assume he passed out and then... well, you saw what happened."

He crossed his arms and stared out at the cows grazing innocently in their pasture. "We don't know the whole story. I wish you'd put up those security cameras like I suggested."

"Me too." I sighed. "I thought trouble would give Runaway Farm a pass for a while."

Kellan turned to glance at the red Corvette and the gravel beneath our feet. "So he got behind the wheel in the middle of the night and did donuts?"

"Looks like it. And there's more." I led him down the lane. "There's a figure eight in the lane. He may have been planning to go somewhere and changed his mind."

"Where would he be going at that time of night?" Kellan asked.

"Home, maybe? It's possible he was ashamed of his behavior at dinner." I watched as Keats sniffed every inch of the gravel. "But I've never known Wilf to be ashamed, and trust me, he has plenty of cause."

Kellan knelt and stared at the spot where the Corvette met the side of my truck. "I hope you have good insurance."

"I do. Thank goodness."

Keats shoved his head under Kellan's arm and drew in the scent of dented metal. The police chief leaned back on his heels and shook his head at the dog. "I mean insurance on the farm, as well," he said.

"Definitely. Hannah Pemberton actually paid the premiums for the first five years. She said after all she'd been through on the farm it would cost me too much to operate the inn at the rate they charged." I gazed around at the property I was so lucky to have. "She gives a new meaning to the word 'generous.'"

"Happy to hear that. Wilf isn't around to sue you but his family might. Is he married? Kids?"

I nodded. "Although things were tense at home. I heard more about that than I wanted."

"Okay." His expression fell into professional lines. "Are you ready to give your statement? I wouldn't say no to a coffee."

"Let me get you a cup and bring it down here, because..."

There was no reason to finish my sentence. The front door opened and five women thundered down the front stairs, shrieking. "Wilf's dead? Is it really true? What happened?"

That was just what I could pick out from the overlapping voices as they ran toward us. Nellie tripped over something and fell. The Raptors leapt over her together and kept running. No one stopped to help Nellie up.

Jilly's mimosas had obviously been quite effective.

I walked over to help Nellie get to her feet but the pack barred my path and swarmed me. "Ladies. Give me a second, please."

Nellie managed to stand. She was still wearing her spa gloves but they were grey with grit now. Staggering over, she said, "Is it true?" Only "it" came out as "ish." She grabbed my hand and clutched it. "He's really dead?"

"I'm afraid so, Nellie. Ladies, please go back inside until the police finish investigating."

Jilly came through the front door, now in capris and T-shirt, and mouthed an apology. Asher miraculously sensed her presence from inside the barn and appeared in the wide doorway. As he jogged across the parking area, his crush was obvious to everyone... except my tipsy colleagues. They moved away from me to block Asher's path before he could get anywhere near the porch.

Kellan rolled his eyes again but couldn't help smirking. Asher was so popular in town that women of all ages specifically asked for him when they called the station to report petty crimes. So many turned out to be nuisance calls that Kellan now deliberately assigned the oldest, most taciturn cop to every report requesting Asher. It was working... for now.

Asher politely and persistently eased out of the Flordale clutches and ran up the stairs to see Jilly. The women turned their attention instead on Kellan. His expression effectively kept them from invading his personal space, but he had to raise his hands to stem the flow of questions.

"Ladies, please. I'll share all I can for the moment." He waited till they simmered down to listen. "Wilfred Darby has indeed passed away. We're not sure how or when it happened but the autopsy will tell us more. You'll all need to stay at Runaway Farm until the investigation is done."

"They're booked for three days," I told Kellan.

He tipped his head and shrugged. "Better get more groceries."

CHAPTER SEVEN

I didn't think anyone could melt Kellan Harper with a glance—in the bad way—but it turned out there was one person with sufficient power. And that person had delivered me into existence.

Mom got out of the passenger seat of Poppy's classic Volkswagen bug and swept toward me on red, faux alligator stilettos. No matter how many hard knocks Mom took, she never staggered on her high heels. She was a survivor. Of course, with six decent kids, she had a pretty good safety net.

Iris clambered out of the small back seat and shrugged at me, whereas Poppy grinned as she leaned on the car to watch the show. Holding Mom back at times like this was impossible, at least without Daisy, our eldest sister. We all adored and respected Daisy, but she'd been avoiding the inn like the plague since being implicated, albeit briefly, in the dogcatcher's death. The incident had forced her to reveal a long-held secret about her family to Kellan that left her feeling vulnerable. She'd gone from bossing me around during the setup of the inn to being the absentee sister. I hoped she'd get over it soon, because I missed her. In all the ways that counted, she was really the parent of the family, even to Mom.

"Kellan Harper," Mom said, pausing to stare up at him with the hazel eyes all of us had inherited except Asher. "We meet again."

"Hello, Mrs. Galloway," he said, taking a step back. Even a murderer couldn't make Kellan step back, but Mom managed it. "You look well."

"Ms. Galloway," she corrected. "Mister Galloway left us to fend for ourselves thirty years ago. If I look well, it's because I had a wonderful vacation. Unfortunately, I came home to discover you seized that opportunity to make advances on my Ivy again. Breaking her heart once wasn't enough?"

"Mom!" It was a chorus from all siblings present, with Asher's voice being loudest of all. He'd left Jilly on the porch to run interference, but I beat him to the punch.

"Please stop, Mom," I said. "Kellan saved my life while you were away. Keats and I wouldn't be here now if not for him."

She shrugged a silent "whatever" and said, "I'm sure you'd have managed. You're a very resourceful girl, Ivy. Your boss—may he rest in peace—nicknamed you the 'grim reaper' for a reason. As inappropriate as it was."

"How about we be appropriate now?" I asked, gesturing toward the guests. "Wilf's staff are all here and they're in shock."

"Some are relieved, no doubt." She nodded at Kellan. "I'm sure Chief Full-of-Himself will get it sorted out quickly."

"Mom!" Asher had never sounded more exasperated. "This is my boss. Show the chief of police the respect he deserves."

She withered Asher with rare disapproval. "Darling, you've gotten so prickly since Kellan came back to Clover Grove last year. Policing our town doesn't require a heavy hand, you know."

"It does when people are getting murdered," Asher said.

All my guests had moved closer, including Ben and Neal, who'd just arrived looking dishevelled from sleeping late. They were staring at my mom with evident fascination. She knew how to command a room, or in this case a large parking area outside the barn. Her red wool suit came from Round Two, a secondhand store in nearby Dorset Hills. Iris' main role in the family was to shuttle Mom around to vintage stores throughout hill country so that Mom didn't risk running into the previous owners of her wardrobe scores.

Walking over, I took my mom by the arm and tugged her away from Kellan. "Leave the policing to the experts, please."

Kellan gave me a grateful smile that morphed into a grin. "What great advice. If only you'd follow it yourself."

"He's right about that, Ivy," Mom said. Her expression said the cost of agreeing with Kellan was high. "I've heard about the unnecessary risks you've taken since rescuing that mutt." She stared down at Keats, now glued to my side. "I don't trust that blue eye. It's like he's looking into my soul."

"Well, I'm sure he likes what he sees there," I said. Strangely, it was true. Keats had a system of grading people apparent only to me. Tail up, ears forward, and sloppy smile all signalled approval. For all her idiosyncrasies, Mom got a five-star rating. My dog and I agreed on almost everything, except perhaps this. "Now, how about you, Poppy and Iris join Jilly for a light lunch? She's making chickpea sloppy joes. A crowd pleaser."

Mom's red lips puckered and she patted her smooth stomach. "Your former boss wasn't right about much, but I share his views on chickpeas. Homesteader hippies have brought some strange passions into this farming community."

"Ivy's raved about your tuna salad," Jilly said, joining us. "Maybe you could show me your secrets."

Her tone was respectful, even deferential—something Mom craved and didn't often get from her own kids. Jilly sensed that and delivered. Her people skills were stellar.

"All right, then," Mom said, heels crunching as she followed Jilly to the front stairs. "A tea would be nice, too, but I don't want to leave Ivy too long in the clutches of the so-called chief. You do know how he practically jilted her at the altar?"

"Oh my god, Mom." Heat surged up from my toes to my hairline. Her statement was not only ridiculous but the opposite of what Kellan believed. We'd broken up during our first year at different colleges because he'd been told I was two-timing him. It wasn't true, but pride, distance and immaturity had kept us from sorting it out.

I couldn't look at him, so I checked on my guests and found they'd closed in a rather tight circle around me. Keats didn't like that at all. His left ear, over the honey-sweet brown eye, had drooped and his tail hung like a flag on a windless day. It seemed like the oxygen had grown scarce as my guests sucked up more than their share.

"Folks, I have a great idea," I said. "How about a trail walk in the meadows? I think we could all use a dose of hill country fresh air."

I heard more crunching of boots on gravel behind me as the police retreated to the barn. Perhaps the gruesome death scene was a welcome break from my mother's theatrics.

Keri clutched my arm. "I don't want to go far till we know more about what happened to Wilf. It feels…"

"Dangerous," Nellie interrupted. "If a cow could stomp Wilf to death under our noses, what could happen in the open fields?"

"Heidi didn't stomp Wilf to death," I said. Now that the initial shock was over, I'd changed my tune about that and I would defend my girl until told otherwise.

"No?" Nellie said. "Then what really happened?"

"Well, it's pure speculation on my part, but I'm guessing Wilf came out here on some crazy, intoxicated mission. He got behind the wheel and thank goodness he hit my truck instead of heading to town and risking other lives on the highway."

"But why was he in the barn?" Keri chimed in. "He hated animals. You know that."

"He was dead set on milking the cows yesterday. Oops." I covered my mouth. "Excuse me. Wrong word. He was *determined* to milk the cows and I forbade it. What happened when you told Wilf not to do something?"

They all looked at each other and finally Keri spoke up. "No one ever told Wilf what to do and got away with it."

"It was a recipe for the opposite to happen," I said. "At least, that's what I found as his second in command. I had to use reverse psychology to get anything done. So, yesterday I should have encouraged him to try milking on the spot. He probably would have decided against it instead of coming out here in the middle of the night to give it a whirl."

"And get attacked by a cow," Neal said.

I shook my head. "I really don't believe it was deliberate. These heifers are young and frisky but they've always been friendly with me."

"I'm sure they wouldn't be as friendly with Wilf," Keri said. "Can't animals smell someone who hates them?"

"I don't know enough about cows yet to comment," I said, sighing. "But dogs certainly know."

Keats was staring up at me with a knowing blue eye. He'd signalled his contempt for Wilf the day before by fully tucking his tail and flattening his ears. It had seemed to take sheer grit for him to stand between Wilf and me. No doubt our old professional grudges created shock waves.

There was a murmur among the guests and I raised my hand. "Folks, again, it's just a guess but I'm thinking Wilf collapsed in the cow stall. Maybe he passed out from liquor. Maybe he had a heart attack. We all know about his unhealthy lifestyle. Or maybe he simply decided to enjoy a nap in the hay. But it's pitch black out in the barn at night, and the cows wouldn't be able to see him. So if—and I'm saying if—trampling turns out to be the cause of death, I really don't think we can blame Heidi and Clara for Wilf's poor decisions."

Once again there was a crunch of gravel and I knew from the

expressions of my former colleagues that the boots belonged to Kellan.

"Interesting theories, Ivy," he said. "And thanks for sharing your thoughts so generously when I asked you to stay out of police work."

His tone took me aback. I thought we'd moved past the animosity. But when I turned, he actually looked more hurt than angry. My mother's words must have struck right in the old heartbreak. She had a talent for finding someone's vulnerability and taking strategic pokes. It helped her keep the upper hand in relationships when she probably didn't feel she'd ever had it in life—at least not since her husband left. I didn't really think of the man as my father, since I had no memories of him at all.

"Sorry, Chief Harper," I said. "I suppose I feel a little defensive of my heifers. I'm sure you can understand that."

He shook his head. "I can understand your being defensive about the dog, I guess. Cows are just—"

"Steak," Neal said, following that up with a nasty laugh.

I turned on him. "These are dairy cattle, Neal. They'll never grace a plate."

He gave a shrug. "I'm vegan, remember? Bring on the chickpea sloppy joes."

Keri gestured for Kellan's attention. "Excuse me, Chief. If Ivy's theories are wrong, what are yours?"

Pressing his lips together, Kellan hesitated. I wondered if he simply didn't want to agree that I was right. But when he spoke, I could tell that he'd chosen his words with professional precision.

"So much depends on the autopsy," he said. "But my forensics expert suspects Mr. Darby was already dead before the cow kicked him."

"See?" I said, triumphantly. "My girls are innocent."

Kellan forged on. "There's a contusion on Mr. Darby's head that seems inconsistent with a cloven hoof."

Everyone gasped and it took a second before Keri continued. "Are you saying someone hit Wilf before the cow got to him?"

"It's impossible to know just yet. I'd ask you to be patient. Rest assured that answers will come."

"Do you think this contusion took place inside the barn?" I asked. "Maybe Wilf hit his head when he smacked the car and then staggered in there confused and collapsed. Naturally the cows would be distressed by the arrival of a body in their midst." I threw a defiant look around. "Heidi and Clara were unfairly accused. Even by me."

"Not necessarily," Kellan said. "They still stomped Mr. Darby, but he may have been unconscious first."

"Did he fall unconscious inside or outside the stall?" I asked again.

"I won't speculate further." He pressed his lips together again to end the conversation and started to turn.

"Chief Harper?" For the first time, Paulette spoke up. "I'm just reading between the lines. That's something I need to do a lot in my job as an admin assistant. But are you saying Wilf may have been hit in the head by someone deliberately?"

"It's far too soon to say," Kellan said.

It was far too soon for *Kellan* to say, but my brother was a different story. He came out of the barn and the truth was written all over his boyishly handsome face. At least, I could read it. Hopefully it was less obvious to my colleagues.

Nellie stepped into the breach and voiced what everyone was wondering. "Did someone club Wilf to death?"

Her bluntness shocked me, but I knew she still had plenty of mimosas in her system.

"Nellie!" Paulette turned on the younger woman and shook her finger. "Show some respect."

"Come on, Paulette," she said. "I'm just asking what we all want to know. Did the real grim reaper finally catch up with Wilf?"

"Ma'am," Kellan said. "It would be best to leave this conversation for a more appropriate time."

"When you're not drunk, for example," Neal said. "All you ladies reek of booze."

I stared at Kellan but his face—even more handsome than my brother's but in a manly sort of way—gave nothing away. So I turned back to my brother and I knew the answer.

"Oh no," I said. "Not again."

"Just relax, Ivy," Kellan said. "There's no need for worry until the autopsy report comes back."

"What do you mean, 'not again'?" Keri asked, her brown eyes full of worry.

"Someone was murdered in Ivy's barn just a few weeks ago," Neal said. "I googled it last night after her mother was blabbering about the attacks."

"You didn't tell us that, Ivy." Keri's voice was heavy with accusation. "If I'd known we weren't safe here, I'd never have booked your inn for our retreat."

"That was an isolated incident that had nothing to do with me," I said. "Someone just picked my farm as a convenient place to do away with the dogcatcher."

"She's right," Asher said, joining us. "It had nothing to do with Ivy."

"Chief?" Keri said, following normal corporate protocol and going up the line.

"The dogcatcher's murder had nothing to do with Ivy," he confirmed. "The subsequent attack on Ivy herself had everything to do with her poking around in an investigation."

"Attack? By a murderer?" Keri said, her eyes wide.

"Someone who's now safely behind bars, partly because of me," I said. "And Keats. Anyway, it was a local issue, Keri, and there's no reason to believe someone from Clover Grove would attack Wilf."

"True," Neal said. "It was more likely to be one of us, right?"

"Neal!" Paulette turned on him now with her wagging finger. "Don't even joke about that."

"Well, who else would want Wilf gone... permanently?" he asked.

Now they all stared at each other with a new expression. Wary. It was dawning on them that one of their own could have perpetrated the crime. Perhaps they even wondered if another attack could follow.

We turned at the clack of heels on wood. My mother was descending my front stairs like an old-time debutante. "Asher! Did someone say murder?"

"Ms. Galloway," Kellan said. "We're all going to stay calm. There's no reason to be otherwise."

She picked her way across the driveway. "Chief Harper. Don't you dare tell me not to worry about my children. If there's been another murder at Ivy's farm, I honestly don't know what I'll do."

"Mom." Asher's voice was pleading. "Leave it."

"Well, really, Asher," Mom said. "This Wilf was obnoxious, as I saw for myself, but who'd have a reason to—" She pulled the decorative handkerchief out of her breast pocket and shook out the fabric with a single sharp flick. "Dispatch him?"

All eyes were on my mother and no one seemed bemused anymore.

Neal, who'd seemingly elected himself team spokesperson, stood a little taller. "Ms. Galloway, you threatened Wilf last night. For treating Ivy like dirt and causing her to go nuts."

The handkerchief came down from her nose and her eyes grew fiery. "My daughter is not 'nuts,' young man."

She seemed to have missed his indirect accusation, but Asher and I didn't. We stepped forward together and each of us grabbed one of Mom's arms. Her heels dragged on the gravel and then clunked on the stairs as we literally carried her back into the house.

Keats followed along, tail held high, as if this were a new and enjoyable game. Kellan wasn't going to take the dog's word for my mom's innocence, but I certainly did.

"Don't be silly, you two," Mom said, flapping and squawking like an angry hen as we crossed the porch. "How could I possibly kill that big oaf? It would have taken a sledgehammer. Not that I wouldn't have liked to—"

Asher's big hand cut off her last words

CHAPTER EIGHT

Senna York's dirty tan Range Rover looked like it had spent hard time chasing livestock in muddy fields when it pulled up on my lawn. The life of the agrarian vet wasn't for the faint of heart, but I guessed the problem I was about to present to her was a new one. At least she didn't need to absorb it all with my mother fluttering around. Jilly still had everyone trapped inside, perhaps with a lunch cocktail or five.

Senna stared around at the police vehicles with a puzzled expression but got straight to business. "Everything okay with Archie?"

Keats circled her boots and herded her toward me. She smiled and let him, having owned sheepdogs herself in the past. Nothing he did surprised her.

"I think so," I said, leading them to the cow pasture. "Heidi seems entranced with him."

The calf was wandering around the enclosure, his spindly legs steadier today, and Heidi was a few paces behind, letting out what sounded like worried huffing.

Senna's grin spread. "Isn't that something? You've got a lucky horseshoe hanging over you, Ivy Galloway."

"Sometimes it comes crashing down on my head," I said. "Like today."

I shared the story in a rapid, hushed whisper. No one was close enough to hear, but Kellan and his team were still in the barn. Yellow hazard tape stretched across the back doorway and the open area outside.

When I finished, Senna's grin had vanished. "That's awful. I'm so sorry this happened." She squeezed my arm hard. "But I don't believe your cows are to blame."

"I don't believe it, either. At first I did, I'll be honest, but they're not dangerous bulls."

Still pinching my arm, her eyes narrowed as she stared into the pasture. "I mean, even if they *were* to blame, they weren't to blame. Their overnight stall isn't huge and that idiot had no right being inside with them." She blew out a sigh. "And with a new mother, yet. I assume you explained to your guests that these are real animals, not plush toys."

I nodded. "In exhausting detail as they signed the waivers. I have a handout with the rules that everyone has to initial."

"Thank goodness you covered your butt. I'm sure this will get chalked up to his drunken foolishness." She glanced over at Wilf's car. "I knew he was trouble when he roared up in the 'vette. Midlife crisis waiting to happen."

"From what I can tell that started when he turned thirty and realized his high school hero days were behind him and he couldn't coast anymore."

"It's a shame he brought this on Runaway Farm, though. You've had a rocky ride already."

We were only a few feet from the gate but she chose to climb the fence and leap lightly into the pasture. I could have followed suit but my limbs still felt as wobbly as Archie's from the shock. No need to add another pratfall, with my tailbone still aching from yesterday's. I handed over Senna's heavy rectangular kit and then opened the gate to join her with Keats.

She tied off Heidi first, and then knelt beside her. Running one hand down the cow's rear leg, she lifted a hoof. Then she moved to the other side and did the same. She signalled for me to bring her the kit and flipped it open. Pulling out a plastic bottle, she used a sterile swab to scrape the cow's hoof and then labelled it. She worked in silence, collecting samples from all three cattle, even little Archie.

I tried to be patient, but Keats poked in with his long muzzle half a dozen times and she just nudged him aside gently.

"Keats, leave it," I said. "Senna's got it covered."

After she closed her kits and stood, I asked, "Well? Did you see any blood?"

Senna nodded. "I'm afraid so. Just Heidi, as far as I can tell. But remember, that doesn't mean she's responsible for what happened. A body in the stall at night would have made the cows agitated. I'm surprised it wasn't worse, actually. And I'm surprised Archie is still welcome."

Opening the gate, I let her out and we walked back to her car, where she set down her kit.

There was a crunch of wheels down the lane and I turned to see a big white cube van coming toward us. "Oh no," I said. "That's the County Animal Services truck, isn't it?"

"Sure is. They've replaced Lloyd Boyce and I hear this one's just as bad."

The driver's door opened and a tall, big-boned woman jumped down. Was it a coincidence that Lloyd's replacement was also a redhead? Did Animal Services have a "type"?

She loped toward us and extended her hand to me. "Tess Blade," she said. "I'm the new field officer for Animal Services."

I let her pump my hand in a crushing grip. "Ivy Galloway,

owner of Runaway Farm. This is Senna York, Clover Grove's new and amazing veterinarian."

Their eyes met for a long second as they took each other's measure. I felt a chill settle over my shoulders. The fall day was warming up nicely, but not here, outside the cow pasture. I glanced at Keats and saw his ears were back and his tail down. He wasn't impressed with Tess either.

She turned to the trio of cows. "So, which one's the killer? Or don't you know yet?"

"Excuse me? The police haven't confirmed my cows are to blame for this unfortunate incident. I'd appreciate it if the County didn't slander my cattle."

She walked along the fence and we all followed. "What I heard was that your cows stomped a man to death last night." She tipped her head toward Heidi. "Not that surprising when we have a new mom."

"Whoever told you that jumped the gun," I said.

"Yeah? Well, we can't be too careful. As you probably know, the County has the power to seize dangerous livestock and send them for slaughter."

Senna pinched my arm again. "It's okay, Ivy. Having the power doesn't mean the County will use it. I'm sure they'll wait for the lab reports on my tests. Won't you, Tess?"

"Field Officer Blade," she said. "Or just Officer."

I wanted to laugh but looked down at Keats instead. His ruff was up and his ears slightly back. Field Officer Blade's character got a big fat fail from my dog. Somehow that didn't surprise me.

"Well, Officer Blade," I said. "It's my duty to protect all the rescue animals on this farm, and I take it very seriously. I'm sure your discussions with Senna and the police down in the barn will give you enough confidence to stand down. The chief said the investigation could take days."

Tess shrugged. "I'll talk to the chief, of course. Just know that *my* job is to protect people from dangerous animals, and I also take it very seriously."

Kellan shook his head as we ducked under the yellow tape and came into the barn. "Ladies. Do I really need to explain the meaning of that tape?"

"Chief Harper," I said. "This is my vet, Senna York, who just examined the cows." Then I nodded toward Tess. "And this is Tess Blade, the new dogcatcher. She prefers to be called Officer."

I thought Tess might be embarrassed, but she was scanning the barn, unfazed. "Where exactly did the cows murder the man?"

Kellan frowned. "Officer Blade, we haven't concluded that's what happened. Perhaps you'll let the police department do its work."

"I can seize those cows now and send them for slaughter, Officer Harper," she said. "If they're a threat to public safety."

"Chief Harper," he said, glancing at me. "You're new, Officer Blade, and I understand you need time to get the lay of the land in Clover Grove. How about I give your director a call and we can discuss due process?"

Officer Blade shrugged. "Knock yourself out, Chief."

While they distracted each other, I looked around, musing. What had Keats been doing when Wilf came down here in the middle of the night and decided to get adventurous? Why hadn't the dog come up to the house to get me? Or at least barked his fool head off? I may not have heard it but the guests at the front of the house would have. There was no way my hypervigilant pup would just stand by while someone hassled his cows. Wilf's unsupervised presence threatened the livestock Keats considered his property and responsibility.

"Check Wilf's calves," I said.

"Calves?" Asher asked, joining us. "Wilf had cattle? And why would we check them?"

Senna laughed and I couldn't help smiling, too. "His legs,

Asher. As far as I know, Keats was here when Wilf barged in drunk. There's a chance the dog nipped Wilf to keep him away from the livestock."

Officer Blade crossed her arms. "So you're saying your dog bites people whenever he feels like it?"

Senna raised her hand. "This would have constituted a threat to his livestock. He wouldn't be a proper farm dog if he didn't protect them."

"I heard he's attacked humans and shredded earlobes," Officer Blade said.

"When he was protecting *me*," I said, crossing my arms and shivering. "From murderers. I wouldn't be here without Keats, in fact."

Kellan stepped into Tess' space, forcing her to back up. "This discussion is beyond the scope of your current investigation, Officer Blade. There's no reason to bring up past trauma."

I gave him a grateful look, which he missed because Tess took a step to close the space again.

"Chief Harper, we both know my predecessor passed away right here on this property. I have every right to ask questions."

"That had nothing to do with my farm," I said. "It's not my fault a crazed murderer chose to end Lloyd's life here."

Tess gave another shrug of her broad shoulders. "Either way, you and your farm and especially your dog are on the County watch list. You already were, before your cows attacked."

My hands went to my hips. "On the watch list? How dare you!"

Senna stepped in front of me. "Ivy, let's stay calm. I'm sure the County is doing its due diligence. This is an inn, after all, where guests are staying. They have to be cautious."

"Exactly," Officer Blade said. "I'm just trying to keep people safe. There's a lot going on at Runaway Farm that raises concerns about public safety."

Sweeping my arm around at Kellan's staff, I said, "There's practically an army here to make sure everyone's safe."

Senna chimed in. "I'm here to attest to the health and character of the animals, and the police can attest to the character of the owner."

Officer Blade kept on firing. "From what I've heard, she may have offed her old boss. Or gotten her mother to do it. They had a grudge against the deceased. Everyone knows that."

"Hey," Asher said. "You're out of line, Officer Tess. Way out of line."

I closed my eyes and literally bit my tongue to stop it from spilling words I'd regret later. As always, the Clover Grove grapevine had churned out the story with lightning speed. Good news never travelled that fast.

"Asher, quiet," Kellan said. "But he's right that you're overstepping, Officer Blade. I'll thank you to reserve judgment and let me conduct my own investigation. Ms. Galloway and her mother will be questioned appropriately."

My stomach sent a little geyser of coffee back up my throat. I had no doubt I could clear my own name but my mom was as tough to manage as Wilma, the sly sow. It's something she and Wilf had in common, although she wouldn't thank me to hear it.

"Fine," Officer Blade said. "I'll stick to my area of expertise, which is problem animals. Obviously, this dog was loose in the barn at the time of the incident. I want to know what he was doing. No way a dog this bossy would just stand by."

"Bossy?" I said. "You don't even know Keats."

She gestured to Keats and I noticed for the first time that he was subtly herding me backward without my even noticing. "Yeah, bossy," she said. "He's taking you somewhere right now. Who's the leader in this equation?"

"It's a partnership," I said. "And if he's taking me somewhere, he has a good reason for it. I trust him implicitly, Officer Blade."

Turning, I followed Keats to a stall that had long ago belonged to a horse that died of old age. Unlike the other pens, the two horse stalls had split doors and grates with metal bars in the top half. Today, the top half was closed and the bottom slightly ajar. To my knowledge, Charlie only used it to store equipment and I'd never seen either half closed.

I ducked under the top half without waiting to open it. Inside, half a dozen wieners lay on the floor covered in flies. Keats followed me inside, and if a dog's lip could curl in disgust, his would have.

Kneeling, I tugged the door closed with one finger and stared at it from a dog's point of view. There were grooves in the wood all the way to the top half. Claw marks. Bloody claw marks, in fact, that focused around the inside latch.

"Keats, shake," I said, holding out my hand. He offered one snowy paw and I examined it. Two broken nails and pads caked in dried blood. The other paw was about the same. "Aw, buddy, I'm so sorry I didn't notice earlier. You tried so hard to protect your herd."

I called for Senna and she knelt outside the stall to examine Keats fully. She'd barely finished when Kellan and Officer Blade came over. He unlatched the upper half of the door and stared down at me. "Ivy, what are you doing? You know better than to crawl all over a crime scene."

"Keats wanted me to see where he was locked up last night." I gestured to the wieners. "These were clearly meant to decoy him. As if that would distract a sheepdog from an attack on his charges. I highly doubt Wilf was coherent enough to find wieners in my freezer and coordinate something like that, Kellan. There had to be someone else in here last night."

"You'll test the wieners, right?" Senna asked. "In case they're poisoned?"

I flopped abruptly onto my butt. "I don't believe any of my former colleagues would do that. Some of them had grievances against Wilf, but they wouldn't make a dog collateral damage."

Kellan shook his head at me. "Ivy, we've discussed this before. Someone capable of murder probably doesn't have the compassion for animals you seem to expect."

I sighed. "I know. I still don't want to believe anyone would deliberately harm an animal. Not that I want to believe they'd hurt other people, but animals are different. Innocent. Pure of heart."

Officer Blade cleared her throat. "I see lots of animals who are far from pure-hearted. My job is to dispose of them."

"Well, my cows are pure-hearted," I said. "Heidi adopted a calf that isn't hers yesterday. That sounds pretty sweet to me. And Keats hurt himself trying to get out of here and protect his herd."

"He's a good dog," Senna said, standing to face Tess. She was much shorter than the brawny redhead, but she had presence. "The County can leave the farm in my care right now. I'll come out daily and check on the animals. If I see any issues at all, I will report them immediately, as is my duty. My reputation rides on my integrity."

Tess stared at Keats for a long moment before finally nodding. "Okay. But the cows and the dog stay on the watch list until this is resolved and Runaway Farm is cleared of murder. Again."

The "again" hit me like a kick to the gut. How could this happen? One murder you could see as an accident, but not two. Why, after 10 years of boring corporate life, was I attracting death like these wieners attracted sleepy, late-season flies?

Kellan waved as if dispersing the flies. "Folks, I need you to clear the crime scene. It's already been contaminated by too many people."

"As if a barn can ever be pristine," I said, hanging back as the vet and dogcatcher left the barn.

"True enough," he said, sighing. "My people are working as fast as they can so that you can get the animals back inside tonight. Can you try to stay out of the way, Ivy?"

"Of course," I said. "You know I have a full house right now. I'm going to be super busy distracting my guests."

My tone must have been less convincing than my actual words, because he said, "I mean it. Stay out of this."

"I hear you, Kellan." I made sure my tone was light. "Relax."

He glared at me. "I'm not here to relax. And I can't do my job properly if I'm chasing you around. You're as nosy as your hound."

"As much as I love being compared to my amazing dog, you must know I was just trying to help the last time."

"I don't need help to find a murderer."

"But I know the Flordale people. I hired some of them and we practically went through war together. I really can help, Kellan."

"You'll get your chance to tell me all about the corporate battles, trust me. But interrupting due process will only slow me down. Would you like to hear how many bodies I've discovered in my career? How many murder cases I've solved?"

"Not really, no."

He stared at me, all fierce blue eyes and squared-off jaw. He'd been a cute teen and now he was a stunning man. I really should have tried harder to heal that old rift back in college. Then we wouldn't need to dance around each other like two spirited alpacas.

I couldn't help grinning. Kellan would hate being compared to an alpaca, since he wasn't a fan of animals or farms.

"I really don't see anything to smile about right now," he said.

"You're right," I said, leaving the stall. My arm brushed his as I passed. A traitorous tingle roared up my arm and made my heart skip like a baby goat again. My brain knew well that this farm-hater was totally wrong for me, but apparently my nervous system had a different opinion. "But I think you're going to regret not letting Keats and me give you a hand."

"Oh, I won't regret it at all, I'm quite sure of that." He walked behind me, herding me now like Keats did. "I don't want to worry about you. Maybe you and Keats won't be so lucky if you throw yourself in the path of danger again. You two pushed your luck far enough."

"You're right about that, I guess."

"I don't guess, I know. Just trust me to do my job."

I did trust him. It was the nest of vipers inside my house I had doubts about. I couldn't stand by and let one of them put Jilly or my family at risk. Not to mention my growing menagerie. I intended to do whatever I could to protect them from harm.

I'd just have to be smarter about it this time.

CHAPTER NINE

M om had insisted that Poppy take her home for a quick change of clothes before our family meeting at Daisy's. Now she was perched on a too-tall stool at Daisy's immaculate kitchen counter with the heels of her black patent pumps clattering against the metal bar she couldn't reach. As always, she saw herself as larger in her own mind than she actually was, even though she constantly had to alter oversized clothing to fit her petite frame. Sewing was one of her talents, but it wasn't a marketable one in Clover Grove, where many homesteaders knew their way around a pattern and quilting clubs abounded. The black wool dress she was wearing now was immaculately fitted, however, and I had to give her credit.

"What's with the funereal look?" Iris asked, leaning on the counter across from Mom.

"Iris, respect," Mom said. "A man died today. The least I can do is dress appropriately."

"After threatening him last night?" Iris said, shaking her head. Like all of the Galloway girls, she had brown hair and hazel eyes. The differences between us were subtle enough that people often confused us. Iris had soft waves in her hair and a scattering of freckles on her pale skin. Violet had curlier hair that she was always trying to tame. Otherwise they could probably pass for Poppy, at least in Poppy's natural state. As the wild child of the family, Poppy had tried every possible hair color over the years, and had more piercings than the rest of us combined. I couldn't really blame her for wanting to stand out, although I'd always preferred to blend in.

"Don't be silly," Mom said. "I was defending my daughter, and no one with half a brain could take what I said seriously." She turned to glare at me. "Does your old boyfriend have half a brain, Ivy?"

"I'll answer that question," Asher said, pushing off the stainless steel fridge he'd been slouching against. "Kellan Harper didn't get the job as chief of police without being brilliant, Mom." He tossed her a grin and added, "Respect, please."

"Respect is earned," she said. "Shouldn't you be over at the farm making sure he finds the killer quickly?"

Mom had all the strength in the world to resist her daughters but one grin from Asher normally melted her into a puddle of maternal doting. Her ability to withstand his charm today told me that something was off with her.

Daisy moved in behind Asher and sprayed down the stainless steel. Then she wiped it with a special cloth. Her flair for interior design meant the house was lovely but keeping it that way was a full-time job with a husband and two sets of teenage twins. The boys—especially the younger ones—took delight in leaving smudges for my clean freak sister to polish away. She was up to the task because she'd been polishing away our family's imperfections all her life. Today was just the next in a long string.

"Mom, I agree that Asher shouldn't stay long," she said. "We just thought it would be good to have a chat about what's happened." Her hand kept buffing the fridge as she glanced over her shoulder at Mom. "You know, get everyone on the same page."

Mom took a long sip from a white china mug filled with herbal tea. There were overlapping lipstick prints on the rim. "Good idea. We need to establish a united front behind Ivy."

"Exactly," Daisy said, leaving the fridge and trying to take Mom's mug. Lipstick stains stressed her out so much that she had a special black mug for Mom. But Poppy had poured the tea and probably chose the white one just to rattle Daisy. That's how things went in our family. "The best way to establish that united front is to get you cleared as a suspect in this man's murder right away."

Mom held onto her mug and Daisy didn't risk spilling the tea. "Me? That's ridiculous, Daisy. Iris was joking."

"Not joking," Iris chimed in, as she came around and joined Violet and me at the kitchen table. Generally she took a back seat in family politics. She was typically the quietest, perpetually overshadowed by Daisy the responsible sister, Violet the popular cheerleader, and crazy Poppy who came next in line. And of course we were all eclipsed by charismatic Asher.

"No one could possibly believe I clubbed that big man to death in Ivy's barn in the middle of the night," Mom said. She waved a manicured hand from her head to her heels. "I'm a delicate flower."

"Untrue," Poppy said. "Dahlias are a hearty species. I have no doubt you could take someone out with the right weapon."

"What *was* the weapon?" Mom asked, deftly changing the subject.

"Unknown," Asher said. "The autopsy will tell us more."

Spritzing vinegar cleanser on the counter, Daisy gave it a wipe. It was so routine that she could continue to pin Mom with the look that withered most people. "Let's not drag this out, Mom," she said. "We need to know where you were last night."

"Poppy dropped me at my apartment around eight thirty," Mom said, planting a lipstick print on the opposite side of the mug. A provocative move. "What is this? An intervention?"

Daisy squinted at Mom before turning a pointed glance on Asher. He stepped forward and straightened his shoulders. He was six foot two and broad-shouldered, which made him quite imposing in his uniform, at least from the neck down. His perpetual smile tended to undercut that impression.

"Mom, come on," he said, dialling up the smile wattage and throwing in a dimple. "We all know you had nothing to do with Wilf Darby's death, but witnesses overheard your threat and you'll need to be questioned. We want to help you prepare so you don't get flustered."

Leaning against the back of the stool, Mom crossed her legs. It wasn't as elegant or nonchalant as she might have liked because her other foot dangled. "I don't get flustered, Asher. Especially not in front of the man who crushed my daughter's heart to smithereens and broke her spirt."

"Ivy has plenty of spirit," Daisy said, wiping the counter in front of Mom. "Too much spirit."

"She'll need it with her farm under investigation again," Mom said, flicking the damp rag away. "How can we help her?"

"By getting your story straight," Daisy said. "You went home at eight thirty and then what? Did you stay home? Can anyone attest to that?"

Now Daisy and Mom had a stare-down, both unflinching. "Who's the matriarch here, Daisy?"

Asher came around and rested a big hand on Mom's shoulder. It was hard to imagine she delivered six of us, particularly this giant. "Like I said, we know you didn't do this. But you're going to need a rock-solid alibi. Help us help you. Please."

"I don't need my children to script my interview with Kellan Harper. I've known him since he played in little league." Mom crossed her legs the other way and pouted. "I never thought much of his mother, by the way. There's no nice way to say this: she was frumpy. Kellan was wise to choose a job that requires a uniform, because his style sense is probably challenged too."

I had sat in silence watching Mom play my siblings like fish on a line. It was truly remarkable how she could handle them all with such ease. But I had more at stake than anyone here and plenty of experience interviewing difficult people. I'd have to step up to get around her shields.

Standing, I walked around the counter, nudged Daisy out of the way and faced Mom. Her smile expanded a little, confident she could handle me most easily of all. As the youngest, I'd always aimed to please, perhaps in hopes of being noticed at the end of the line.

"Mom, I really appreciate that you see how important this is to me," I began. "Obviously another death at the farm will send my reputation into the gutter. But you know what would completely decimate it? If *you* got pinned for the murder. So that's why we need to know your alibi. Did you stay in your apartment after Poppy dropped you off?"

Her smile contracted slightly. "I don't care to be interrogated by my children. I'm a grown woman."

"An evasive woman," I said. "Please answer the question."

"I'd just gotten home after a lengthy trip," she said. "Obviously I was exhausted, Ivy." She fluffed her meticulously colored hair with one hand. "Still am. I barely slept for worrying about you dealing with those... *vipers*, I think Jilly called them. She's delightful by the way. You found yourself a good friend there."

"Interesting digression," I said. "My question needed a simple yes or no, but I'll rephrase it. Did you leave your apartment after Poppy dropped you off?"

"As I said, I was exhausted and—"

"Mom, stop." I shook my head in exasperation. "Kellan Harper isn't going to fall for these games. Let me read between the lines here. You left your apartment. So we'll move on to where you went and what you did."

She let out an exasperated breath herself. "I needed a few things. The fridge was empty and Poppy was in too much of a rush to take me to the store. She seemed to have pressing matters of her own to—"

"I offered," Poppy said, adding her exasperation to the mix.

I raised my palm to Poppy. "Red herring alert," I said. "Mom doesn't want to tell us where she went for some reason. But Kellan Harper will find out, Mom, and it'll look worse for you than if you cough it up yourself. What are you hiding?"

"You were always my sweetest child." Mom looked genuinely perplexed. "The big city stole my little girl and sent back this—"

"Mom!" Daisy's voice took on the sharp note normally reserved for her younger twins, a rowdy pair of kind-hearted ruffians. "Do not add to Ivy's stress. She's still getting over her concussion, remember? You could set her back with your silly games."

"Silly games?" Mom swelled like a puffer fish and her eyes turned to dark buttons. Stinging words would follow if I didn't intervene.

"Mother. Please." I closed my eyes and rubbed my aching head, preparing for the next round. "Here's what's going to happen. You're going to tell us the truth or every single one of us is going to walk out of this house right now and leave you to your own devices. Think about what that means."

Her mouth worked as she considered the support that could dry up. I didn't know exactly how much my siblings tossed in for Mom's maintenance, but I was pretty generous. And then there were all the drives, not to mention the recent trip to Disneyland. If she had to think that hard about it, what she didn't want to share right now must be significant.

Finally she pushed her mug away and let Daisy seize it. "Fine, if you nosy parkers must know, I met up with a friend last night."

"What friend?" I asked. "Chief Harper will need to know."

"A gentleman friend. I have a social life that I don't feel the need to share with all of you. If I need to share a name with Kellan Harper, I will."

I leaned my elbows on the counter, risking Daisy's spray. "I have news for you. Keats and I are pretty good sleuths. You might as well give me the name of your big date so that I can focus on other suspects."

"You promised Kellan you'd stay out of this," Asher said. "He told me."

I raised my hand to silence him. I was winning and I wasn't slowing down. "Mom, who was your hot date?"

She squirmed on the stool, looking as uncomfortable as I'd ever seen her. "I really hate to tell you this, Ivy, but since you insist... I went to The Tipsy Grape for a drink with Charlie. Your farm manager."

"Charlie! Mom, really?"

"What? Charlie's a lovely man."

I pushed myself upright and crossed my arms. "Oh, I know Charlie's wonderful in every way. But he's also a confirmed bachelor. I hope you know that. I don't want any trouble if he breaks your heart. I will never fire the best manager a farm owner could have just because my mom got in the way."

"Well, I guess I know where I stand," she said. "Behind the farm staff and probably the swine, too."

I sighed. "On the bright side, Charlie will give you an alibi and you'll have witnesses at The Tipsy Grape, too. What time did you go home? I'm guessing the murder took place around two or three in the morning." I looked at Asher and he nodded. "Did Charlie see you home?"

She pressed her lips together. "He did, yes. Around midnight. I think it's fair to say that a woman of my age would retire for a good night's sleep at that point. Particularly after a tiresome trip."

"Tiresome? What part of a free ride to Disneyland is tiresome?" Poppy asked.

My hand shot up again. "Another red herring. Don't take the bait." I never took my eyes off Mom, noting her eyes darted to Asher again and again, perhaps seeking rescue. "Yes, that is totally fair to say, Mom. But is it true? Did you stay home after Charlie dropped you off?"

Again she squirmed on the stool, and this time she almost slid off. Violet jumped up from her seat at the kitchen table and braced her. Six kids meant someone was always ready to prop you up.

"Yes," she said at last. "I stayed home after that. Chief Harper will need to settle for my word on that."

I continued to stare at her. "What else aren't you telling us? Did Charlie stay over?"

She blinked rapidly. "No. Charles and I are just dating. He's a godsend, really. So many men want to get serious right away. At my age, they're looking for a caretaker."

"Good luck with that," Poppy said, with a snort of laughter. Mom had never been much of a caretaker. That job had fallen on Daisy.

Mom spun on the stool and faced Poppy. "Poppy, you should try dating. You'd be surprised how many lovely men there are in Clover Grove. I've been having such fun lately."

"There are others?" Iris asked. Like Poppy, and even Violet, she'd had trouble finding good men in Clover Grove. Or maybe our upbringing just made relationships difficult.

"It's called a rotation," Mom said. "I learned about it online. You find several prospects and enjoy dating them all. No one gets serious, no one gets hurt. Honestly, I've wanted to tell you about this, girls, because I think it would be wonderful for all of you. You're not spring chickens anymore, so marriage is probably off the table. Why not just have fun?"

A silence fell over the kitchen like a black drop cloth. None of us wanted to think marriage and family were off the table and Mom had hit too close to home. She'd trumped me in her game and she knew it. Hopping off the stool, she headed for the door. Swaggered, actually.

Asher's eyes rose from the floor and he shook his head. "I did not want to know about this."

I shrugged. "We'd have heard about Mom's rotational dating eventually. I'm surprised we haven't already."

"Asher," Mom called from the front door. "I'll take a ride home please. You need to go back to the farm and keep an eye on Kellan Harper. I think he's out to get Ivy."

Daisy looked up from scouring lipstick off the white mug and smiled for the first time. "I hope so," she said. "He's a good man. But no match for Dahlia Galloway, I'm afraid."

Asher shook his head and turned to go. "Don't underestimate the chief. He likes a challenge and her sordid love life won't repulse him like it does us."

Poppy was the first to laugh but we all joined in.

"That noise is at my expense, I'm sure." Mom's voice faded as she stepped outside. "But I'll have the last laugh. Count on that."

CHAPTER TEN

The long white Flordale van carried us all into town that afternoon. Ben Miller took the wheel and it was a relief not to be jolting around in my truck for a change. Keats perched on my lap, after outright refusing to get in the back with the others. He was blocking my view but I didn't really need to see my hometown to navigate around. Much had changed but the layout was the same.

Once we'd parked, I jumped out and rolled open the side panel to release my guests. "Listen up," I said. "We need to stick together today. I practically had to beg the police chief to let us off the property at all. He finally accepted my assurance you'd act like ducklings and follow me closely."

The description was apt, because they hopped out of the truck one by one and gathered around me looking a little dazed. That was no doubt partly due to the lingering impact of Jilly's mimosas and a high starch lunch that included several desserts from Mandy McCain, the superb baker who now ran the Clover Grove Country Store. Mandy delivered to the inn now, which saved me a trip I didn't want or need.

Pulling me aside, Jilly leaned in and whispered, "You owe me for babysitting, my friend."

"I owe you for so much more than that," I whispered back. "I hope I can get you on the payroll soon. Not that I could ever afford what you're worth."

She grinned at me. "Especially when you factor in the murders. I want danger pay."

I looked from her to Keats and back. "Speaking of murder, I want to circulate and ask a few questions. Can I count on you two to keep everyone together while I take a moment to chat to the guests?"

Jilly nodded and Keats offered a swish of his tail. "Work fast," Jilly said. "Because the carbs will wear off and they'll get harder to herd."

"Understood." Turning back to the crowd, I said, "Welcome to Clover Grove. I used to be embarrassed by this town, but after ten years in Boston it was a relief to come home. Right now, it's in transition from average and boring to quaint and charming." I pointed from an old gas station that hadn't changed in decades, to the cutest little knitting store called Needles in a Haystack. "It'll take a few more years to transform fully, but in the meantime, there's plenty to see."

"I can't wait," Paulette said. "I'm hoping to find a few gifts for my family."

"Have I got stores for you," I said, letting Keats gently separate her from the rest of the flock as we started walking along the sidewalk on Main Street. When we were far enough ahead, he circled back and blocked the others from catching up, giving me a moment of privacy with Paulette.

"How are you doing?" I asked her. "I know what happened to Wilf hit you hard. You've been his assistant for three years."

"Yes, but just between us, Ivy, he was the most difficult boss I ever had." She shook her head slowly. "Not that I wished him ill, but I suppose a change in the office won't go amiss. After you left, there was no buffer. Things were tense."

"I'm sorry to hear that, but glad I was missed by someone," I said. "After ten years, it hurt when the door hit me on the way out."

"I definitely missed you," she said, smiling. "Honestly, I think Wilf did, too. Things seemed to unravel fast and he got... erratic. It felt like the senior VPs were breathing down our necks. They kept asking for briefings and showing up unexpectedly."

"Huh. That's odd. They never paid that much attention to the HR department before. What changed?"

"I hate to speak ill of the dead, but I think Wilf lost their trust after you left. People really respected you."

"That's kind of you to say, Paulette. I honestly felt no one noticed me."

"If they didn't notice you before, they noticed after you left," she said. "Because work didn't go smoothly anymore. It became very clear who'd kept that department running. I don't think Wilf had a clue how much you covered his butt until it was hanging out in the breeze."

I couldn't help laughing at the image. Paulette had always been the soul of professional discretion. Jilly's mimosas must still be lingering in her bloodstream, which meant I should push on. "He did seem more extreme," I said. "I wasn't sure what to make of it."

She leaned in and whispered. "Stress. He split from his wife and she was taking him to the cleaners. I really didn't blame her after— Well, I shouldn't speculate."

Her discretion had kicked back in at the most inconvenient time. "After what? Was Wilf having an affair, Paulette? I admit I had my suspicions."

She gave a single, quick nod. "There were expenses that didn't reconcile. The odd text I happened to see over his shoulder. But he was super secretive about it so I figured it might be someone on the team." She gave me an apologetic look.

"Paulette, please don't say you thought it was me!"

She laughed. "Just for a little while, and only because he kind of fell apart after you left. I thought you might have been forced to leave because of an affair and that his heart might be broken."

"First, I'm not sure he had a heart." I glanced at her. "Sorry to be so blunt, but I need to be very clear, Paulette: I would have preferred kissing one of my crabby donkeys to Wilf Darby."

She laughed even harder, and that was enough for Ben Miller to push past Keats and join us. "The fun's obviously up here," he said. "Everyone else is so glum." He seemed to catch himself and added, "For obvious reasons."

I glanced back and saw that Jilly was circling the others with Keats' help. She was almost as good at herding as he was, and she needed to be because Nellie kept trying to break away.

"Everyone's in shock," I said, staring up at Ben. "Plus I'm sure no one slept well."

"I slept like a rock," he said, scanning the street. The sidewalks were still busy with foot traffic. At this time of year, people started stocking up like squirrels gathering nuts for winter. "I guess the stress of that dinner knocked me right out."

"Me too," Paulette said. "You and Jilly went to such lengths to make us feel comfortable and special and Wilf was so embarrassing."

"It's okay," I said. "You know he's embarrassed me plenty before. I slept well, too—at least till about four. I'm surprised I didn't hear a thing after lights out. How about you guys?"

"Nothing," Ben said. "Not even the Corvette roaring around and hitting your truck."

"That was weird," I said. "Where do you think he was trying to go?"

"Home to Boston?" Paulette suggested.

"In his pajamas?" I asked. "Without his things? I can't believe he'd leave his laptop behind."

Ben shrugged. "I've never seen him so drunk, and I've seen him drunk plenty of times. Especially lately."

"Why lately?" I asked.

Ben hesitated and glanced at Paulette. She gave him a nod and he continued. "After you left, the crap hit the fan, Ivy. Senior management was fed up with him, or so I heard. You were next in line to be promoted and all your knowledge was suddenly gone." He shrugged his broad shoulders. "I half wondered if Wilf had finally messed up enough to get axed."

"Ben," Paulette said, softly.

"Not literally." He looked startled. "Just professionally. I wouldn't wish what happened to Wilf on anyone, but I won't pretend that working with him was easy. He was a bully."

"That he was," I said. "Especially to you. I think he was threatened."

"Threatened?" Ben's eyes widened. "I was just a recruiter. So far beneath him."

I looked up at him and grinned. "You're not beneath anyone, Ben Miller. On top of being very good at your job, you're tall, handsome and well-liked. That's threatening to a guy like Wilf."

A flush crept over Ben's collar and soon his face was red. I didn't recall seeing him blush before, but he had never gotten enough positive reinforcement. Wilf watered his professional garden with vinegar so that nothing could grow.

"Thanks, Ivy," he said. "You don't know how much it means to hear you say that. I just wanted to do a good job, and Wilf made it so difficult. He belittled me constantly, even at meetings. I actually started to doubt myself."

Anger squatted heavily on my chest. My eyes fell to Keats and I saw his hackles had risen at the same time. He couldn't know that it wasn't a real threat—that I was just furious at Wilf for breaking the spirit of so many good people, including mine. Finally I said, "Ben, you, Paulette and Keri were my very best hires. I was so proud of all of you. Don't you dare let anyone erode your confidence."

I stopped speaking suddenly, noticing that Nellie had managed to slip away from Jilly and was close on our heels. Was she eavesdropping on us? I hoped she hadn't heard me praising my favorites, because our road together hadn't been easy. I'd have to make time to bolster her confidence, too. It sounded like everyone needed a shot of joy.

Ben stood a little straighter, casting a long shadow on the sidewalk. "Ivy, you were always so kind. We missed you. A lot."

"That's so nice to hear, but I'm sure Keri is doing a great job. She's very capable."

"Did I hear my name?" Keri said, falling in step with us, as Jilly managed to reclaim Nellie.

I nodded, smiling. "I was just saying that you, Ben and Paulette were my best hires. As hard as all this is, I know you're going to bounce back and flourish."

Keri's serious brown eyes filled with tears. "I've done my best, Ivy, but I couldn't fill your shoes. Wilf told me so every day." She pulled a tissue out of her pocket and patted her eyes. "I wondered if I was going to end up in the next round of cuts."

"Me too," Ben said.

Paulette pressed her lips together and looked down. She knew too many of Wilf's secrets to be let go. In fact, she probably had dirt on a lot of people in the company. With Wilf gone, they'd no doubt retire her before long with a very generous package.

Keats circled and gently urged us back to Jilly, who looked frazzled. Her hair had been in a neat twist earlier, but loose frizzy tendrils flew around her face now. Neal was crowding in too close to her. Meanwhile, Nellie, Kate and Macy had forged on ahead despite Jilly's efforts to keep them together.

"Ladies," I called after them. "Ducklings, remember?"

Nellie called back, "The only thing that helps when I'm stressed is to spend money. Please tell me this sad little town has something to offer."

I gestured to Keats. "Bring them in, buddy. No wandering allowed."

His ears came forward and his posture changed. Sinking closer to the pavement, he rushed toward them, circling a large planter filled with fall flowers and emerging a few yards ahead of the women. In typical sheepdog style, he cut a wide arc and then pressed them back with his presence and confidence.

"Get away from me, you scraggly mutt," Nellie said, trying to duck around him. In her stilettos and tight short skirt, she couldn't compete with Keats' smooth moves. He used his signature figure eight to bring her together with Kate, and then repeated it to unite Macy with them. They stood bunched and motionless on the sidewalk, unsure what to do.

"Ivy," Nellie said, turning on the spot. "Call off your dog. This is not my idea of the grand tour."

"It's not what I had in mind, either, Nellie," I said. "But we're making the best of it, and that means staying together all the time. Keats and I are just following Chief Harper's orders."

Jilly snickered beside me and whispered, "As if."

"It's true," I said, grinning at her. "I mean, basically."

"Interrogating people is following Chief Hottie's orders?" she whispered.

"That was just some idle chitchat with old pals," I said. "And I'm done for now."

Turning, I saw Keats was staring from one woman to the other. He was trying to mesmerize them with his gaze in typical sheepdog fashion, and it appeared to be working. All of them were frozen on the spot like lambs.

"Leave it, Keats," I said, snapping my fingers. "Ladies, start your engines. We're going into my favorite store in Clover Grove."

Teri Mason looked up from her laptop when the bell rang as we walked into Hill Country Designs. Her hair was streaked in vibrant colors that conveyed both her love of art and her independent spirit. We'd hit it off right away and were well on the way to becoming friends. It didn't hurt that she found Keats so compelling she'd asked to paint his portrait. She'd taken some photos of him in front of the barn at Runaway Farm and promised to have the painting installed over my mantel before the next group of guests arrived.

Since there was no one else booked, she'd cleverly given herself a generous deadline.

"Welcome," she said, coming to greet the crowd. "You must be the Flordale staff. Ivy's told me so much about you, and it's an honor to welcome you to my store."

I could tell by the way Teri's normally fixed smile flashed on and off that she'd heard about Wilf. Of course she had. The Clover Grove grapevine would be on fire with the news, especially with both my mother and I included as possible suspects. It was like Christmas in October for our gossip-loving community.

"Teri, I need your help," I said. "These ladies have credit cards screaming for action. Could you hook them up with some quality hill country souvenirs to remind them of their stay?"

"Like we could ever forget it," Nellie muttered. "I'll have nightmares forever."

Teri scanned Nellie from her immaculately straightened hair to her deathtrap shoes, and finally her smile stayed on. "I love your style," she said. "I have a one-of-a-kind pendant I've never put on display because no one in Clover Grove could pull it off."

"Flattery will get you nowhere," Nellie said, rolling her eyes. "But I'll take a look at this rare piece and decide if it makes the grade for Boston."

All the Flordale women crowded around the display case to see what Teri had to offer, while Neal and Ben roamed around the store looking uncomfortable.

"This feels like an art gallery," Neal said. "It gives me the creeps. Is there a sports bar around where we could wait for you?"

I shook my head. "Keeping the herd together, right? But as soon as we're done here, I promise we'll sit down for a drink."

"My testosterone might be gone by then," Neal said, grumbling as he paced. "This place is a chick store."

"No worries, I have plenty for both of us," Ben said, giving Neal a playful shove.

"Big isn't better, buddy," Neal said, faking a punch to Ben's gut.

"Careful of the art, guys," I said, although I was relieved to see them starting to joke around as they used to when we worked together.

Not that I missed those days one bit. It would take a lot more than two deaths on my property to make me regret my move to Runaway Farm. My eyes drifted to Jilly, who'd perched on a bench by the window with Keats by her side. We'd get through this together, just like she said. But I couldn't deny that a murder hit you harder when you knew the victim well. Wilf was no saint but he'd been part of my life for years. A whole lot of hot air just got sucked out of the world and it was impossible not to feel the vacuum.

At least, for me. My female colleagues, on the other hand, were kibitzing as they argued over Teri's trinkets. I'd never heard Macy and Kate talk so much, and for once they were on opposing sides. Ultimately, everyone left with something, and most with multiple items. It made me happy to help a friend and the local economy.

Their credit cards got another workout at Miniature Mutts up the street. Although none of the women seemed to be pet lovers, they had friends or family who were, so there was a great deal of cooing over Mabel's tiny hand-painted dogs, cats and farm animals.

Ben and Neal wilted further, until I had to call it quits on the shopping. I promised the women we'd return as soon as Kellan gave us more freedom.

Outside, people started scattering again and I got Keats to round them up so we could take a break at the Berry Good Café, one of the more popular spots in town. Since the day was bright and unseasonably warm, we sat outside on the patio. Keats took his place to my left, like a black-and-white statue, staring around with his eerie blue eye as people ordered tea, coffee, scones and other treats.

"You promised a drink, not a tea party," Neal said, tapping his fingers on the table.

"I figured we'd all done enough day drinking," I said, lumping myself in, although I'd steered well clear of Jilly's mimosas. "Some caffeine will revive everyone. It's been quite a day."

"Thanks for trying to make it a little better," Ben said, giving me a warm smile. "I think I can speak for all of us in saying we missed you."

There was a murmur of dissent somewhere down the table, where Nellie sat with the Raptors, Kate and Macy.

I gave them an HR-approved smile and said, "Well, our department was like family to me for years." If piranhas could be family. Some of these corporate fish could pick a corpse bare in two minutes. But they weren't in a corporate setting now and already they were starting to seem like run-of-the-mill goldfish. Clover Grove—or murder—had mellowed them.

Keri mirrored my smile. "Although we've missed you, it's clear you did the right thing. You've created a wonderful new life for yourself. I mean, except for... Well, you know."

The waiter arrived with a tinkling tray and we fell silent as he put cups and plates in front of us. After he left, I poured tea into my mug and then raised it.

"Let's take a moment and pay tribute to Wilf. Maybe we can each share something good about him." The silence continued, so I said, "For example, he never rewrote my slide decks. I really appreciated that."

"I'll go next," Paulette said. "He always gave me flowers on Secretaries Day."

Keri looked as if she were digging deep but finally spit out, "He didn't dock me for sick days when I got that nasty virus during a business trip."

"He let me have the last turkey sandwich in the cafeteria once," Macy said.

"I got to take an extra long lunch on my birthday and only make up half the time," Kate said.

Nellie raised her hand. "Once he complimented me for getting back to my desk so fast after a fire alarm, especially in heels. I think the stairs almost killed him."

"Nellie!" Paulette sounded horrified.

"What? I didn't mean it that way. Do we have to watch every word now?"

"Yes," Keri said, simply. "Every word."

"My turn," Neal said. "I'm grateful Wilf didn't fire me. Even though he threatened to pretty much weekly."

"Weekly?" Ben said, with a bitter laugh. "It was daily for me."

"Aw, guys, that was just his way," Keri said. "You know he threatened me with the same thing just last night. I'm sure he wouldn't have followed through."

"I always took him seriously," Ben said. "Every day I went home and counted my blessings that I was still on the payroll."

"He was all bark, really," Keri said. She twisted her serviette, visibly upset that her staff was so stressed.

"Except when he actually bit," Nellie called down the long table. She was carefully scraping all the icing off a cupcake and piling it on the plate. I never understood that. Wasn't icing the whole purpose of a cupcake? "Let's be a bit more sensitive to Ivy. He only threatened us, but he actually fired her."

Everyone froze. Spoons stopped clinking and china stopped rattling. A heavy silence hung over the table as Nellie continued stripping her cupcake.

"It's okay," I said, quickly, as Keats crawled under the table to sit on my feet. "I don't know what you heard, but I had my letter of resignation ready. That's why my desk had been cleared out even before Wilf let me go. I'd hoped to make a graceful exit, but after what happened with Keats, I never got the chance."

"Wilf burned you with that package," Neal said. "It took some guts for him to come here and face you, I bet."

I shrugged. "He didn't seem fazed, did he? I guess he wanted to let bygones be bygones, just like I did."

Neal stared at me over the rim of his mug. His nose was pointy and his eyes a swampy sort of green. "He stiffed you for what... a couple hundred grand? Not to mention pride. I bet that still smarts, but you always had a good poker face, Ivy."

I summoned that very poker face now. "Maybe that's why they called me the grim reaper."

Ben glared at Neal. "I don't know what you're getting at, but I'd just like to say that Ivy was great to me at Flordale, and probably to all of you, too."

"We're all on edge," Paulette said. "But there's no reason to make insinuations, Neal, if that's what you're doing. It's disrespectful."

"Well, *someone* killed Wilf," he said. "At the moment, everyone's a suspect, and from where I sit, Ivy had the most motivation. Maybe she set her mom up to help."

Jilly slapped her hand on the table hard enough to make the china and cutlery rattle. "How dare you, Neal Fife? Ivy's my best friend and she's incapable of killing so much as a fly."

"Oh, I kill flies," I said. "The ones that bite. But thanks, Jilly."

Lifting her hand off the table, Jilly signalled me to pipe down, and then continued her attack on Neal. "I suggest you stop throwing accusations around, because your reputation isn't spotless, Neal, is it?"

He set his mug down so clumsily that coffee sloshed over the rim. "How do you know that?"

"Headhunter grapevine. And you just confirmed it with your reaction."

"What did he do?" Keri asked. "I'm head of HR at Flordale. I should know."

"I'm afraid I can't divulge that information," Jilly said. "Just like I can't divulge what I know about anyone else."

I figured Jilly was bluffing to divert their focus from me. She'd certainly grabbed my interest and everyone else's.

"Whatever," Neal said, flicking his fingers at Jilly as if she were one of the biting flies. "You gave up a sweet job to slave in the kitchen. Steve is running your firm now."

She gave him a cold smile. "My name's still on the masthead and my reputation is still on the line. So don't worry, I'm not sharing stories from the headhunter grapevine. But it's worth noting that most people at this table probably have something to hide."

The mumbled protests grew, and I had to raise my voice to be heard. "I highly doubt any of you had a big enough grudge against Wilf to want him gone. And I had nothing at all to gain from it. So let's just put all that aside right now and have some fun, okay?"

"Fun?" Kate said, picking up her spoon and clinking it around in her cup. "Here? This place is dead."

There was a long awkward pause and then Ben started laughing. The rest of us followed.

Kate's thin face flushed and she said, "I didn't mean it like that."

"You know what?" I said. "I've changed my mind. More day drinking is exactly what's needed. Let's stop to refuel on the way home."

CHAPTER ELEVEN

E dna Evans had a permanent pucker that probably predated my arrival on earth. I remembered it from her visits as a school nurse to administer vaccinations with far too much glee. It seemed to be the only time her lips unfurled to permit a small smile. When she had to chase kids down—as she always did my brother— she let loose a wild cackle that many of us probably still heard in nightmares.

When I arrived at her house the next morning, the smile and the cackle were locked away and the pucker deepened as my closest neighbor, a shameless snoop, stared down at Keats. He sat by my feet with his tail wrapped neatly around his paws, white tuft on display.

"Again?" Edna said. "We talked about this weeks ago, Ivy Galloway. No vermin in my house."

"Miss Evans, this dog saved my life a few weeks ago and he might very well have saved yours. It's anyone's guess who the killer may have come after next."

"I'd like to see someone try," she said, resting her hands on the hips of a yellowed, old nursing uniform. "I'm not easy to kill. I can't tell you how many nasty infections I caught from you kids at school."

"Well, I suppose the murderer wouldn't have threatened you," I said. "You were friends, after all."

"Friends! That is slanderous overstatement." Her fingers twitched as if she'd like to slap me. "We'd crossed paths over the years, of course. It's a small town. But we were never close."

Kicking off my boots, I invited myself into the living room and took a seat on an overstuffed chair. Keats took his post at my left, sitting as erect as he possibly could, ears forward, nose twitching. He was taking Edna's moral temperature, and judging by the way his ears flattened, he didn't like the results.

She was equally unimpressed by him. Her lips looked as if someone had stitched them up and pulled too tight on the thread.

"I heard you went to school with Lloyd Boyce's killer," I said. I avoided speaking the name aloud, partly because "killer" made more of an impact and partly because mentioning the incident still made me flinch. I wanted to stay composed, because Edna played a good game—especially for someone close to 80. "Plus you had a standing bridge night and were in the sheepdog herding club. That sounds pretty friendly to me."

"I can see that it would given you're an outsider, Ivy. We do things differently in Clover Grove. It's quite possible to attend social gatherings together without linking arms and skipping like girls in the schoolyard."

Now *my* lips puckered as I tried to hold in a laugh at the idea of Edna and Lloyd's killer skipping today.

She took a seat in her recliner and pushed it back with a clunk. "I don't see anything funny about this, Ivy. You brought a very warped sense of humor home from Boston."

"Thank goodness I've kept any humor at all given what's been happening." I rested my fingers on the soft fur between Keats' ears, which always had a powerful grounding effect on me. "Edna, let me be frank. The killer told me you two were in cahoots together. That you provided information, in fact, that nearly got Keats and me killed."

Keats let out a little whine. I could tell from the angle of his head that he was pinning Edna with his eerie blue eye.

The stare didn't faze Edna one bit. "Oh, don't be dramatic," she said, waving a gnarled hand. "I'm sure you'd have thrashed your way out of that situation just fine without the help of that dog. You Galloways are like vermin yourself, come to think of it. Very hard to keep down."

This time my laugh escaped. "Why thank you, Miss Evans. That's quite a compliment. I'll be sure to pass it along to my mother."

"You do that. I never had much respect for Dahlia, although she was a very pretty girl. She could have done so much better than the deadbeat she married. After churning out six kids, she hadn't a particle of sense left in her head."

"Now who's being dramatic?" I said, although I couldn't really argue the point. My father was a deadbeat whose departure left Mom permanently rattled. "We did just fine, in no small measure due to your excellent nursing care at school."

She prepared to fire back, but her lips hung slack for a moment as she searched for the pill in the jam. "I wasn't born yesterday, Ivy. Obviously you want something from me, so you'd best spit it out. My standing bridge game is in an hour."

I moved to the edge of my chair, which wasn't easy since the puffy cushions were like quicksand. "I do, actually. Since you keep such a sharp eye and ear on the community, I'd like to know if you noticed anything amiss on my property the night before last."

The pucker loosened as she gave a sly grin. She knew something. Edna regularly spied on Runaway Farm with binoculars. That annoyed me, but it had also given me a valuable lead on the previous murder. The police told her to desist but I suspected she hadn't. Why would she give up her fun?

"Possibly," she said. "It's hard to know what's normal and what's not at Runaway Farm. There's always something going on."

"It's a busy place, yes. Especially with my first guests in residence."

She crossed her fuzzy slippers and snorted. "I saw that chubby man—the one who died—trying to climb in with the alpaca. You flapped around so much I thought you'd lift off."

"Wilfred Darby," I said. "My old boss. I'm trying to figure out how he died, Miss Evans. The County's pinned it on my cows."

"Oh, the County. That bunch of fools." She plucked at something on the arm of her recliner. "But I guess they're aware you don't know a cow from a sow, Ivy, and both have ravaged my garden to the point where I might well starve."

"I am sorry about that. Charlie has new protocols in place and so far, so good." I pushed out of the chair and stood with my arms crossed. "I sense you know something, Miss Evans."

Giving a little shrug, she pushed the chair upright and stood, too. All the better to see my reaction, I suspected. "Well, I know Dahlia made rash threats and she's first in the perp lineup."

"The perp lineup?" I nearly laughed again. Giddiness was always lurking around the corner today, waiting to take me over. "You know my mom isn't capable of killing Wilf Darby."

"She would have needed help from someone with brains, I'll grant you that. But you're one sharp cookie, Ivy. Perhaps you worked together to make it happen."

"To what end, Miss Evans? I love my farm and inn. How would killing off a guest help me?"

"I don't know. Insurance scam, maybe? Or just the satisfaction of ridding the world of one nasty man."

"He was that. But he didn't deserve to die in my barn. So please tell me what you saw."

"How could I see anything? It was the middle of the night and I need my beauty sleep, Ivy."

"I'm sure you have information of value to me. It's written all over your well-rested face."

The little grin was back. "Oh? Well, first let's chat about what you can do for me."

She had some nerve asking me for anything after implicating my sister in Lloyd Boyce's murder. No doubt she'd slandered us far and wide to divert attention from her own actions. But there was no denying she held the cards here. I had nothing at all to go on with this case.

"Tell me how I can help you, Miss Evans," I said, offering my sweetest smile. It wasn't that sweet, I knew, being rusty from disuse.

"That's better, Ivy. As I've said before, you were the softest of the Galloway hooligans, and the brightest, too. I suspected you'd respond to reason."

I drew on my well-honed negotiation skills from a decade in HR. Time to establish common ground. "Of course, Miss Evans. We both want the same thing: to feel safe in our homes."

"Exactly. I haven't had a moment's peace since you took over Runaway Farm. Or Hannah Pemberton before you, for that matter. At my age, I don't need stress like that."

"How can I ease your stress and restore peace at the border?" I asked.

"For starters, you can take my chickens."

"Chickens!" That was unexpected. But it was only her first demand.

"I don't get enough sleep anymore and that blasted rooster never shuts up. And it's too much upkeep at my age." She crossed her arms. "You'll collect them all and start dropping off fresh eggs. Don't be stingy, now. My award-winning sponge cake requires a dozen yolks."

"Done. I'll send Charlie over to shut down your coop. Is that it?"

She shook her head. "I hear your chef is talented, and while I've always been a good cook myself, I'm too busy for anything fancy these days. So I'll take delivery of gourmet meals on occasion. None of those new-fangled chickpea dishes, though. I can't handle much fiber anymore."

Again laughter threatened to explode and I had to hold my breath for a few seconds. Finally I said, "Gourmet to go. Done. You must have some very good information."

"I think it might be of value to you, yes. And you'll be the first to hear it, since the chief of police hasn't bothered to pay me a visit." She walked over to the big windows facing Runaway Farm. Her house was on a hill and she'd cleared trees to get an unobstructed view of my property. "I guess I'm just a nosy old woman to him."

I joined her at the window. "Whereas to me you're a vigilant neighbor who might help me protect the people and animals I love."

"Don't suck up," she said, turning to give me a cold stare. "It's unnecessary. We struck a deal."

"Believe it or not, I'm being honest," I said. "Now, spill it, Miss Evans. There's a lovely chicken pot pie and apple cheesecake on the menu tonight."

After milking the moment a little longer, she turned to a cedar chest in the corner and lifted the heavy lid. "No judgement, Ivy," she warned, pulling out a pair of goggles.

"Are those night vision goggles?" I asked. "You're sitting up all night spying on me now?"

"I said no judgement."

"*After* we struck the deal. Sorry, but I'm totally judging. I deserve privacy, too."

She put the goggles back in the chest and crossed her arms again. "You can't have it both ways, so get off your high horse. With two murders on your property in a month, I have every right to look out for myself. You make Hannah Pemberton and her circus look like a Sunday church service."

"Fine," I said, mirroring her pose. "Tell me."

"No guarantees, but I may have insight into what happened with your boss."

"Former boss," I corrected. "I left Flordale months ago."

"You'll go back." She lifted her chin and sniffed. "You still smell like city under that stench of manure."

I gritted my teeth. She was relentless in trying to get a rise out of me and if I didn't move things along she'd be successful, too. "Miss Evans, how do you stay so chipper when you're up all night spying?"

"I hydrate," she said. "And I gave up indulgences years ago. You should try it, Ivy. You look older than Daisy now. How do you expect to land a handsome man like Chief Harper if you let yourself go?"

Jilly's advice surfaced at the right time and I counted to seven as I drew in my next breath. "Let's exchange beauty tips when I deliver your dinner. Right now, we'll stick to the story. So... you were up that night at around two a.m., I assume? What woke you?"

She ended her game of cat and mouse. "I heard that loud sports car roaring and got up to take a look. The car's lights were on at first and I saw it doing circles in front of your barn."

"Then what happened?"

"Someone jumped in front of the car waving their arms and the car stopped. The door opened and I saw your boss get out of the car. It was quite a production because he was clearly drunk and his bathrobe got stuck. The other man came over to help free him and they struggled for a bit."

"You saw the other man?" I asked.

"Oh yes. The car lights went on and off and I had to switch back and forth between regular binoculars and night vision goggles. Either way, it was hard to miss the other man. He's a veritable giant.

I saw him with you in town yesterday. Six foot six by the looks of it."

"Ben?" I couldn't hide my shock. "He was with Wilf?"

"Don't make me repeat myself, Ivy, or I'll miss my bridge game." She walked to the front hall and collected her jacket. "The giant got Wilf out of the car and probably saved lives for it, so I wouldn't be too hard on him if he lied to you about it. Then he and the other man tried to get your boss back to the house. It was like a crazy dance, and pudgy as he was, your boss outmaneuvered them both and ran to the barn."

"There were *three* men?"

"I can count, Ivy," she said, pulling out a black patent leather purse that looked straight out of the 60s. "I still have my faculties."

"No question there, Miss Evans," I said. "What happened next?"

"The smaller of the two men threw up his hands and left the circle of light. I assume he went back to the house but I kept my eyes on the real action, which was the giant man grappling with your boss outside the barn. I've always enjoyed wrestling, you know, even though it's mostly theater. There's something about the costumes that—"

"Miss Evans?" I grabbed her sleeve. "What happened then?"

She stared at my hand until I released her sleeve, then continued. "Your boss slipped out of the giant's grasp like a greased pig and literally rolled into the barn. His robe must have been a mess."

"It was, actually. I saw that myself."

Her eyes sharpened. "You found the body?"

"Keats did. But I saw enough."

Settling a broadbrimmed hat on her gray curls, she kicked off her slippers and replaced them with sensible slip-on shoes. "I don't know what happened in the barn, obviously. I watched for a long time and didn't see them come out. Doesn't mean they didn't, of course. You have a back door, too, as I recall."

She slipped the handles of her purse over her shoulder and reached for the doorknob. I stepped in front to block her. "Did you happen to hear anything?"

"Well, I could only hear things if I went outside, and that would be foolish, wouldn't it?"

I stared at her. "A calculated risk. They were too caught up to sense you watching from afar."

"True. Which is why I *did* stick my head out the back door. And to answer your question, I could hear yelling."

"How many voices?"

"I have goggles, Ivy, not a microphone. There were two men for sure." She gave an exaggerated shudder. "Honestly, Ivy, you've brought some frightening people into our community. It's almost enough to make me move."

"But then you'd miss the gourmet meals," I said, managing a smile.

"I haven't tasted them yet. I'll be the judge of whether it's worth risking my life here."

She gave me a sharp jab in the ribs and I stepped back. Keats moved into the small space between us. This time there was no question he was giving her a heavy dose of his blue eye.

"It's okay, buddy," I said.

Shaking her finger at the dog, she said, "You'll have to do worse to scare me, sheepdog. Now, outside, both of you."

"But—"

She shoved me out the door and onto the front porch, and shut the door behind her. "I can't do all your work for you, Ivy. Go into town and figure out why your boss came to Clover Grove a day early in his mid-life crisis car. He didn't seem to care who saw him."

"He was here early? Where?" I asked, following her down the stairs.

"At the Summit Hotel, among other places," she called over her shoulder. "I've never liked the owner, Chantelle. She acts like she's special because her mom was French. The accent is fake and pathetic."

"Miss Evans," I called after her. "Let me drive you to town so we can talk a bit longer."

She turned and then gave that cackle that still haunted me. "I've seen how you drive, Ivy. I'd rather take my chances on the bus or even hitchhiking." She tapped her head. "I have a nice long hairpin if someone gets fresh."

"But I—"

"Social interaction keeps people my age alive," she called back. "And bridge waits for no woman."

Only as she rounded a curve in the lane did I realize she'd put me out of her house without my boots.

CHAPTER TWELVE

Edna had vanished by the time I drove to the end of her driveway. I had no idea if she'd truly hitched a ride on the highway, was hiding in the bushes to avoid surrendering my boots, or more likely still, had hopped onto a broom and flown into town.

Luckily, I didn't have far to drive because the pedals felt strange under my socks and my gear-shifting deteriorated even more. I stalled twice in the relatively short expanse between her driveway and mine. It was particularly unnerving because there was a long curve in the road. If any of the town's crazy teens came hurtling around too fast, they'd be flossing my fender out of their teeth.

"Seriously, Keats, I think that old witch cursed me," I said, turning the key in the ignition yet again. "Did you see that creepy little grin? She knew full well she was evicting me bootless."

He turned his blue eye on me as I started the truck again.

"Don't give me that look. I was flustered, okay? I can handle most people and you know it. Edna gets under my skin. Maybe that's because my actual skin is still scarred from the vaccines she gave me as a kid. If you saw her coming at you with a needle, you'd be traumatized, too."

If border collies had shoulders, he'd have shrugged. Instead he mumbled something that sounded quite judgy.

"Oh, please. You're not such a big guy at the vet's, are you? You tried to claw your way off the table when the rabies shot came out." I couldn't help chuckling. "That reminds me of the time Edna hauled Asher out from under the gym bleachers by his feet and dragged him on his back down the hallway kicking like a feral cat. The woman is fearless—even about public opinion. Off she goes to play bridge when everyone knows she helped a murderer. Can you believe that?"

Keats' grumble turned into a whine. It was louder than his usual commentary. He was trying to tell me something.

"I know, I know. I can't stall again and risk injuring someone. Plus the truck is already a mess thanks to Wilf's drunken joyride."

Bracing one white paw on the dashboard, Keats turned to look behind us and whined again. This time there was a note of urgency.

"I'm going, I'm going." I got the truck in gear, finally finding the right balance between gas and clutch with my socked feet. The truck moved along briskly for about 20 yards, during which Keats continued to mumble what sounded like a warning. He was still looking over his shoulder, so I glanced in the rearview mirror myself.

Flashing lights had swept around the bend and the police SUV was gaining on me steadily. The siren gave one bleep, telling me to pull over.

"Oh, for pity's sake," I said. "Can I not catch a break today?"

My foot slipped off the gas and I stalled yet again. The police car braked behind me, lights still flashing. I took a deep breath, and then another and turned the key in the ignition. "I can do this. I can do this."

Amazingly, I *did* do it. The truck took a telling and let me glide smoothly off the highway and onto the small gravel road that led to a farmer's field. I managed to put the truck in park and turn it off before it died on me. That gave me just enough dignity to roll down the window coolly. I'd hoped to see my brother in the side mirror—or any of the other 10 officers in the Clover Grove police department. But no. Of course not. It had to be Kellan Harper.

"Hello, Chief," I said, with feigned nonchalance. I dug deep for my old HR blandness and slapped a businesslike smile on my face. "What can we do for you today?"

He peered into the truck at Keats. "Well, the dog can't do a thing for me. But you could do me a huge favor and stay off the road till you learn to handle that vehicle. You stalled four times."

"Three," I said, realizing it was ridiculous to argue that embarrassing point. Keats offered a mumble of disgust, which I ignored. Acknowledging the dog's contributions always rubbed Kellan the wrong way. Long ago when we were seeing each other, I was just a typical teenage girl. Or at least I was better able to hide my quirks. Now they were on display so frequently that it probably gave Kellan mental whiplash.

"It's a safety hazard, Ivy. You could hurt someone—including Keats, who shouldn't be riding shotgun by the way. Aren't dogs supposed to be in crates, or at least wearing a seatbelt?"

"Probably. Not a bad idea, actually." I glanced at Keats, who was staring at me full on. He gave a sharp yip of protest. "He wouldn't like that very much."

"Get out of the truck," Kellan said. "I'll drive you home and walk back here. We need to see about getting you a car with an automatic transmission, at least until you get the hang of this."

I wondered who "we" meant. Kellan and me? Or Kellan and Asher? Or the County road safety committee? I sighed. With all that was going on, I shouldn't be wasting time thinking about the "we" that used to be. At this point each of us had a full plate.

"I'll just slide over," I said. "Keats, get in the back, please."

Kellan opened the door as the dog vacated the passenger seat.

"Don't climb over the gearshift. You could hurt yourself. Just walk around the truck, Ivy."

"I'm good." I swivelled in the seat to try to get my feet into the well of the passenger seat before he could notice that—

"Excuse me? Are you seriously driving without footwear, Ivy?"

I tried hoisting myself over the stick but it was awkward and risky. Eventually I reversed course, clambered onto my knees and crawled over, with my socks—and my butt—practically in Kellan's face. Some clumsy contortions helped me land my plane safely in the passenger seat. By then I was puffing from exertion and humiliation.

Staring straight ahead into the field that was plowed under for winter, I said, "I left my house in boots."

He shook his head. I barely caught the movement but I felt the disapproving breeze. "And where did you lose those boots?"

"In Edna Evans' front hall," I said. "She shoved me out without them and vanished before I could catch up with her on the drive-way. I can only assume she left by broom or teleportation. She was running late for a bridge game."

He slid behind the wheel and started the truck. "We really need to talk."

"I've been doing so much better with my driving."

"If that's better, I'd hate to see worse." He backed out of the gravel road and onto the highway with ease. I had no doubt that he could pilot the big old red tractor behind the barn with equal panache. Or a bulldozer, if the need arose. He didn't even have to think about it. I knew this because he kept turning to give me serious glances with his dark blue eyes, yet the truck hummed along like it recognized its new master.

If he decided I couldn't drive at all right now, I'd really be stuck. I spent half my time running errands for the farm and inn. On top of that, I'd be facing the same shame as my mother at being taken off the road by a cop for public safety. Suddenly, I had more compassion for her.

"I'm a little rattled by the murder," I said. "I mean, the second one. As any normal person would be."

"True. But those people wouldn't be driving a big farm truck with a manual transmission. They'd be home meditating or something."

I couldn't help laughing. "Like that's possible with the Flordale vipers crawling all over."

He passed the lane for Runaway Farm and kept going. "Don't vipers slither?"

"I stand corrected. These people are all legs and on the run. Even Keats has a hard time rounding them up."

"You'd better improve your herding skills or I'll confine them to the property until the murder is solved."

"Don't say that. Or at least say you're close to figuring it out."

He laughed. "Ivy, it's been less than two days. I'm good, but I'm not that good."

Keats gave a yip from the back seat that sounded so much like agreement that Kellan turned quickly to the dog and added, "No one asked you."

"He doesn't wait to be asked." I stared around as we headed for town. "Where are we going? To find a nice, safe sedan?"

"Not today. I have a more peaceful destination in mind."

Just before we reached the town limits, he turned right and headed toward the hills. I sat a little straighter and I didn't have to see Keats to know he was doing the same. A walk in the hills would do wonders for my nerves, and Keats could afford to blow off steam, too. Besides, it would be nice to spend a little time with Kellan alone —even if it was grossly unfair to Jilly to leave her one hour longer than necessary babysitting our guests alone. I told myself she'd be happy that Chief Hottie wanted to spend a little quality time with me.

Finally, Kellan rolled onto another gravel road and down a long lane. The arching sign seemed to be of similar vintage and style to the iron sign at Runaway Farm. This one said *Clover Grove Gardens.*

"I totally forgot about this place," I said. "I haven't seen it since..."

I trailed off. Kellan and I used to ride our bikes over here a lot when we were dating. With an overprotective sister like Daisy, a meddlesome brother like Asher, and three other sisters hanging around, the opportunities to be alone were few and far between. Only on summer evenings when Daisy worked at the grocery store could we steal away to watch the sun go down from this small, quaint County-owned property. More than once we had to climb the fence to get back out after old Mr. Burnside locked the iron gates early.

"You always loved it here." His voice was still clinical—all Chief Harper—but the fact he was taking me down memory lane had to mean something. Keats must have thought so, too, because his white paw landed on my shoulder, perhaps cautioning me not to get my hopes up. Well, I wouldn't. I wasn't that naïve girl anymore. I was a seasoned executive with 10 years experience firing people and breaking their hearts. More recently, I'd seen ugliness and violence. I wasn't likely to fall prey to schoolgirl fantasies anymore. The paw lifted, as if Keats felt his work was done. I knew that if I turned, he'd be giving me a dose of the kinder, warmer brown eye.

"I did," I said, hopping out the minute he stopped the truck. "And it looks like it's been kept up. More or less." Staring around, I realized it looked quite different now. Some of the beds were overgrown with aggressive tiger lilies or various types of chrysanthemums, whereas others were completely barren. But it was autumn, so I couldn't expect the sweet blooms of spring and summer. At least the old stone benches were exactly where they should be.

Kellan got out and came around the front of the truck. "It had gone completely to seed, I'm afraid, but the town struck a committee two years ago to dig the place out. Being next door to Dorset Hills means we have to keep up or die trying."

"It'll take a few years to bring it back to its former glory, I suppose," I said, reaching for the back door.

He pointed to a sign featuring a dog with a big X through it. "No dogs allowed."

"Oh, please," I said. "Keats is not a dog."

"He's a smart dog, no question, but he's definitely in the canine family."

"No one else is here anyway. If someone joins us, I'll put him back in the truck."

"See, the problem with the law is that you have to abide by it even when no one's around," he said. "It's inconvenient, but it does help maintain order."

"I understand you have to take a hard line because you're in uniform. So I'll accept a ticket from you if the need arises." I let the dog out of the truck and he raced around the paths as if he'd been locked up for days. Yet he didn't touch a single plant. "See, he's impeccable."

Keats looked directly at Kellan before cocking his leg on a sundial.

"A perfect gentleman," Kellan said, laughing.

"When a dog's gotta go, he's gotta go. At least he didn't wither the mums."

Kellan led me around the garden, and the grand tour didn't take long. There were small cards sticking out of the soil to indicate where the plants had been earlier in the season. The days were so short now that the sun was already low in the sky.

"Poppy," he said. "There were lots of them this year, just as unruly as your sister." He pointed to another card. "Iris. Quiet, elegant and totally overshadowed by the poppies. And here, we had the sweet yet hardy violet, loved by all for heralding spring." He made a sweeping gesture to tall, multicolored flowers still in bloom. "Outlasting them all, we have the resilient and persistent dahlias, which pretty much dominate everything else. Isn't that something?"

"Very clever, Kellan," I said, laughing. "Very clever indeed." I peered around. "Is there some ivy lurking in a corner cowering under an ash tree?"

"That's exactly what you'd expect of ivy, isn't it? Quiet lurking," he said. "But nowadays, ivy is far less subtle than it used to be. Sometimes it even upstages the dahlias of the garden. It's the new age ivy."

I shook my head, still grinning. "I don't remember you having such a way with words when we were in school."

"People change, I guess." He led me on another lap around the garden, seeming to forget I was only in socks. I didn't complain about the sharp pebbles stinging my feet, either. "We couldn't have imagined then what we'd witness in life. Together and apart."

"No." I sat down abruptly on the stone bench. We used to sit there as teens, our fingers laced together, watching dusk fall and the fireflies magically ignite. "It's shocking, isn't it?"

He nodded. "Clover Grove hadn't seen a murder in years, which is one of the reasons I wanted to come home. And now there have been two, back to back."

"Coincidence or conspiracy?" I was joking, but he turned quickly to stare at me. "Oh, come on, Kellan. You can't think I'm bringing trouble on Clover Grove. The only witch that's cursed me is Edna Evans, who's holding my boots hostage until I deliver gourmet cooking."

He raised his eyebrows. "Food delivery now?"

"It was the only way she'd tell me about—" I stopped abruptly but it was too late.

"I knew it! You were snooping again. Edna's on my list to question but you got to her first."

"Well, she wanted to talk, Kellan. She complained you hadn't been over sooner."

He rubbed his forehead and then ran his hand through his dark hair. "Oh, Ivy, you are a dangerous vine. Tell me what she said and don't spare a word."

Shifting into lotus position, I rubbed my sore feet and shared everything Edna had witnessed on the night of Wilf's murder. "If she's right," I concluded, "Ben lied to me earlier. He said he slept like a rock the entire night."

"Do you believe Edna?" he asked. "Or is she just trying to get free meals out of you?"

"It fit with what we already knew, about Wilf doing donuts in his Corvette. She guessed correctly that his bathrobe must be ripped from getting stuck in the car door. But that doesn't mean Ben killed him, even if he lied about being up with Wilf."

"What can you tell me about Ben? Did he have a beef with Wilf Darby?"

I told him about Wilf's management style, and how Ben had been feeling lately. "Honestly, Kellan, they all had beefs with Wilf, some bigger, some smaller. But if you bully and diminish people enough, someone could eventually blow." I traced a pattern on the stone bench. "I suppose that's what happened to me, in a way. The day I discovered Keats."

The dog came out from under the bench and jumped up beside me, resting his long muzzle on my lap.

"I'll get to the bottom of this," Kellan said. "Just leave the questioning to me."

"But I know them better than you do. I know the hot buttons. Whoever did this must be unhinged, and if you go poking around, the inn could explode from the tension. People already suspect each other, including me."

"I didn't become one of the youngest chiefs of police in the state by blundering around and blowing things up, Ivy. Give me some credit."

"I know, I'm sorry." After a few quiet moments of stroking Keats' ears, I glanced at him. "I'm not really a suspect, am I? I was sound asleep. What kind of alibi can I have?"

He looked like he might string me along but finally shook his head. "You'd have nothing to gain and a lot to lose. And while you're impulsive, you're not unhinged."

"Why thank you. I guess." After a moment, I pressed my luck. "And my mom? Obviously she wasn't wrestling with Ben in the night. Edna would love to implicate her if she could."

Kellan stared over at the flower bed full of dahlias. "I'm afraid I can't rule her out just yet, Ivy. She wasn't exactly truthful about where she was last night when we spoke earlier."

"Where did she *say* she was?"

He turned to glare at me. "I know you guys coached her, and it must have taken a Herculean effort. I've never seen her so subdued. It was like she was medicated." After a pause, he added, "She wasn't, was she?"

"No, we didn't medicate our mother, Kellan, although I kind of wish I'd thought of that." I grinned at him. "Mom says and does some very silly things, as you well know, but she's quirky, not unhinged. You know she can't be corralled, so whatever statement she gave you is all on her."

"Well, it was quite a story. Full of intrigue."

"I know she's dating Charlie, if that's what you're alluding to. And that they met for drinks at The Tipsy Grape last night before she went home to attend to her chores."

"She may well have attended to her chores... after her second date."

"*What?*" Mom had clearly ended things earlier with Charlie than she'd let on and then squeezed in another meet-up. Where did she get the energy? "My mother is a floozy."

He laughed out loud at my reaction.

"She's rotational dating," he said. "It's all the rage."

Now my face was flaming. "I want to throw myself into the thistles right now. But regardless of her wanton ways, you know my mom's not a murderer."

"I know she has a record."

"She does not. Asher would have told us."

"Okay, it's an unofficial record. We've never formally booked her. But that's only because she's lucky and very charming when she wants to be. Her unofficial record is not insignificant, and there are some rather peculiar incidents I promised Asher I'd never mention."

"You had better mention them, Kellan Harper. This is my mother we're talking about."

"All I'm saying is that your mother is capable of extremely impulsive behavior when she's fired up. And Jilly said she was fired up about Wilf Darby firing you."

"You spoke to Jilly? When?" Normally we shared everything, and I didn't know about this. For a second it was like the bench shifted under me.

"Probably when you were interrogating Edna. I went to the farm to see you and since you weren't there, I took Jilly's statement instead." He smiled at my expression. "I think you'll find a text or three. She was trying to do it discreetly while making some very strong coffee."

"Well, fired up or not, Mom didn't cab it out to the farm to take out Wilf Darby. She still hopes I'll go back to Flordale one day, so she wouldn't destroy my chances."

"Time will tell," he said, getting up. "Let's get going. It's nearly dark, and one of us has police work to do."

"Kellan, I have a right to know about my mom's involvement with the police."

He started walking back to the truck and I hopped behind him trying to avoid sharp pebbles.

"No, you don't," he said. "You get to know what she tells you.

And I get to find out why she's not telling you everything."

"This isn't fair. Ow. Ow. Ow!"

Keats circled me anxiously and then raced out ahead of Kellan and closed in gently to slow him down. The move was so subtle Kellan barely noticed. In fact, he turned and came back for me as I picked my way along the path.

"See how you're walking?" he said. "That's what investigating a murder is like: a minefield. Yet today you were off again, tiptoeing around without protection."

"But I shared good information from Edna today."

"I would have gotten the same information, and without promising her free meals," he said. "As for the Flordale staff, all we know is that Ben and likely Neal tried to stop Wilf from driving into town drunk. This afternoon, I'll be at the farm talking to everyone, one by one. I'm sure I'll hear enough about corporate politics to make me grateful to be on the frontlines of police work."

"Guaranteed," I said.

He opened the passenger door of the truck for me, and Keats jumped through to the back. "Stand down, new age Ivy, or I'll take whatever recourse necessary to halt your creeping."

"A threat is still a threat when it's couched in flowery metaphors, Kellan."

He helped me into the truck and I tried to ignore the fireworks detonating from head to foot simply from feeling his hand on my back. I wondered if he felt the same. His eyes met mine and for a second I thought—*hoped*—he might kiss me.

Instead, he smirked. "I've got another metaphor. Clover Grove is my garden and it's my job to yank out weeds by the roots."

He closed the door and I rolled down the window. "Well, I've got a load of fertilizer I can sell you cheap."

"You're full of it all right," he said, grinning as he walked around the truck.

CHAPTER THIRTEEN

Jilly was covered in flour up to her hairline and surrounded by all the Flordale guests when I walked into the kitchen. The whites of her eyes didn't make the usual impact when she rolled them at me and mouthed, "Where were you?"

"Chief Hottie," I mouthed back, knowing that might be the only get out of jail free card I held. Out loud, I asked, "What are we cooking today, aspiring chefs?"

"Jilly's teaching us to make tourtière," Paulette said, dusting off her apron. "I voted for quiche but Ben and Neal refused to join us if there was no red meat involved." She gave them a disapproving look. "They're as bad as Wilf."

"Hey now," Ben said, giving her a rare frown. "Those are fighting words, Paulette. No one here is as bad as Wilf."

Except Wilf's killer, I thought. That might very well be Ben if what Edna saw was correct. She may not be good-hearted, but I couldn't see any reason she'd lie about it, and Ben was unmistakable given his size.

Paulette flushed and put a floury hand on Ben's arm. "I only meant about being a carnivore. Real men *do* eat quiche, you know."

Jilly rapped the granite counter lightly with her rolling pin.

"The tough part is mastering pastry," she said. "Once we've done that, we can easily toss a quiche together and everyone will be happy."

"We're all happy as it is," Paulette said. "You've been so kind and fun, Jilly."

"What I really crave is some exercise," Ben said. "I'd love to go for a run."

"No runs today, Ben, I'm sorry," I said. "The police chief is spending the afternoon here taking statements. But if you don't mind some hard labor, Charlie's down in the barn and would love some help. I've been slacking off on my chores since you guys got here."

"Not till my lesson is over," Jilly said, giving me a significant glance.

"Of course," I said, realizing she was probably doing a little questioning of her own. "Pastry before pasture."

"This fancy meat pie had better be good," Neal said. "Because kitchen and barn chores weren't on your list of resort activities."

"It's all part of the farm experience I promised," I said. "Plus, I have good news. Chief Harper gave us permission to go to the Clover Grove Harvest Fair tonight. It's a big deal around here."

Neal rolled his eyes. "A fair. Wow. I can hardly wait."

"There are rides," I said, remembering his interest in theme parks. "Good ones. They've hired one of the best travelling midways in the country and split the bill with Dorset Hills. If it's thrills you want, Neal, you'll get your chance tonight."

"We'd better eat early," Jilly said. "Or it'll be a sad waste of tortière."

"I can't handle more than a merry-go-round anymore," Paulette said.

All of the other women chimed in with agreement.

"I guess it's just you and me, Ben," Neal said.

Ben laughed. "I exceed the size requirements on most rides.

They can't strap me in properly. Getting flung off a roller coaster is more thrill than I can handle."

I signaled Keats and started backing toward the door. "Save me a piece of the fancy meat pie, folks. I've got to run into town on some errands."

Jilly gave me another "you owe me" look and I just shrugged. My tab with her was higher than I could repay in a lifetime, so there was nothing to do but love her hard and thank her often. Best friends like her were harder to find than a needle in a haystack. I knew someone was looking out for me the day we met. I just wished that same someone would stop dropping murders in our path to test us.

Outside, I stared at the truck for a moment. Kellan's message had been loud and clear, but who knew when a mild-mannered sedan might arrive. I couldn't be without wheels in the meantime, so I'd have to shoot into town and get back here before he arrived.

The truck itself seemed to have settled just from being under Kellan's control for a while. It didn't stall once on the way into town and Keats relaxed a little. I rolled down the window for him and he stuck his nose out.

"Life is still good, buddy," I said. "There's never a dull moment, but you like that." He swept his tail in an affirmative, brushing a little flour off my coat sleeve. "I'm starting to wonder if I do, too. I mean, I came home for tranquility but maybe I'd have been bored. After all the stress at Flordale, I'm probably an adrenaline junkie now. That said, murder is more adrenaline than I can handle ever again."

His tail swept harder and I marveled as always at his capacity to understand me, or at least the intent of my words. There was no denying our ability to communicate got stronger by the day. Although it felt downright magical to me, I knew border collies were bred to read the subtlest signs from both their handlers and their herd. Keats wasn't even looking at me so I guessed my intona-

DARK SIDE OF THE MOO   121

tion or energy gave him the cues he needed to look like the most intuitive dog on the planet.

Musing about my relationship with Keats calmed me, and that showed in my ability to handle the truck. I travelled through town without the hippity-hop that usually drew attention to me. Today my truck was just like any of the other black trucks on the main drag.

Just the same, I left the pickup in the parking lot at the grocery store and walked the rest of the way to the Summit Hotel in case Kellan happened to drive by, as he so conveniently managed to do. I'd forgotten to tell him what Edna had said about the hotel, which he would say *I* conveniently managed to do. It would probably turn out to be nothing, and I'd have saved him a trip.

The small hotel wasn't on the summit of anything, but I couldn't blame the new owner for wanting to exploit the best marketing angle. I'd have to do the same once the Flordale crew left and I was looking for new guests. I didn't expect them to fall into my lap, especially with the farm's recent history.

I walked up the broad front staircase and into the small-but-classy foyer. Chantelle Blaise had spent a lot refurbishing what used to be a medical office in an old mansion. The mansion itself had belonged to one of Clover Grove's founding families and there'd been a scuffle with the County over whether to designate it a heritage site. Filthy commerce won out, and Chantelle probably had to make some big promises for that to happen. Politics in Glover Grove were still relatively clean but everything got more complicated as the town grew.

Pinging the bell on the old oak desk in the foyer, I whispered to Keats, "Best behavior, okay? Both of us."

A woman with classic features and dark hair in a smooth knot pushed open a door and joined us. "Sorry, I didn't quite catch that."

The French accent Edna had mocked was almost undetectable and sounded more Quebecois than France itself. "Just having a word with my dog. I didn't want him embarrassing me in your lovely hotel."

Keats shot me a look as if to say I was more likely to embarrass him, which was so true that I couldn't help smiling. Luckily, Chantelle smiled back, instead of giving me the "crazy lady" look that so often came my way in town.

"He's a lovely dog," she said, introducing herself and offering her hand over the counter. "Keats, I believe?"

My eyes widened. "How did you know? I hope people aren't talking about us all over town."

"Not at all," she said, laughing. "I overheard a guest talking about Runaway Farm and the dog's name came up." She leaned in. "I shouldn't have been eavesdropping but there was no one else in the lounge at the time and it was hard to miss. Plus, you were on my radar as we're both new to the hospitality sector in Clover Grove."

"We *are* the hospitality sector, I guess. Other than the Have a Nap Motel and a few bed and breakfasts."

"Exactly," she said. "I've been wanting to meet you so we could share our experience. I'm new here, and I know you're new again."

"It would be great to talk shop, Chantelle. I feel overwhelmed by the whole thing sometimes, especially with all that's happened. I'm sure you've heard."

"You've had a rough start," she said, nodding. "But in a few months, that will all be a grim memory. I hope we both have a constant full house by spring."

"Come out to the farm in a few weeks and I'll show you around," I said. "My best friend, Jilly, is an amazing cook."

"I've heard that, too," she said. "The grapevine is quite something around here."

"It sure is. That's why I'm here, actually. Someone mentioned seeing a red Corvette outside four days ago, which is a day before my guests arrived. My former boss, Wilf Darby, drove a red

Corvette. I'm sure there are other cars like that around but it seemed like a coincidence."

Chantelle picked up a pen and started doodling on a notepad. Her eyes flicked up at me and then away. "I need to respect the privacy of my guests, Ivy. You know how it is."

"Privacy's been hard to come by since Wilf died," I said. "The police are prying into my guests' lives and my own. All I want to do is help get to the bottom of this quickly so that people can go home and forget their farm experience ever happened. As you can imagine, my reputation has taken quite a hit from this."

Her face creased with sympathy, and Keats confirmed the sentiment was sincere by fanning the white tip of his tail. He was a master of fraud detection, and Chantelle passed his sniff test.

"There *was* a red Corvette here," she said. "The driver parked at the paid lot down the street, but he dropped off a guest twice and spent some time here with her."

My HR mask dropped into place. Showing too much interest often stopped the flow of valuable information. "Do you think it was my boss?" I asked. "Big guy, kind of chubby, with thinning blond hair and a ruddy complexion?"

"Sounds about right." I could tell she was uncomfortable. The pressure of her pen on the notepad almost tore the paper.

"If it helps, I know Wilf was seeing someone," I said. "He told me about the split with his wife while I was working for him. I'm guessing he brought a lady friend to enjoy some romantic drives between the teambuilding activities at the farm."

"They did go on a nice drive," she said, brightening. "I told them the best routes for fall leaves and they seemed happy when they came back."

"Wonderful," I said. "I'm truly glad Wilf found some moments of joy before... what happened. Is his lady friend alright?"

Now the paper did rip under Chantelle's pen. "I don't think so. My chef told her the gossip yesterday at breakfast and she left her meal untouched. She was out most of the day and I'm afraid she cried during the night."

"Is she here now?" I asked. "Maybe she'd like to reminisce about Wilf with me. There are stories from our work travels she's never heard. He was quite a character."

Chantelle shook her head. "She left again this morning without eating, I'm afraid."

"On foot?" I asked. "Any idea where she went?"

She tore the sheet off her notepad and crumpled it. "I heard she spent some time on the patio at the Berry Good Café yesterday. You might try there. She's petite and blonde, and last I saw, wore sunglasses inside and out."

"Thank you," I said, as Keats trotted ahead of me to the door. "I promise I'll reveal nothing you've told me. You can hold me to that, because with our small hospitality sector, we need to have each other's back."

"Good luck, Ivy," she called. "With everything."

CHAPTER FOURTEEN

Leaving the Summit Hotel, I wove through the surprisingly heavy foot traffic on the sidewalk. It was a beautiful day and people had come out in droves to enjoy it. We all knew how long and bleak a winter here could be. The rolling hills sheltered Clover Grove from the worst of it, but they seemed to act as a shield to spring, too.

Keats usually walked beside me like a normal dog when we were in town and I didn't need to leash him. Today he picked up on my impatience, however, and tried to herd me through the crowd to the café. He circled in front of me, created some space, then eased behind me to push me forward before that gap closed. It worked all right, if you didn't mind being treated like livestock. I had enough on my mind that it was a bit of a relief to leave the navigating to him. That left me free to wonder about Wilf's affair. It must have been serious if the woman had cried all night. I suppressed a shudder. Wilf had been repulsive to me in every way. His faded football star looks could never make up for his flawed personality. But like my mom always said, there's a lid for every pot.

When we reached the café, I walked down the alley to the

patio. With a jacket to shield against the breeze, you could sit outside, and if I were grieving, I'd want to be away from the crowd.

There was only one woman out there, and her blonde hair and sunglasses fit Chantelle's description. She was sitting in the corner seat where Kellan and I had bickered while sharing a scone a month ago. The table held bad memories because that's where he threatened to seize Keats from me if I didn't back away from his investigation into the dogcatcher's death. We'd moved far enough past that now I could almost convince myself he wouldn't mind if I had a little chat with Wilf's girlfriend. *Almost.*

The woman turned to look up at me and gasped. "Ivy!"

"Avis!" I couldn't think of another thing to say to the woman I'd last seen on the day I literally fled Flordale's head office during a meeting to announce global downsizing. Avis Arron was a senior vice president of the company and the one who told me I'd need to travel for the better part of a year to downsize hundreds of staff. It was the straw that broke this camel's back, and ultimately led to my owning several camelids, specifically an alpaca and two llamas.

I stood in the middle of the patio, paralyzed. I wanted to turn and run from her again, but now my farm's future hung on helping to solve Wilf's murder. I couldn't run away from Flordale trouble anymore; I had to run toward it.

Keats brushed against my leg to give me courage, and somehow my boots—the ones caked in manure, since Edna still had my good ones—carried me the last few yards. My mouth had dried up, however, so I simply obeyed her gesture to sit down across from her. I was used to obeying Avis' wishes, even if they came through Wilf's lips.

"I heard about what happened," she said. "It was terrible news for Flordale. I've been on the phone with the president and executive ever since."

I stared at her, trying to make sense of her presence here. Maybe Chantelle and I were wrong about their being in a relationship. It was quite possible Avis and Wilf were staging a coup that was better planned away from head office. There were always schemes afoot at the senior levels and grunts like me took the fallout.

But that wouldn't explain the crying Chantelle heard in the night. And it wouldn't explain Avis' chapped, red nose.

Tapping my temple, I said, "You've got something right here. It looks like dried blood."

She lifted her glasses quickly and scratched at the spot I'd indicated, revealing bloodshot, puffy eyes. "Gone?" she asked, dropping the glasses.

"Gone," I said. "Avis, it's obvious you're heartbroken over Wilf's passing, and I'm sorry for your loss. I was aware he was in a new relationship. I just didn't know it was with you."

Shoving the shades up on top of her exquisitely highlighted hair, she stared at me with fierce blue eyes. "I know what you think of him, Ivy. But that wasn't the man I knew. He treated me like a queen."

"I'm happy to hear that," I said, waving the waiter away. Avis still had tea in her big mug and I couldn't swallow a thing if I tried. "I'm sure there was a side to him that we never saw. And I'm truly glad he found happiness after his divorce."

Her lips pressed into a thin line and she twisted the diamond eternity band on her left hand. "We were going to make it official after his paperwork was done," she said eventually. "I have teenage children, so I wasn't in a rush to disrupt their lives." She took the band off and set it by her phone. "Now I won't have to, I guess."

"Did your husband know, Avis?"

"No, we were always very discreet. Why?"

Driving around in a red Corvette seemed the opposite of discreet, but I didn't contradict her. "I'm helping the police figure out what might have happened to Wilf."

Her blue eyes grew frosty. "Your cow kicked him in the head and broke my heart. That's what happened."

"My cows are innocent and that will be proven in time. The forensic team suspects Wilf was dead before he was kicked."

She hooked the ring with her index finger and spun it in little circles. "That's impossible. Wilf hadn't an enemy in the world."

"Oh Avis," I said. "You may be grieving, but you're a smart woman—smart enough to be Flordale's first female senior VP. So you know Wilf had plenty of enemies. One of them might be your husband if he knew Wilf was threatening your happy family."

"He didn't know. And no one at Flordale knew."

"That's almost never true, no matter how discreet you think you are. I saw literally dozens of affairs exposed over my decade in HR. For Wilf, the VP of HR, getting caught in a relationship with his superior would be a career killer."

"Untrue," she said, snapping her glasses back down on her nose. "It's only a problem when the man is in the senior position. It could hardly be said that he exploited me."

"I doubt the president would see it that way. Regardless, one of you would have been asked to leave the company, I'm sure."

"You don't know everything, Ivy Galloway," she said. "We had a plan and it would have worked out just fine if your cows hadn't stomped all over it."

"Let's assume the police are right and it wasn't my cows," I said. "Who else might have ended Wilf's life?"

Lifting her glasses again, she tried to intimidate me with the executive stare. "I heard your mother threatened him. How about you interrogate her?"

Now I smiled. "Trust me, I did. And the police did, too. How about the other members of my team?" I shook my head. "My *former* team. I can't believe any of them would be capable of such a thing."

She gave a huffy sigh. "If it comes to that, all of them probably had motive, including you. That's because you misjudged Wilf. He just wanted the best for the company and you took it so personally.

Wilf and I were totally committed to Flordale. Meanwhile, the second you heard you'd have to deliver bad news for the company, you bolted. I was so disappointed in you. It was terribly unprofessional."

A mixture of fury and shame percolated in my gut but my mask was locked in place. "You were thinking about the company, whereas I was thinking about the staff I'd have to fire. The lives I'd have to ruin. You do know Wilf called me the grim reaper, right? Avis, I just couldn't do that anymore. It was a personal decision."

Her hand left the ring and gave a dismissive wave. "All of you were constantly whining. Ben Miller complained about bullying— as if anyone could bully a giant. The two that look like birds of prey complained about harassment—as if Wilf could ever be interested in them. And then there was the bubble gum popper who wobbled around in tight leather and griped because she wasn't promoted fast enough. Optics are everything if you want to be taken seriously as a woman in a man's world." She smoothed her hair. "*You* understood that. I always respected your professionalism... until your breakdown. And over a dog, no less."

She looked at said dog and he stared back. Something startled her, and she pushed her chair back. Keats never moved a muscle.

"What about Neal and Paulette?" I asked. "You've lumped everyone else into the category of suspects."

"Paulette's a sweetheart," she said, which told me our admin assistant had been covering for them. "But Neal Fife should be the cops' first stop. Wilf found out he was sharing Flordale trade secrets with the competition. He was going to fire him right after the retreat."

"Really?" I tried to conceal my surprise and likely failed. "Did Neal know?"

She put her ring back on her finger and shook her head. "Wilf didn't want to ruin the party for the rest of you. He was so thoughtful that way."

"Well, he was pretty drunk the first night at my farm," I said. "Maybe it slipped out, either before or after he rammed his Corvette into my truck. I assume he was on his way to see you."

"We didn't have plans." Her voice was crisper than the fall air. "In fact, I explicitly told him not to come over."

"And yet he was behind the wheel in his pajamas, bathrobe and slippers. A lover's quarrel, perhaps?"

She let her shades slip down her nose. "Don't make something of nothing, Ivy. He was tipsy when he called and I told him not to drive. It's a shame he hit your truck and visited your cows in that condition but regardless, this is all your fault."

"*My fault?* How is it my fault?"

"How could it be anything *but* your fault? He was so distressed that you left the team he wanted to come and win you back to Flordale."

I gasped. "That's not true! He did nothing but insult me from the time he arrived."

"Oh, you know how men are," she said, rising from her seat. "They hate to admit they were wrong." She was halfway across the patio before she added, "You should never have let him drink that much, Ivy. You have a responsibility as an innkeeper to keep your guests safe. I am holding you personally accountable for all of this. Trust that I'll share my views about your new venture widely if you share any of your ridiculous notions."

"So now you're threatening me?" I called after her.

She stopped and spun around. "There you go, getting all emotional again. You were of so much more use to us when you behaved like a robot. Flordale needs more people like the old you. Honestly, I can't wait till artificial intelligence takes over routine operations like hiring and firing. Now, go back to your farm and try to keep the rest of my staff alive, will you?"

CHAPTER FIFTEEN

The Clover Grove Harvest Fair had been an institution since long before I was around. I'd loved it as a kid, until deciding at 12 that it was "lame." That happened to every local teen, but probably earlier for me because of having so many older siblings who aged out of the fair. Poppy, in particular, heaped scorn on the event, from the haybale maze to the pumpkin patch portraits. Back then there was no real midway, just an old merry-go-round and an even older Ferris wheel that was more terrifying than modern rides simply because it seemed ready to collapse at any moment.

Tonight, as we hopped out of the rental van, voices overlapped in a comical mix of delight and disdain.

"Oh, how quaint. I bet there's fudge."

"Do I smell cotton candy?"

"Do I smell cheesy?"

"If there's a kissing booth, I'm all over it."

"Let's all bob for apples."

"Take my money, Clover Grove."

I was too stunned to say anything until the clamor died down. Eventually, as we walked out of the field that served as parking lot, I turned to Jilly. "You have no idea how much this has changed in ten years. I'm both impressed and appalled."

"I think it's wonderful," she said. "Perfect for a romantic date. Don't you wish you could ride the Ferris wheel with Kellan?"

After hearing about our trip to the public gardens, Jilly had silently started planning our wedding. I could see it in the calculating way she scanned the farm, and hear it when she spontaneously asked me about my favorite finger foods. She was a diehard romantic waiting for magic moments to happen.

"I prefer to keep my feet on the ground," I said. "So much safer."

Keats wasn't listening, for a change. He trotted between us, tail up, eyes bright, tongue lolling. There was nothing this dog loved more than a new experience.

I was pleased to see most of the old harvest fair favorites were front and center, including the haybale maze and the pumpkin patch photo opp. There were carts nearby selling candied apples, fudge, caramel corn and cotton candy, and the promise of fried food hung heavily in the air. Where there used to be just a few games and booths, however, now there were long rows of clanging, banging contests. Other rows offered handicrafts, local produce, cheese, preserves and baked goods. In the distance, I heard the various vocalizations of sheep, cows, horses, goats and probably far more. Their fine bouquet mixed with the sweet and savory food smells and whisked me back to childhood on a roller coaster of emotions.

In the next field was a legit roller coaster so high that it took my breath away. I'd seen the flashing neon lights from the farm the evening before, but I couldn't quite believe it. It took up the most prominent real estate in the fairground, but there were other equally terrifying rides that elicited screams that probably echoed down the range of hills. Judging by the shrill pitch, there was no shortage of teens tonight. These rides had chased a lot of the cheese away from this old tradition.

"Who's going on the roller coaster with me?" Neal asked, immediately.

There was a chorus of "not me." My voice was loudest. I wasn't a fan of heights or speed and I certainly didn't need to embarrass myself in front of my former colleagues with shrieking or crying.

"Fine, I'll do it alone," he said. "This one's nothing compared to the rides I've taken all over the world."

Theme parks were Neal's passion. When we worked together, he was always trying to show people videos and photos, but few could relate. Even I couldn't feign interest, and I normally did my best to find common ground with my staff.

"You're a thrill seeker," Ben said. "And I've had enough thrills for one week."

Neal shook his head. "You guys have lost all sense of adventure. Wilf beat it out of you."

"No speaking ill of the dead," Paulette reminded him.

"Look, Paulette," Neal said. "You're the only one here who liked Wilf. Obviously, he was nicer to you because you kept his secrets."

"I kept everyone's secrets, remember?" She cast a sheepish glance my way and added, "Not that there were many."

"I'm sure you shared them all with Chief Harper in your one-on-one," I said. "At least I hope so, because your company confidentiality agreement doesn't apply to police matters."

"Of course," she said. "Whatever I know, he knows, and it isn't much. He's no closer to solving this crime, I'm afraid."

"What *I'm* afraid of is getting stuck in this hick town forever," Nellie said. I wondered if she'd brought any casual clothes with her to Clover Grove, because she was wearing a flimsy dress with sparkle and stiletto ankle boots that might well break *her* ankle before the night was out. At least she had a leather jacket to block the breeze. There was a nip in the air that would bring on the full colors in the hills before long.

"You need your spa gloves tonight, Nellie," I joked. "It's a cool one."

She flicked her hair at me. "I gave up on my manicure days ago. I'll need a mani 911 the second we're home."

Ben leaned down to whisper, "I'd give us a week on the farm before it turned into Lord of the Flies."

Normally I would have laughed at his comment, but I was miffed with him for lying to me about what happened with Wilf. Or at least, lying by omission. "I'm sure we can all stay civil," I said. "Getting this crime resolved depends on it."

"What's wrong?" he asked. "You used to love speculating about the corporate descent into chaos."

"Times have changed, Ben. Wilf's death could spell the end for Runaway Farm if the police don't figure out what happened soon. Even then my reputation will be in tatters with two murders hanging over my new inn. Mostly, I worry about my animals. You have no idea how it feels to be responsible for so many creatures."

"Just be patient. Things will sort themselves out in time," he said.

"I don't have time. Remember, I didn't get a decent package from Flordale to fall back on. I need to line up my next guests soon. And yet, I get the sense some of you may not be telling me the full story."

His eyes left my face and darted around the fairground. "What do you mean?"

Watching him closely, I took my chance. "I heard through the grapevine that you were outside with Wilf on the night of the murder. Struggling with him, actually."

Ben's genial smile melted away. "Who told you that? I thought our police statements were confidential."

"They are. But in a small town, word gets around. My source is reliable."

Edna Evans was anything but reliable, but Ben had confirmed her story with his reaction.

He stopped walking and caught my sleeve till we fell behind the Flordale crowd. "It's true that I held back some details about being outside with Wilf in the night. I was worried it would sound bad when I was only trying to keep him from doing anything stupid. He bumped into my bedroom door on his way out and I followed him. Sure enough, I found him behind the wheel. He circled me twice. I was the center of his donut."

"Go on," I said.

"Your source was right about the struggle. Wilf was out of shape but it was like wrestling a slick hippo." He shook his head. "I was too easy on him because I worried about repercussions. But eventually I managed to take away the car keys and get him back to his room. Obviously he went out to the barn again later, after I fell asleep."

"What did you do with the keys?" I asked.

His handsome face drooped almost comically in shame. "I put them on his dresser in the morning before joining Jilly for mimosas. At that point I had no idea what had happened."

My intuition said Ben was telling the truth and a quick glance at Keats showed the dog agreed. His ears were forward and his tail at half mast. The signs said he wasn't a huge fan of Ben but he didn't dislike him, either.

"Who else was with you?" I asked, pinning Ben with my own intense stare. I didn't have Keats' almost mystical eye game, but I was a good observer of human behavior. "My source said you weren't working alone."

Ben scuffed the well-trodden grass underfoot and sighed. "Neal. He came out to see what all the fuss was about, but he wasn't much help. Wilf yelled some threats at him and he went back to the house before I did."

"What kind of threats?"

"The usual... Professional annihilation. Maybe dialed up a notch." He stared at the Ferris wheel for a second and then added, "Something about corporate treachery and that Neal 'deserved what was coming.' Nothing I wouldn't expect from Wilf in that state. He was a mean drunk."

"That I know." I turned to find Jilly and then raised a finger to ask her to wait for us. "We'd better join the pack, Ben. Thanks for filling me in."

"Ivy, I'm sorry," he said. "I hope you'll forgive me. Things have just been... difficult since you left Flordale."

There was something in his eyes I couldn't quite read. Keats tipped his head and stared quizzically at Ben. His tail gave a delicate swish and then drooped—a new sign I hadn't witnessed before.

As we merged with our group, I decided to believe that was the extent of Ben's involvement, at least for now. We had a good history. Besides, the thought of sharing a roof with a six-foot-six killer who could successfully wrestle a slick hippo was unnerving. He didn't look threatening now, stooping to take a bite out of Nellie's bright red candy apple. Even the cool girl had caught harvest fair fever and sweetened up.

Neal was my next target and I didn't relish the challenge. I'd never particularly liked him and that's why I hadn't hired him when he applied for the role of IT specialist in our department. His references were tepid, and he'd seemed shifty to me. But technology experts were hard to find, and in the end, Wilf went around my back. One day I came to work and found Neal giving me a sly smile from behind a bank of monitors. As the consummate professional, I welcomed him warmly to my team. Now, based on what Avis Arron had said, my assessment of Neal turned out to be accurate. Mind you, I wouldn't have predicted he'd share company trade secrets. A skilled IT guy should have been able to cover his tracks better.

If I wanted to learn more about Neal's activities, I was going to have to make some sacrifices. What I had planned felt like an almost intolerable risk. But it also felt like the most expedient route to get some answers. Keats nudged my hand and I whispered, "I know, buddy. I'm worried, too, especially because you can't come with me. I'm sure once I get over the initial shock, it will be child's play."

A snicker made me look up, only to find Neal crowding my space. His energy had always made my hackles rise, even before I knew what the hair on the back of my neck was telling me. Tonight, Keats' ruff came up, too.

"I never would have pegged you as someone who talked to dogs, Ivy," he said. "That bump on your head really did knock a few screws loose."

I gave him a mischievous smile. I'd accumulated quite a collection of smiles I could pull out to suit the occasion, but that one didn't get used often. "Oh, Neal. The screws were always loose in here." I tapped my temple. "I just hid it better. On the bright side, 'old Ivy' would never go on a roller coaster, whereas 'new Ivy' is up for it. What do you say?"

"Really?" His muddy eyes brightened, but it wasn't enough to offset his pointy nose or the weak chin behind the wispy beard. "You said no earlier."

"Changed my mind. You only live once, right?"

Jilly took my sleeve and yanked me away from the crowd with none of her usual finesse. "Ivy, are you nuts? You had a brain injury a few months ago and it can take a year to recover. Getting whiplash on a roller coaster is the last thing you need."

Leaning in, I whispered, "I think Neal may have killed Wilf, so I want to soften him up for questioning."

Her blonde ponytail snapped from side to side in a brisk protest. "That's Kellan Harper's job. Let the police chief get on a roller coaster and rattle *his* brain. He gets paid the big County bucks to do that."

I laughed. "As if Kellan would ever ride a roller coaster. Can you imagine? I don't think there's an ounce of fun left in him."

"Well, I don't think there's an ounce of *sense* left in you."

"These rides are perfectly safe. There's plenty of padding and there's never been a serious accident." I grinned at her. "I googled before offering."

"Ivy, let *me* take the ride, then. Just tell me what you want me to ask."

Reaching out, I squeezed her arm. "You're the best friend ever. But all I want you to do is watch over everyone, including Keats." I hooked up the dog's leash and handed it to her. "He won't like this."

"Of course not. He wants a busy, full life with someone whose brain still works."

"That's why I need to clear the farm's name, and if it takes a thrill ride to do it, I'm willing."

Before she could wear me down with her logic, I slipped away and beckoned Neal.

"Everyone's a stick-in-the-mud except for us," I said, as we joined the lineup for the ride. "They don't know how to have fun."

"You didn't know how to have fun, either," he said.

"Like you said, a blow to the head changes everything. I vowed not to let another roller coaster pass me by." Clasping clammy hands, I stared up at the ride. "I won't pretend I'm not scared, Neal, but it's important to take chances. I took plenty in my career and it paid off." I grinned at him. "Until the end, anyway. But everything works out for the best, right?"

The train rolled in, and Neal shrugged as we watched people disembark laughing, squealing and clutching each other. "I guess so," he said. "I hope so."

"You've got to have faith," I said. "If I hadn't taken a huge chance I wouldn't have my amazing farm. No regrets here... other than Wilf's passing."

The ride operator gestured for the line to start filling the seats. Neal selected the very first seat on the train. Fabulous. Now I could see every detail as we catapulted into the abyss. For all I knew, this could be the only one to soar off the tracks of this death machine.

After someone else strapped us in, Neal said, "Wilf deserved to go."

I dug my fingernails into my palm to keep my emotions in check. "Well, he bullied all of us. That's pretty clear."

"It wasn't just that," Neal said. "Wilf lacked vision. There were ways to help the company grow that he wouldn't take. He was determined to stay small."

A laugh tickled my throat, so I coughed instead. Wilf was a large man, and Neal a scrawny one. Scratch the surface, however, and they were probably both overcompensating for low self-esteem.

The roller coaster started moving, gliding slowly toward the first massive hill. "I don't think Wilf listened to you enough," I said. "You're more than just an IT guy."

He leaned forward, as if trying to urge the train on. "I kept asking to move up the ranks and he shot me down every time."

"Me too." I looked down at my hands squeezing the safety bar, trying to focus on the conversation instead of the terrifying view. "I wanted to grow and he held me back."

Neal jiggled in his seat like a kid as we approached the crest. "He was a jerk. I'm glad someone took him out. I just wish I'd been there to see it."

The train stopped at the peak so that we could take in the sight of Clover Grove spreading beneath us. I dared to glance around and saw glittering points of light all the way down the range of hills. It would be gorgeous if the circumstances were different. Luckily I had something else to keep me focussed. I had to speak now because words might fail me after our descent. "I heard you *were* there to see it happen."

Neal turned to me just as the train started its perilous roll down the steep tracks. His voice was almost blown away but I heard the indignant, "I was not."

My screams drowned out anything more until we were ascending the second, even larger, hill. "Sorry," I said. "I was just repeating what I heard on the Clover Grove grapevine. You and Ben were seen struggling with Wilf near the barn that night."

His eyes were on me instead of the awesome escapade. "After we got him subdued, we all went back inside. Wilf passed out and I went to my room. I have no idea what happened after that." He faced forward again. "That's what I told the police, too."

As the train paused at the second peak, I tossed out, "I believe you, Neal. But since I knew you were about to get fired for just cause, you had... MOTIVE." My last word came out as an unintended shriek and the roller coaster surged forward.

"Who said that?" he yelled back.

"Senior management," I gasped, as we bottomed out and sped toward the full loop. "I have friends."

"Your friends are wrong."

"They said you were sharing trade secrets." I closed my eyes in hopes that it would quell the rising nausea. If I couldn't *see* what was happening, maybe my brain would believe I was lying in a sweet meadow with Keats beside me.

"Exchanging good information," he said. We kept rolling until we literally hung upside down in our harnesses. "And Flordale wouldn't have fired me for it. I had leverage."

"I wish I'd had leverage," I yelled, eyes still closed. "What did you have on him?"

Rolling into the downward spiral, my breath got sucked out into the fall air.

"An affair," Neal yelled. "Never mess with IT guys. We know everything."

When my breath came back, I choked out, "I figured. My money's on Kate."

"Wrong," he said. "Think bigger. I was still gathering proof when they locked us all out of the system yesterday."

"Keep up the good work," I said. "You're a brave man."

"Everyone loves an underdog," he said.

Not necessarily, I thought, as we moved into the last death-defying incline. If I could keep my stomach calm, it would surely be a miracle.

We made it through alive and coasted to a stop. Neal jumped out and didn't look back, but a young male worker took one look at me and offered his hand.

"I'm fine," I said, although I clutched his arm gratefully as we walked down the few steps. Jilly reached out and took my arm from him. "I'm fine, Jilly, really."

"You look terrible," she said, as Keats circled, poking me with his long muzzle as if taking my pulse at various points of contact.

"That she does," a familiar voice said.

I turned to see Kellan Harper coming down the stairs from the roller coaster platform. Hanging from his arm was a pretty woman who could be Jilly's twin, unless I was seeing double. She wobbled on high heels, making peeping noises of distress.

Who was this woman? And why was she clinging to Kellan as if she had a right to? If she *did* have a right to, why did it feel like we'd shared a moment in the garden the day before?

Whatever feeling I was trying to recall vanished as another wave of nausea rolled over me. I had just enough time to seize Jilly's half-empty box of popcorn and turn quickly away from everyone before losing both my dinner and my dignity.

CHAPTER SIXTEEN

Jilly, Keats and I walked through the meadow in silence. It was a cloudy, cool morning with a breeze that made us tuck our hands into our pockets. The grass rustled a bit under our boots, and a few stray moos, bleats, neighs and brays drifted out to us.

Asher had arrived in civvies in time for a generous breakfast that he followed with a generous offer to take the guests on a drive through the hills to see "the hotspots." It was a surprise to me that we had any, and I may have gone along to be edified had I not been so desperate for downtime in nature with my two favorite souls on the planet.

After a long stretch of marching, Jilly laughed out loud. "It was fun seeing Asher walk Ben and Neal out to the van, wasn't it? They couldn't have been less interested in the autumn landscape but he was determined to give us a break."

"Maybe he's afraid I'm cracking under the pressure," I said. "No doubt Kellan told him what happened last night in the fairground. That was the single most humiliating event of my life. The way I'm going, there will be worse."

She patted my shoulder. "Don't be so hard on yourself. Throwing up after a roller coaster ride is so common they keep barf bags at the gate. I guess you didn't notice that or my popcorn would have been saved."

"I was too busy thanking the good Lord for getting me off that ride alive. Maybe I'd have been okay if I hadn't seen Kellan with his date."

The pat on my shoulder firmed into a reproof rather than a comfort. "All you know is that he took a ride with a woman at the fair."

"With a gorgeous blonde woman."

"Not that gorgeous. Her makeup was doing the heavy lifting." She shook her head. "I don't like to be catty about people I don't know. All I can say is that Kellan was very solicitous of your health after your... episode."

Indeed, he'd wanted to call an ambulance, and Jilly had to work hard to dissuade him.

"Thank you for convincing him it was just motion sickness," I said. "I'm sure you had your doubts, too."

"Keats told me you were fine," she said, bending to pick up a stick to throw for him.

That made me smile. "Did he now?"

She nodded. "If you pay attention, that dog has a lot to say."

Keats wagged in agreement. He wasn't inclined to frivolity but after her vote of confidence, he raced after the stick, tail high, white plume showing above the long grass.

I stopped and pointed. "See that? Just before we spoke to Keats' former owner, a vision just like this popped into my head. It's my dream come true." I turned to look at Jilly. "Except for the murders."

She waved her hand to disperse a few gnats that had braved the chill. "Kellan will get this one sorted and the dream will get back up and running. We'll bring in some cool new guests. Like a book club. Or a quilting society. Or oenophiles. Wouldn't it be nice to learn about wine?"

"That sounds like heaven. But we can't count on Kellan to get to the bottom of this anytime soon when he's slacking on the roller coaster with his almost-gorgeous date."

"Kellan's not dating that woman," she said. "You know I'm pretty much an expert on affairs of the heart. I didn't see the signs on either one of them. Maybe it's his sister."

"He doesn't have a sister," I said. "But I do have news to share about another affair. I found out Wilf was having an affair with Avis Arron."

Jilly stopped dead, letting the gnats swarm around her. "Avis, the senior vice president at Flordale?"

"The same. And she's here in town. They met up two days early to enjoy the sights... and each other."

Her green eyes narrowed. "How do you know all this, Ivy? Have you been off sleuthing while I babysit the vipers alone?"

"I poked around a bit when I was running errands, that's all. Then I ended up at the Berry Good Café having a chat with Avis."

"Oh my god," Jilly said, as Keats dropped the stick in front of her hopefully. "You confronted Avis? Are you nuts? You're supposed to call Kellan and let him do the dirty work."

"Well, I was in the neighborhood and I know Avis personally. Do you want to argue or hear what she had to say?"

Her hand started fanning the gnats again and her boots moved forward. "Of course I want to hear every detail. Right after you assure me you told Kellan about this."

"I left him a voicemail. And he left me one this morning saying that the autopsy results were back, and confirmed Wilf died of a blunt force injury. The cows are off the hook."

"That's a relief," she said. "I'm getting fond of little Archie. I went into the barn to see him yesterday, you know."

"Aw, Jilly, we'll make a farmer of you yet."

"Unlikely. I'm still far too interested in corporate politics. So get to the good stuff."

I filled her in on my discussion with Avis, and when I got to the end, I said, "I wouldn't rule out an angry husband in Wilf's death, although her money is on Neal. Meanwhile, Neal seems to think his evidence about their affair would counter any move Flordale might make against him for leaking trade secrets."

Her feet stopped moving again and she closed her eyes. "You cornered him on the roller coaster, didn't you? That's why you got sick."

"Well, *you* try interrogating someone during a gravity-defying loop. I couldn't keep my mind on that and my stomach at the same time."

"Ivy, you are too much. I saw you whispering to Ben, too, and he looked very sheepish."

Picking up the stick, I tossed it for Keats. He practically rolled his eyes because I didn't have much of an arm, or aim for that matter. But he graciously trotted after it and retrieved it, making it clear he was just being nice.

"Ben admitted he lied to me about sleeping through the night of Wilf's murder—although he claims he was honest with Kellan. He and Neal tried to stop Wilf from driving and they eventually got him back to bed. Obviously Wilf got a second wind and tried again, but Ben had his keys. The big question is who went out the second time and struck Wilf? And what did they hit him with? There's no sign of a murder weapon yet."

"Maybe Keats will find it out here," Jilly said.

I shook my head. "No way this dog would be chasing sticks if there were clues to be found. He only plays when there's no work."

After a brief pause, Jilly said, "I hate to admit this, but I've been working on the women. Baking is so therapeutic. You'd be surprised what people will say when they're up to their elbows in flour."

"Why, Jilly Blackwood," I said, grinning. "Do tell."

The sun emerged suddenly as she grinned back at me. She took the stick and gave it a toss worthy of Keats' effort. "Well, Kate and

Macy really aren't that bad. They became codependent in a tough environment to survive and don't know how to break apart. Believe it or not, Wilf's comments at that dinner were a wakeup call. They've asked for coaching on how to improve their corporate game."

"Huh. And Nellie?"

"Immature and insecure," Jilly said. "She's had to fight for every break in life and it shows. Right now she's not receptive to coaching, but give her time. I planted the seed."

"That's good of you, Jilly. I guess I should have done more when I worked with them. That last year was all about survival."

"You did the best you could at the time," she said. "At any rate, for all our heart-to-hearts, no one has made a single suspicious comment. They all seem truly glad to spend time together."

"Just don't let your guard down," I said. "Paulette told me she didn't know about Avis, and Avis said she did. So even my sweet admin is capable of lying. I understand why, but still... We're not hearing everything."

A long loud honk made us both jump. By this point we were on the crest of a small hill and I could see the farm below clearly. There was a black car in the parking area that looked fancy.

"Expecting someone in a Porsche?" Jilly asked.

"Nope. And I didn't expect you to recognize a Porsche at a distance, either."

"I've had some nice dates," she said, as we started back. "Hot little sports cars like that are too hard to get in and out of in a skirt and heels." She gave a little laugh. "I guess I'm not the Porsche type anymore."

"I'm afraid not. If you're dating my brother, you're the pickup truck type."

"I'm not dating your brother... yet. We hang out a little when we both have time, which as you know is not often. Maybe some day... When the murders end and the book clubs take over the inn." She glanced at me with a sly grin. "Have you seen the hotties on his basketball team? Some of them make Kellan look merely average. If we ever get a night off, we could double date."

It gave me a little pang that she was proposing new options for me. The mental wedding planning for Kellan and me had obviously screeched to a stop with the arrival of her roller-coaster-riding twin. There was nothing I could do but roll with it, so I did.

"I'm not permitted to date Asher's friends, remember? Bro code."

"Asher can't enforce that if he's dating *your* best friend. Just think about it. We could go square dancing. I saw a sign in town for it."

I laughed. "Right. Because I'm so coordinated." Keats was out ahead, trotting with purpose toward the new arrival. There was no sign of the stick-chasing pup now. "For now, I'll stick with my good buddy, Keats. When I'm ready, I could pick up some tips about rotational dating from my mom."

"Don't even," Jilly said, as we got closer. "Oh no. Is that who I think it is?"

Standing beside the low-slung Porsche coupe was a distinguished, silver-haired man in a dark suit. His arms were crossed and his face severe. Once, that frown had chilled me so much that I had to resist submissive peeing.

"What is Piers Frankel doing at Runaway Farm?" I said. "I can't believe Flordale's president would come all the way out here himself just for a staff murder."

"Play it cool," Jilly said. "He doesn't own you anymore, Ivy."

I swallowed hard. For 10 years, I watched this man in awe from the audience as he delivered motivational speeches. In fact, I'd never seen him outside the work context. It didn't surprise me at all that he drove a black Porsche. What did surprise me was that the car gleamed in the sunshine despite the long gravel lane. Most vehicles arrived coated with dust. Were there advances in dust-repel-lants, or had he polished it himself while waiting for us?

"Why, Ivy Galloway," he said, as we walked toward him. He forced his frown upside down, looking like an eerie marionette. "I've never seen you look better."

I glanced down at my overalls and boots, wondering if they'd magically changed into Cinderella's ball gown and glass slippers. My hair was bunched in a knot and there were dark rings under my eyes that would have defied makeup had I been inclined to apply it.

"Welcome to Runaway Farm, Mr. Frankel," I said. "If I've never looked better, that's sad to hear."

"It must be the country air," he said. "You're practically glowing. I guess I expected something different, considering what's happened since our team arrived."

Ah. So I was supposed to be sitting in a puddle of tears over the public relations slam to Flordale, not hiking through the fields as if the world still turned on its axis.

"Mr. Frankel, have you met my friend, Jilly Blackwood? She's the owner of the best headhunting firm in Boston and supplied many of your best recruits. Lucky for me, she's also a gifted chef and has been helping me start up my new inn."

He scanned Jilly from head to foot with cool, pale blue eyes and glanced away. "I'm familiar with your firm, Ms. Blackwood. Perhaps we'll chat later, after Ivy gives me a tour of the property."

Summarily dismissed, Jilly squeezed my forearm for luck and walked toward the house. It felt like a gust of frosty air hit me as she left, but I still had Keats. He was practically sitting on my feet, his posture erect, his ears folded back. I didn't need to see the dog's tail to know that Piers Frankel got a failing grade in the character department. That was no shock. Piers was known for being even more ruthless than Wilf, but without the clumsy buffoonery. In battle, Wilf's choice of weapon would be an axe, whereas Piers would slice you with a dagger before you ever saw the blade.

And now he wanted an exclusive tour of my farm. Well, Piers Frankel used to be top dog in my corporate life, but here at Runaway Farm, I was top dog and I had a great dog backing me. I could do this.

I patted the bulky front pocket of my bibbed overalls to make sure my phone was there. It had become a repository for everything I might need during the day, from a leash to sunglasses, making my outfit of choice even less flattering.

"Let's start with the barn," I said, pulling out my old corporate team player smile.

"Must we?" he said. "My shoes... They're Italian leather."

"Don't say that in front of the cows," I said, before realizing how it sounded. "Oops. That's nothing to joke about after what happened to Wilf. I'm sorry, Mr. Frankel."

"Call me Piers," he said. "And it's okay, Ivy. I heard you got hit on the head, too."

"I do blurt things out sometimes, I'm afraid." I led him in through the wide double doors. "Your shoes should be fine. Charlie's already mucked out. That said, my animals produce constantly. Did you know that there's money in manure, Mr. Frankel? I'm thinking of starting a Runaway Farm black label. But manure management can't be taken lightly. There's an art to it."

He turned and his pale eyes widened at my nervous babbling. "You were always so reticent, Ivy."

"Guess it's that fresh country air." More like past trauma. In just a few months the memories of my misery at Flordale had faded considerably but they rushed back now. He was there the day Avis Arron told me I had to do the mass firings. He witnessed my epiphany, when I realized I couldn't be Flordale's grim reaper anymore. He saw me lay down my metaphorical scythe and bolt.

My breathing was fast and shallow until Keats shoved his head under my left hand. It was like a life buoy and time slowed down again. After a few seconds, he moved out to circle and stare at Piers.

The dog was fast, low and definitely uneasy—as if there were a coyote near his sheep pasture.

More like a wolf, because Piers was no scruffy coyote.

I started to introduce Florence, the blind mare, but Piers kept walking, straight through the back door. His eyes were on the floor to preserve his footwear.

Outside, he scanned until he found his target. "There they are: the cows that killed my vice president."

"They've been cleared, sir. The autopsy showed that Wilf was struck and killed by a human, I'm afraid."

His pale eyes darted to my face. "With what? And by whom? Why am I just hearing about this now?"

As president of a large firm, he was used to being catered to, but it didn't work that way out here. "The police are under no obligation to keep us posted about their findings, sir. The chief of police was kind enough to share that information this morning. My cows had been unfairly threatened with slaughter by the County, you know."

His brow furrowed. "You really have suffered impairment, Ivy. What are cows compared to a man's life?"

I pressed my lips together for a moment to lock my professional filter into the "on" position. "Sir, I'm distraught that someone struck and killed Wilf Darby, and on my property, too. I have no idea who's behind this terrible crime, or the weapon they used. But I'm confident that our chief of police will resolve the matter quickly."

He let out a huffy snort and straightened his shoulders. The man knew how to wear the heck out of a suit, I'd give him that.

"It must be a crazed local," he said. "I know Wilf could be... polarizing. Perhaps he insulted your farmhand?"

"He managed to insult quite a few people during his short time here," I said. "Wilf was a bulldozer when he'd had a few drinks, unfortunately. I think a few people held grudges against him."

"Like your mother?" Piers said, with a sly smile.

Keats paused in his circuit and his ruff came up. I quelled him with a glance and a slight movement of my right hand. The last thing I needed was for a powerful man like Piers to take issue with my dog.

"Mr. Frankel, it serves no one to throw accusations around. Obviously, I'm as anxious to have answers as you are. The future of my farm and my new inn hangs in the balance."

He walked up to the fence securing the cow pasture and crossed his arms over the top rung. "Quite. In fact, it's time you gave up this foolish notion and came back to the firm, Ivy."

I took a step backward and my boot landed in a mudpuddle with a splash. It had rained hard overnight but the sun shone now as if Piers had arranged it. "Pardon me?"

"You heard me. I know you needed to make a grand statement and you've done that. So it's time to get back to your real job. We need you at Flordale."

"Sir, I couldn't even imagine—"

"Of course you could. We both know this is a negotiation. State your terms."

"It's not that at all. I could *never*—"

"You could *always*. For the right price. State your terms."

"There's nothing that would—"

"There's always *something* that would tempt you. Don't be coy. I assume you'll want Wilf's job with a very hefty raise. We're prepared to accept your request."

Keats' head arrived under my left hand and my fingers touched his soft ears, groping for calm. "That's not my request. I want—"

"I can't promote you directly to senior vice president. I'm sorry, but it would cause unrest. But I can pay you more than you ever dreamed of making."

"It's not about the—"

"We'll announce it today, while everyone's gathered here. I know how much they respect you. We all do."

I stomped my foot in frustration, which made quite an impact because my boot was still in the puddle. The dirty water splashed Piers' pant leg and he gave me a look of such loathing that I knew instantly that he didn't want me back at Flordale at all. Not for my skills, anyway. There must be another reason.

"I can't," I said, simply. "People and animals depend on me here." He tried to speak over me again and I lifted my foot, threatening another splash. "I appreciate your kind offer, sir, but there's no way—"

"There's always a way." He shook out a snowy handkerchief and dabbed at his pant leg. I was surprised to see an artfully disguised bald patch on his crown. Even a man like Piers couldn't control thinning hair.

"Not for this," I said. "Even if I wanted to sell—and I don't—my contract with the previous owner stipulates that she has to review and agree to the sale. I got a very good deal on the place. I couldn't have afforded it based on my buyout from Flordale."

"Ah, so that's it," he said, straightening. "You want us to review your buyout. Consider it done. And if we have to help finance this... dung heap... we will."

I shook my head, completely baffled. "Why on earth would you want me back that badly?"

He rolled his eyes. "Have you really forgotten how important reputation is to a company? Ever since you stormed out of that meeting in a tantrum it's been one PR disaster after another. The only thing to do—the right thing to do—is bring you back on board. I sent Wilf Darby here to make that happen. It's his fault you went rogue after the ten years we invested in grooming you. You should have been made vice president before him, actually, but Avis wouldn't hear of it." He shook his head. "Wilf was a liability to Flordale and she shielded him."

All his mixed messages swirled in my head. He thought Flordale had wronged me and wanted me back. But he despised me for who I was, or at least who I'd become. And he was prepared to give me carte blanche to clear this ugly blot from their corporate record.

Maybe all of this *should* have felt good, but it didn't. The only thing that felt good in this moment was Keats' head under my fingers. The only thing that smelled good was real manure, versus the corporate crap he was shovelling out. The only thing that sounded good was the contented grunts Archie made as he followed Heidi around the pasture. And the only thing that looked good was the path up to the house, where my best friend sat waiting on the porch swing.

"If you'll let me speak for a moment, sir, I can clear all this up," I said. "As much as I appreciate knowing I was valuable to the firm, I have no doubt I made the right move in coming home to Clover Grove. I belong here and nothing—truly nothing—could bring me back to Boston and Flordale. But thank you for your very generous offer."

He brushed dust off his sleeves with evident revulsion and shook his head. "You can't carry on with this silly plan, Ivy. Your inn is doomed. Like I said, reputation is everything. With two murders hanging over this dung heap, you're dead in the water."

"I'll recover. I have faith."

Shaking his silver head, his frown returned. "You're dangling off a precipice and one little push will send you over."

Was he threatening me? It sure sounded like he was trying to buy me off and silence this whole incident. There was no question in my mind that he would do what he felt necessary to protect his company. In retrospect, I was surprised it hadn't happened earlier. Maybe Avis was supposed to take care of it but was too overcome with grief.

Regardless, there was also no question in my mind that I'd do what I felt necessary to protect my farm, and especially all the creatures that depended on me. So I brought out a completely different smile to try on Piers. A conciliatory one.

"Sir, you've given me so much to think about. Maybe I was too hasty in turning you down. Please give me some time to think about your kind offer and how this might work for both of us." I started ahead of him to the Porsche and he followed. "Like you said, there's always a way."

I opened the car door and he folded himself rather elegantly into the driver's seat.

"Think fast, Ivy," he said. "I'll be staying at the Summit Hotel for a couple of days to meet with the staff and help them through this ordeal. I'll need your answer before I leave."

"Of course, sir," I said, starting to close the car door. "And please, let me pay for your dry cleaning."

I could only see one of his eyes as he peered out. It looked eerily like Keats' blue eye.

"The car will need detailing, too," he said. "This place is appalling. I don't know how you can—"

I closed the door before he could finish. It was a small act of defiance that lifted my heart and Keats' tail. I followed up with a corporate-quality smile and something like a salute as he drove off.

"See what you rescued me from?" I said, turning to Keats. "I'd take a conk on the head over Flordale any day of the week and twice on Tuesdays."

CHAPTER SEVENTEEN

J illy ran down the front stairs to join me while Piers Frankel was still a cloud of dust in the lane.

"How did it go?" she asked.

"You will not believe this story, Jilly," I said, standing on tiptoe to see the last of the Porsche. "Wait a second... what is going on down there?" I watched and then groaned. "Oh, no."

The big white County Animal Services truck had practically rolled into the ditch to give way to the sports car that had stopped beside it.

"Are they fighting?" Jilly said.

"Probably. He'll ask the County to cover detailing from all the dust the truck is kicking up."

I pulled my phone out of my front pocket and texted Senna York to come over as soon as she could to play mediator.

Before long, Tess Blade pulled the truck into my parking area and backed it around skillfully. Then she leapt out like a superhero ready to take on crimes against the County. Her red hair was in a long braid and her coveralls with the Clover Grove crest were crisp.

"Good morning, Officer Blade," I said. "What can I do for you today?"

"Just checking on the livestock, per my orders from the County. I've stopped by a couple of times but you're never here, it seems."

"It's only been two days since I saw you," I said.

"Animals need constant care and supervision," she said. "Especially feisty heifers like these."

She pointed at Heidi and Clara, who were contentedly grazing in their pasture while Archie frolicked and kicked up his heels.

"Charlie's doing his rounds, but they've had plenty of attention from both of us today," I said. "Which is why they look so darned happy, I suppose."

"I'll be the judge of that." She practically catapulted into the pasture with them. I was no slouch at fence navigation now but Tess seemed to have springs in her regulation boots. She bounded over to the cattle and circled them. The girls didn't look up from their grazing, but Archie came sniffing around.

"Do you mind if I ask why you were talking to my former boss in the lane?" I called.

She looked up from the calf. "You mean the jerk in the ego car? He complained about the dust and I told him to call the County if he wanted your lane paved."

Senna's Land Rover hurtled toward us. She pulled right up to the fence and jumped out. Her feet were a blur as she scaled the fence and joined Tess Blade.

"Hey Officer Blade," she said. "Remember I represent these heifers. You're not supposed to get near them without me."

"The County never agreed to that," Tess said. "You do your job, I do mine. Is there any reason for you to be worrying about the health of these cows?"

"About their physical welfare, no. But I certainly don't want them to be further traumatized by you pestering them."

"They're under County watch, remember? That's what I'm doing: watching."

"Excuse me," I called. "My cows have been cleared of wrongdoing, Officer Blade. The victim had already passed away when they, uh, stepped on him. Sharing a small pen with a corpse in the dark probably made them antsy."

She raised a big hand in my direction to block me. "We got the police report. Cattle shouldn't be kicking anyone, alive or dead. I've been told to continue to monitor the situation closely. You're not in the clear yet."

Senna shook her head. "Seriously? With all the complaints that truly require your attention, you're going to hassle Ivy and her livestock? I've called in more than a dozen cases myself in the past month. Neglect, improper breeding, improper feeding, failure to protect, failure to vaccinate. That's just for starters. Don't even get me started on castration practices that are abhorrent and downright cruel."

"We're checking into your reports one by one," Tess said. "Doesn't mean I don't have time to drop by when I'm in the neighborhood."

Senna advanced on her. "Look, these cows are happy and very well cared for. And that calf is prancing around today because I castrated him humanely and early, unlike many of the people I told you about." She glanced over at me. "Remind me to check the barn again for my cutters, Ivy. I'm always leaving things behind."

Tess looked as if she might back down for a second and then thought better of it. Towering over the vet, she said, "Senna, how about we hammer out where your job ends and mine begins?"

"That's Doctor York, Officer Blade."

Jilly came up beside me. "No one needs to be hammering anything. Why don't you both come up to the house? I've got a blueberry coffee cake fresh out of the oven."

There was a momentary standoff, and then both women took a single step backward.

"I don't eat cake on the job," Tess said. "But thanks." She jumped the fence and loped back to her truck. "I'll see Heidi and

Clara tomorrow, and will continue as long as the County tells me to do it."

"I'll take the cake," Senna said, grinning from the top rung.

"Me too," I said, but when my phone buzzed, I added, "Make mine to go. Plus a spare. I've been summoned."

Ten minutes later, I drove over to visit my neighbor with a slab of blueberry cake on the front seat, while Keats reluctantly rode in the back.

"Oh, lighten up," I said, when he mumbled a complaint. "You ride shotgun unless it's Jilly or her gourmet grub. Seems fair to me."

Edna was standing at the door when we arrived, wearing her usual yellowed nursing uniform. It was loose on her now, although she was still robust for her age. I wouldn't be surprised if she could take me in a fistfight.

"What's going on?" I asked, handing her the cake as I stepped into the front hall. "And don't ask me to take off my boots so that you can pretend to lose them for two days, Miss Evans."

"I forget things," she said, with her sly smile. "I'm no spring chicken, Ivy. And how are my chickens doing, by the way?"

"Settling in nicely. Now, I assume you've observed something important. Or is this a social call?"

"I don't socialize with people who drag dirt and dogs in here," she said. "But we have an arrangement. You bring me meals and I bring you information."

I noticed that the occasional food drop-off we'd agreed upon had expanded to be "meals," in general. Seeing her every single day was more of a commitment than I wanted to make, but we could renegotiate after Wilf's murder was solved. "Jilly's serving beef bourguignon tonight, and I hear it's delicious."

She gave a curt nod, to signal the meal worthy of her intel. "I noticed you chatting with the bigwig in his black Porsche earlier. I've never trusted a man who likes Porsches. There are understated cars that still signal virility for insecure men, don't you agree?"

"I'm not one for fancy cars, period. The Porsche belongs to the president of the Flordale Corporation. He came down to check on the staff, but they're out on a drive with Asher."

"I'd never drive anywhere with Asher," she said. "Did you know he had more speeding tickets than any teenager in Clover Grove? He set a record."

"I didn't actually," I said. "But I guess it was good practice for police work. Now, what piqued your interest in Piers Frankel and his sports car?"

"I thought you might be interested to know that I saw the same car sitting outside The Tipsy Grape the day before your guests arrived. I was in town getting my toenails clipped at the podiatrist and couldn't help noticing the Porsche as I passed. We don't see a lot of flashy cars like that, and it completely outclassed the red Corvette sitting beside it."

She crossed her arms and smiled, waiting for my reaction. I blinked a few times and swallowed before speaking. "You saw my boss's car and his boss's car sitting together outside a bar? Before my guests arrived?"

"Ivy, have you been getting enough sleep? You're slow on the uptake, even for you."

"Why on earth would Piers and Wilf Darby be in a bar in Clover Grove together before our team retreat?"

"I don't know. Aren't you corporate types always scheming up takeovers?"

Recovering from the surprise, I said, "How come you didn't mention seeing Wilf's Corvette there the last time we chatted, Miss Evans?"

She shrugged. "I assumed he was just having cocktails with his lady friend until I saw the bigwig today. Besides, information is currency, isn't it?"

"Apparently. Did you go into The Tipsy Grape, perchance?"

"Now, why would an upstanding woman like me go into a den

of iniquity like that? Spirits have never touched these lips, Ivy. How do you think I've lived so long?"

I had a few good comebacks for that, but I tamped them down. "I'd sure love to know what they were talking about in that bar."

"Then you'd better ask your mother," Edna said. "I saw her boyfriend walk in as I was passing. It was broad daylight, mind you. Some people don't care about appearances."

"Mom's boyfriend?" My poker face was certainly getting a workout today.

"One of them, anyway. Dahlia's been getting around these days. It's hard to keep up."

"Could you describe this man?" I asked, as a flush tried to fight its way over my collar.

"Tall. Thin. Nicely trimmed grey beard a shade lighter than his hair. I don't like beards on principle, of course. You never know how long food particles have been stuck in there."

"Interesting," I said, summoning Keats. The dog had slipped behind Edna to do his own investigation. He must have come up empty because his tail drooped in disappointment.

"I appreciate your sharing this information, Miss Evans, and I'll pass it along promptly to Chief Harper."

Smirking, she pulled the door open for me. "You don't want to talk to your mom about her dating life? Can't say as I blame you."

"Oh, you'd be surprised how frank we are in our family sometimes," I said. "But I've had a few lectures from Chief Harper about not sharing leads quickly enough."

"Me too," she said. "But Kellan doesn't scare me. I vividly remember vaccinating that boy. He wasn't squirmy like your brother. Asher could become boneless and practically slide into a crack to escape. Kellan was stoic. Never made a peep."

I could tell she preferred thrashers like Asher. There was probably more satisfaction in finally nailing them. Maybe she thought Kellan was the weaker for his stoicism, but she was wrong about that. Asher was brash and bold, but Kellan was strategic and dogged. I'd rather he had my back in any battle.

That's why I planned to contact him promptly about everything that had happened today. It had nothing to do with Mom and how her rotational dating was lighting up the town's gossip lines. I'd leave that in Daisy's capable hands.

As if reading my mind, Edna said, "How's Daisy doing after the Lloyd Boyce fiasco? I'm surprised her husband didn't divorce her."

That comment hurt far more than her digs about my mother, but my blandest smile had locked itself down automatically. Maybe the effects of my concussion were abating.

"All's good with my family," I said, passing in front of her and walking down the front stairs. "How's bridge club these days? I'm impressed with how well *you* bounced back after the Lloyd Boyce fiasco. Nicely done, Miss Evans."

I felt her caustic gaze withering me from behind and didn't turn till I got to the truck.

"You seem moody these days, Ivy," she called out. "I hope it's not because Kellan Harper has taken up with that blonde. If it makes you feel better, she's got nothing on you... other than the fact that she's not bogged down by a million pets. Kellan's more genteel than the average Clover Grove man. You'd do better to find someone who can tolerate all your manure." She waited a beat before firing the last shot. "It won't be easy. But there are worse things than being single. I'm a role model for you."

My foot slipped as I tried to get into the truck and I did a face-plant into the driver's seat. Keats, who'd jumped in ahead of me, leaned over from the passenger seat to lick my hair. "It's okay, buddy, I'm fine," I said. "A kick in the prides never killed anyone."

"It's a shame about Kellan but at least you have your mutt," Edna shouted. "In the long run, dogs are probably a better invest-ment, no matter how handsome the police chief is."

I managed to swing into the truck without mishap on the second try. "Enjoy the blueberry cake, Miss Evans," I called. "I'll be back with the beef bourguignon later."

"Out here, we just call it stew, Ivy. The sooner you drop the affectations, the sooner you'll be accepted and find an appropriate match. No man wants a snooty outsider."

I stalled twice backing out, which was no surprise. Her comments had completely deflated me. I felt so small I could barely reach the pedals.

"One day she'll get what's coming to her, Keats," I said, gunning it out of Edna's driveway just for the satisfaction of sending dust whirling up into her face. "Sometimes you just have to trust in karma."

CHAPTER EIGHTEEN

"Please tell me this isn't another intervention," my mother said, looking up from her seat at Daisy's kitchen table.

"It's another intervention," I said, slipping into the seat opposite her. "But just between you and me, this time."

"Plus Daisy, obviously." She rolled her eyes toward my sister, who was scrubbing the kitchen counter with extra verve. Mom had already left a semicircle of lip prints on a white china mug she'd chosen herself, no doubt to aggravate her firstborn. With every fresh application of scarlet, Daisy spritzed the counter with vinegar solution. She was itching to decontaminate the mug but she'd have to wait.

"I don't want to drag this out, Mom," I said, cradling my own cup of tea. "In fact, I'd prefer never to hear about your dating life again."

"Good," she said, raising a manicured hand. "Let's leave it there, then, shall we?"

"We shan't and can't," I said, following her gaze to the crescents of dirt under my own fingernails. No matter how many times a day I used soap and a nail brush, the grime was nearly always there.

"Edna Evans told me you have a longer string of suitors than we imagined."

"I explained the concept of rotational dating, Ivy. I'm simply enjoying the company of several men. One likes to dance, another to walk in the hills, a third to enjoy the limited cultural events this town has to offer, and so on. I don't like to be pinned down and variety is the spice of life."

It looked like Daisy might snap her arm in two from the pressure of scouring.

"No need to debate your approach," I said. "Even if it's not for the rest of us. I really just want to speak to you about one particular man. Tall, thin and bearded, Edna said. You've been seen at The Tipsy Grape with him, apparently."

"Thaddeus, yes. He's from Dorset Hills and joins me for a cocktail from time to time. Lovely man, although too much of a dog enthusiast for anything serious, I'm afraid." She flashed her teeth at me. "What about him?"

"Apparently Edna saw him go into the bar around the same time the president of Flordale met with Wilf Darby. It was the day before the rest of the guests had even arrived in Clover Grove. I'm wondering what they were talking about, and knowing how loud Wilf was, I thought your friend Thaddeus might have overheard something useful."

Daisy looked up from her cleaning. "Couldn't you just leave that legwork to Kellan, Ivy?"

"I told him about it," I said. "I figure he has his hands full and the least I can do is help out where Flordale politics are involved."

Mom pulled out her phone and tapped a text, her long nails clicking. "I don't blame you for wanting to advocate for yourself, Ivy. We won't be able to relax in this town until Asher is chief of police."

I nearly spit out my mouthful of tea. "Mom, come on. Asher has many wonderful qualities, but if he were chief, all the criminals would run free. He's too nice."

"There's nothing wrong with nice," she said. "In fact, there's everything right about it. Kellan could learn a thing or two about nice from your brother."

"Mom, Kellan's a good guy," Daisy said. "Cut him a break."

"I will not. He's made life difficult for me on numerous occasions. And he broke Ivy's heart, too."

I considered mentioning all the ways Kellan had helped Mom, but it would create too much of a diversion.

"There's nothing wrong with Ivy reconnecting with Kellan," Daisy said. "Although seeing a cop would be difficult. Their job is so dangerous."

"That's right," Mom said, although I was pretty sure that hadn't factored into her thinking. "Plus he spurned her once already, and no man gets a second chance to do that with the Galloway girls."

"Except my husband," Daisy said, with a pained smile.

"You have children. That's different," Mom said. "Although I'd never have taken your father back in a million years."

"Let's come full circle and talk about Thaddeus," I said.

Mom pushed her chair back and stood, smoothing the creases from her royal blue A-line dress. It looked more appropriate for high tea than a mug of pekoe in Daisy's kitchen.

"Are we done?" Daisy asked, swooping in to collect the mug with the waxy red stains.

"Yes, darling. Now, go get yourself ready, and lend Ivy something presentable to wear. We're meeting Thaddeus at The Thirsty Grape in an hour."

"Why do I have to go?" Daisy whined, carrying the mug to the sink.

"Because I want my favorite daughters to meet my gentleman friend," she said, with a tinkling little laugh. "Now, please don't mention my rotation to Thaddeus, or Charlie for that matter, Ivy. I'm sure they're dating others too, but there's no reason to be crass about it."

"Charlie and I have more important things to discuss than your love life," I said, following Daisy out of the room.

Half an hour later, Daisy and I slunk into the bar behind our mother. She waved gaily at the bartender and walked directly to a table in the darkest corner. Gesturing for me to slide into the booth ahead of her, she said, "I don't want Thaddeus to see that your pants are too short."

"Then you shouldn't have made me wear Daisy's clothes," I said. "I'm four inches taller than her."

"Well, you couldn't walk into a nice bar like this in bibbed overalls," she said.

"Overalls suit my lifestyle now," I said. "I wore suits for ten years and it feels great to expand my lungs. Which I currently can't do in Daisy's blouse without popping the buttons."

"Then don't breathe too much," Mom advised. "Slow and steady wins the race. I'm sure you know that. You've always been my calm one."

The door opened and we all looked up, expecting tall, thin and bearded. What we saw was tall, brawny and clean-shaven. Kellan Harper.

I waved and he walked toward us.

"Why is he here?" Mom asked. "I don't need the chief of police chaperoning me."

"This isn't about you, remember? It's about finding out who killed Wilf Darby, and I let Kellan know what we were doing."

He slipped into the booth beside Daisy and opposite my mother. "Ivy, giving me a heads up about what you're doing is an improvement," he said. "But you shouldn't be doing anything at all. Don't you have enough work with your farm and your guests?"

"Jilly's got it covered," I said. "She's doing career coaching and a resume workshop today. I don't think any of them want to stick around Flordale after what's happened."

Mom tapped her nails on the table to get Kellan's attention. "Ivy discovered one of my sources might have information," she said. "I was happy to make the introductions."

"I thought we should move quickly on this because Piers Frankel is only in town for another day," I told Kellan. "He wanted my answer about his proposition by tomorrow."

"Proposition!" Three voices overlapped.

"Not *that* kind of proposition," I said. "Although it was equally distasteful. He wants me to come back to Flordale in Wilf's position with a huge salary increase. He'd hoped to announce it to the team while they're here."

Mom gasped, covered her mouth, and then clapped her hands. "Oh Ivy, that's wonderful news. I'm so happy for you." She reached for my hand and squeezed it hard. "I always knew they'd regret the way they treated you and come crawling back. And the president himself, no less."

I shook my hand loose. "He regrets the optics and the bad press, Mom, that's all. His contempt for me—or at least my new lifestyle— was quite obvious."

"But that's understandable," Mom said. "Running a hobby farm is a ridiculous lifestyle choice. Kellan thinks so, too."

"Don't bring me into this," he said. The light was dim but I could still tell his face had flushed. "Ivy's lifestyle choices are her own to make."

"But isn't that why you chose the other girl?" Mom asked. "I assume she's no farmer."

My gasp of horror burst not one, but two buttons on Daisy's blouse. Looking down, I realized my sports bra was now on full display. I don't know if I was more mortified that my bra was showing, or that it was the ugliest bra in the world. Either way, I clutched the edges of the blouse together and felt my face ignite. Luckily Mom didn't notice because her sights were still on Kellan. But Kellan certainly noticed. His eyes dropped to my chest again and again, either hoping or fearing the free show would repeat.

"A mother cares about these things," she continued. "I heard Ivy was so shocked to see you and your lady at the harvest fair that she threw up."

Holding the blouse with one hand, I grabbed her hand with the other and squeezed until she yelped. "Mom, Kellan's lifestyle choices are *his* own to make."

"True," he said, a small smirk playing on his lips. "Although I'll clarify for the record that the woman in question is the fiancée of an old friend. They're thinking about moving here, so I showed her around."

I appreciated the clarification, even if he wasn't meeting my eyes. Even if he disapproved of my farm. The clarification, not to mention the smirk, told me there might still be hope. And to my mind, the best way to move ahead was to stick to the matter at hand.

"Kellan, don't you think it's odd that Piers Frankel arrived at my farm when his staff were all away to make me this grand offer? He said Wilf made a mistake in letting me go, and further, that Wilf was supposed to woo me back during the team retreat."

Kellan shrugged. "I don't know how companies work. Happily, I've never had to work for one."

"Then you'll just need to trust me that it's odd. It was clear to me that he wanted Wilf Darby gone. He said Wilf was a liability to Flordale."

"Well, I doubt he'd kill Wilf, if that's what you're implying," Kellan said. "There are easier ways to get rid of a vice president. Like a huge buyout. He was willing to throw money at you to get what he wanted."

"Yeah, well, there's something fishy going on. Piers lied about just arriving in town, when he's been here for days. What else is he covering up? I'm hoping Mom's boyfriend overheard something when Piers and Wilf met up here."

"Thaddeus is not my boyfriend, Ivy," she said. "He's just one of many gentlemen I spend time with on occasion. Please don't give Kellan the wrong idea."

"Mom, enough. Let's stick to business."

"All right," she said, jerking her hand away from mine. "Let's talk about your promotion, then. When do you start?"

"Never. Never is when I start, Mom. Right now I have a houseful of possible suspects in my former boss's murder. Do you really think I'd want to step into his shoes and put myself on the firing line? On top of that, Wilf's boss might be a suspect, not to mention his girlfriend or possibly her jealous husband. Working in senior management at Flordale is dangerous. I'd rather take my chances with my vicious pig."

Kellan laughed, and it was a welcome sound, even if it was at my expense. "Avis Arron and her husband both have alibis," he said. "So strike two off the list."

"Even so, I'd never go back to work there again."

"But darling, with the black cloud hanging over the farm—"

"I may need to find a job to help support the farm till the clouds clear, and I'll do that locally if I need to. Dorset Hills would have work for people with my skills."

She tried to grab my hand again. "Just think about it, that's all I ask. You were the only one of my children to escape this small-minded town, and now—"

"And now I'm back and I love it," I said. "Keats and I are settled here for good, so you'd better get used to it."

We glared at each other long enough that Daisy threw herself into the breach. "Any sign of the murder weapon yet?"

Kellan shook his head. "My team's combed the property thoroughly and come up with nothing." Staring at the door, he added, "I assume Keats hasn't found anything?"

A genuine smile—my first in what felt like forever—spread over my face. "Are you saying you'd welcome Keats' help, Chief Harper?"

"No, but I do believe that if the murder weapon was on your property your dog would probably find it. He has a good nose, no question about that."

"We haven't walked the fields much lately, but if you're deputizing Keats, I'll make it a priority."

He pulled his eyes back from the door to stare at me. "Ivy, I'm repeating—this time in front of your mother—that I want you to avoid any further involvement and stay safe. You shouldn't be walking the fields alone, even with Keats."

"Here's the thing: it's quite possible—even likely—that the killer is sleeping under the same roof with me."

"If so, they don't have motive to make a move against you. Don't give them one by poking around."

"Listen to him, Ivy," Daisy said. "Please. It's dangerous for you, Jilly, the guests and even the animals."

"I agree," Mom said. "And I want you to give that Flordale offer more thought, darling. Once Kellan catches the killer, I'm quite sure it will be safe to go back."

"Doing my best, ma'am," he said.

"Do not call me that in front of Thaddeus," she said, her hand flying up in a wave. "There he is now."

Thaddeus was exactly as Edna described him, and his beard looked clean and well kept. He squeezed in beside my mother and kissed her cheek, unintentionally driving me right into the corner of the booth. Kellan glanced at me and his lips twitched. He was quite sure this was going to be a bust, I knew, but at least he'd get a laugh out of it.

"It's so good of you to come, Thad," Mom said, introducing Daisy, Kellan and finally, me. "I know this may seem a little odd, but we really just want to know whether you happened to notice two men from Ivy's company meeting here the last time you visited."

I leaned forward and described Wilf and Piers. "One drove a red Corvette and the other a black Porsche. I heard from a neighbor that you were here at around the same time."

He nodded. "I was meeting someone for lunch, actually. A friend."

Mom patted his arm. "It's all right, Thad. We're all dating here. No need to feel awkward about it."

Smiling in relief, he went on. "While I waited, I noticed the two men you described because they were arguing. The younger one got so red I thought he might have a heart attack. The silver-haired guy was cooler, but he leaned across the table in a threatening way. He knows how to take up space."

"Could you hear what they were arguing about?" I asked.

"Ivy," Kellan said. "Leave the questions to me, please. Thaddeus, go on."

"Not all of it, because the silverback was soft-spoken. But the red-faced guy said over and over, 'You can't fire me. I gave my life to this company. And my marriage.' Then the silverback said, 'You're a disgrace.'" Thaddeus shuddered. "It hurt just to hear that. The red-faced man's pride must have been shattered. He made all kinds of excuses that silverback shot down one by one. Red ended up actually pleading with him. He said he'd lose his lady and maybe even his kids and asked his boss to let him 'make it right.'"

Kellan had pulled out his notepad and was writing furiously. "And what did the older man say to that?"

Thaddeus' brow furrowed and he sighed. "He said, 'You'd better make it right. Or you won't like what happens next at all.'"

"In your opinion, did it sound like a serious threat?" Kellan asked.

"I'm no expert, but I'm afraid so. I'm quite certain Red was going to be demoted or fired."

"Is that it?" Kellan asked.

"That's all I heard, because my friend arrived, and I always give a lady my full attention."

Mom patted his arm again. "He most certainly does. A perfect gentleman." She turned to Kellan. "Men of your generation could learn a thing or two from ours, Kellan."

"No doubt," he said, taking Thad's card and sliding out of the booth. I'd never seen a man make better time getting out of a bar.

"Was it something I said?" Mom asked, with the tinkling laugh that grated on me.

I gave her a little shove so I could make a similar exit. "If you'll excuse me, I have to go rake my manure pile. Did you know it can explode if it's not turned regularly?"

"Oh, Ivy." She fanned her face as she got out of the booth after Thaddeus to release me. "Don't pretend to be funny in front of Thaddeus."

"Pleasure to meet you, Thaddeus," I said, still clutching Daisy's blouse together. "I can hook you up with fertilizer anytime. Runaway Farm has the best combination of dung in Clover Grove. I'm creating a black label brand."

"*Ivy!* Stop that right now."

Finally, I'd managed to mortify her. It was a very proud moment, and I wasn't ashamed to admit it.

As I left, I heard her tell Thad, "She was always the good one, you know. The concussion did terrible things..."

Outside, I climbed into the truck, happily submitting to an exuberant greeting from Keats. "I don't know how long we can ride on the concussion excuse, buddy, because I think it's the new normal. Some days life feels really wobbly, you know?"

He treated me to a steady look from his warm brown eye, put

one paw on my leg and mumbled some reassurance. Confidence flowed back into me.

"Okay, you're right," I said, as he propped himself on the dash, ready to take on the next challenge. "We'll get this figured out together. Like we always do."

CHAPTER NINETEEN

Jilly and I barely said a word as we drove to town that afternoon. Asher had once again offered to take the Flordale guests on a drive down the range of hills to Brenton, a town that boasted a cute little museum and art gallery, plus some high-end gift and clothing stores. I wasn't sure whether he was looking out for me, trying to impress Jilly, or following Kellan's orders to keep everyone well occupied and supervised. I accepted gratefully and without asking questions.

Even the truck was inclined to cooperate, and we got to the outskirts without so much as a hiccup. That gave us a chance to enjoy the companionable silence only a true, longstanding friendship allows. Keats was subdued as well, simply staring out the back passenger window instead of roving around to monitor the world from every angle, as he usually did.

That's why, when he gave a sharp little yip of what sounded like alarm, Jilly and I instantly snapped out of our trance.

"What is it, buddy?" I asked, trying to follow his gaze while staying in my lane. "Oh. *Her.*"

I geared down carefully to avoid stalling and we watched the big white cube van with the County logo on its side turn right, and then pull over near the corner. Tess Blade hopped out, ran around the back of the truck and opened the rear doors.

"Careful," Jilly said. "Any slower and you'll—"

I stalled the pickup. But the time it took to get going again was enough to see Tess pull out a dog catchpole—a long fiberglass pole with a noose on the end of it. I shivered and Keats let out a long, keening whine. We had both experienced what a catchpole could do when it was in the wrong hands. Could a catchpole ever be in the *right* hands? Surely there were ways to help stray dogs that didn't involve choking them.

Jilly's hand was on my right arm and I hadn't noticed. "Pull over until you catch your breath," she said.

I hadn't noticed I was gasping like a drowning woman, either. "Bad memories," I said.

"I know. Let's just take a moment before we go on." She waited till I'd pulled ahead and onto the shoulder before saying, "It wasn't Tess Blade's fault, remember? The person who did that to you is gone."

"Gone," I said, pulling even further ahead, until the truck was surrounded by scrub bush on the side of the road. We were still outside town limits, where the roads were wide. "I don't want to see what she does with that pole."

"Me either. We'll rest a minute and then go on, okay?"

Keats was pacing back and forth across the back seat, a breathing, black-and-white embodiment of my unease. He paused for a second when I turned and stared at me with his blue eye. His warm brown eye would have calmed me, if he'd wanted me calm. I got the distinct impression he wanted me to do something. But what?

"Is there something I should know about Tess?" I said.

Jilly shrugged. "How would I know?"

"I was asking Keats," I said. "He's trying to mesmerize me like he does the livestock. That's what sheepdogs do, you know."

She turned and watched, shaking her head as she saw him work his magic. "He is, too. Totally fixated. What is up with him?"

I tore my eyes away from the dog and focussed on the County truck instead. And that's when it hit me. "Jilly, I've got to look inside that truck."

"What? No! Are you crazy?"

"Maybe, but I'll explain later. For the moment, you need to stand watch while I take a quick look. It'll take Tess time to seize and wrangle a dog. I can get in and out in that time, no problem."

"No way," she said, crossing her arms. "I am calling Kellan right now if you even try it, Ivy Galloway. I'm sure whatever you have in mind is dangerous. On top of that, you could get in trouble with the County. You're already on the watch list."

"I won't get in trouble if I don't get caught. All I need to do is take a quick peek into the truck. No big deal." I was already opening the driver's door. "All you need to do is stand watch with Keats for three or four minutes. I've had an epiphany, thanks to Keats, and I need to see if we're right."

"Ivy, you'll be the death of us all," she said. But she opened her door and jumped down.

I let Keats out, hooked him up and handed her the leash. "Here's your cover," I said. "You're just out walking the dog. Nothing to see here."

We walked around the corner to where the white truck was parked at the end of the long driveway of a mansion that had seen grander times. There was no sign of Tess Blade. She could have been inside, or behind the house. Either way, I probably had a good few minutes before she emerged. On the other hand, the woman always moved at a run.

The back doors of the County truck were still open, practically inviting me to hop inside.

"Stand a bit closer to the gate, where you can see her coming," I said. "Code word bluebird."

"Code words death wish," Jilly grumbled. "This had better be worth it, Ivy."

Keats grumbled as I hoisted myself into the truck and I hushed him. "Just stand watch, Keats. It's a critical role." I poked my head back out. "Come up with a stalling tactic just in case, Jilly."

"Oh right," she said. "Maybe I'll pretend to faint and see how that goes."

"Perfect." I gave her the thumbs up and turned on my phone light. What I was looking for should stand out in all the normal equipment a dogcatcher might carry.

Except that this particular dogcatcher carried a lot of stuff. There were two big metal dog crates near the back door that I had to skirt around without bashing my shins. Behind them were a couple of smaller plastic dog carriers, some baskets overflowing with bungee cords and rope, and a pile of tarps.

The walls were covered in hooks holding even more apparatus, including three ladders, a long poker similar to the one I used to manage Wilma, and a shepherd's hook. There were extra coveralls, hip waders and even a full scuba suit. It seemed like she was ready for anything, whether it be a cat in a tree, runaway livestock, or even Noah's ark sinking in one of the nearby streams, since there was no large body of water within county limits.

With all of this equipment neatly arranged, I still didn't see what I was looking for. That left me no choice but to clamber over everything and go right to the back of the truck.

That's when I heard Jilly's voice ring out loud and clear. "Bluebird. Oh look, buddy, it's a BLUEBIRD."

Cursing softly, I flashed the light into each back corner. In one corner, there was a pile of towels and the tip of a silver handle poked out from under them. Bending, I carefully lifted the corner of one towel and gasped. I'd expected to find this—*knew* I would find this—and yet I was still shocked.

No matter how many times Jilly chanted "bluebird" I wasn't

leaving without this valuable evidence. If I did, I was quite sure it wouldn't be here when Kellan's team came to investigate. Tess Blade would dispose of it quickly, because it didn't belong to her and it sure looked incriminating. I was surprised she hadn't done so already. For all her officiousness, she didn't seem stupid.

Now I was stuck. There was no getting out of the truck without an explanation, and I could hear Tess and Jilly talking now. Jilly's voice had taken on a high sing-song quality and I only picked up a few words like "dog walk" and "gorgeous weather."

Tess was getting closer to the truck and barking that didn't come from Keats told me I'd soon have company in the back. Wrapping the towel around the metal device, I tucked it inside my coat. Then I got down on my hands and knees, grabbed a tarp and draped it over myself. The plastic dog carriers would shield me from view unless she hopped right inside. She should be able to get the stray dog into the metal crate without doing that, and she probably wouldn't want to waste time. Then, after she closed the door and went around to climb inside the cab, I could release myself and jump out before she started rolling.

It was a good plan, if I could just stay calm and move quickly at the right moment.

There was growling behind the truck from the stray dog, and Tess spoke with soothing sweet talk. I hadn't expected her to be so kind, but I guess it was part of her training.

"Just hop in here, honey," she said. "Let me put the ramp down for you because I know it's scary. But it's all going to be fine. We'll get you back to headquarters and see if we can find your owner. And if we can't, well, a pretty dog like you will find a new home. I can guarantee you that. Now, up you go."

There was a scrabble of claws on metal and then another metal clatter as the crate door closed.

"Good girl. Now you're safe. You hang tight back here. I'll drive nice and slow so it doesn't freak you out, okay?"

The double doors slammed one after the other, leaving me alone in the back of the Animal Services truck with a terrified stray dog and a bloody murder weapon.

CHAPTER TWENTY

Tess had lied to the stray dog twice.

First, she said the dog was pretty. When I threw off the tarp and shone my phone light into the crate, however, I saw the big crossbreed wasn't attractive at all. She was a peculiar mix of bulldog and possibly shar pei, with cropped ears and loose folds of taupe skin. But then we all have "a type," I supposed, and my type was border collie.

Second, Tess didn't drive slowly. In fact, she took off like a rocket long before I could get to the door, taking corners so erratically that the metal crate slid around. The dog whined and I crawled over to comfort her. The poor thing licked my fingers through the bars and I murmured, "We'll be okay, girl. Let's just hang on for dear life."

Bracing my boots on the side of the truck, I pushed the crate back and sat that way to prevent it from sliding. It prevented me from sliding too, so it was a good strategy. It also left my hands free to text Jilly.

"Follow me," I wrote. "I've got a plan."

"I don't drive stick, remember?"

"You've seen me do it."

"Forget it. Hailing a cab," she said.

Hailing cabs was one of Jilly's superpowers. Back in Boston, I'd thrash my arm around to no avail, only to have Jilly lift a finger and have a taxi magically appear. Here in Clover Grove, however, cabs were few and far between.

Nevertheless, a few minutes later she texted that she was cabbed up and in pursuit.

"Here's the plan," I wrote. "Get Teri Mason to call in an animal emergency. Tell her to throw the word 'rabies' around. Tess will rush over there, and when she goes inside I'll escape."

There was a long gap in texts but I didn't need Jilly to tell me it had worked. The truck screeched to a halt, pulled a heart-stopping U-turn and took off again. Tess had to slow down in town, and that gave me a chance to clamber back to the pile of tarps and bury myself again.

Soon, the truck stopped and I felt the vibration as the driver's door slammed shut. I had just enough time to turn my phone off before there was a loud click and the back doors opened. Cool air poured in and it was all I could do not to gasp audibly. The poor dog was so terrified she'd ejected from all orifices and in close confines, it stank something awful.

"Oh girly, you've had an accident," she said. "Or three. But you're going to have to sit tight for a bit because we've got an emergency. A serious one." There was a pause and she mused, "What should I take for a rabid raccoon? I've got the catchpole and the long gloves. I need the plastic carrier."

Oh no. The plastic carrier that was right beside me.

I heard the thump of boots as she sprang into the truck and clomped toward me. She grabbed the first plastic crate, slid it out and then dropped it over the side of the truck with a clatter.

"I'll take the poker, too," she said, coming back my way.

The poker that was right beside the murder weapon now tucked into my jacket.

There was a long pause, during which I held my breath and prayed. Finally I heard her pick up the poker from the floor. It whacked me in the shin as she turned and I bit my lip to keep from yelping in pain.

The pole clunked against the door before she tossed it out on the asphalt and then she jumped down after it. "Stay calm," she said. "I'll leave the door open to air it out a bit. If there's a rabid raccoon here, we'll figure something out for you. Chill, sweetheart."

I waited for the rattle of the plastic crate to fade away and added an extra minute or two in case she forgot something.

Then I threw back the tarp and moved faster than I probably ever had in my life.

JILLY SAID nothing as we rode in the cab back to my pickup. Absolutely nothing. It was no longer a companionable silence but an angry one, and I'd felt nothing quite like it in our 15 years of friendship.

Keats on the other hand could not have been more delighted with me. There was room between Jilly and me in the back seat of the cab, but he insisted on sitting in my lap. It wasn't terribly comfortable given what I was concealing. He wriggled, licked my face and fanned his tail in a low wag that told me how worried he'd been about me. Jilly had worried, too, I knew, but she certainly wasn't going to give me the big sloppy smile Keats had on his face.

"I can explain," I said.

"Good." Her green eyes were as cool as a frozen pond. "Because Kellan is meeting us at your truck."

"Perfect." I let out a huge sigh of relief. "I don't want to hold onto this thing one second longer than necessary."

She gestured to the cab driver in front of us. "Let's talk about it in a few minutes."

It really was only a few minutes. Tess had been heading for the Animal Services building that sat on the far side of town when she got called to Teri Mason's store, which wasn't far from where we'd left the truck. Poor Teri was probably busy explaining right now how the rabid raccoon had mysteriously vanished. Hopefully she'd be able to convince Tess it was all a big mistake so the stray dog wouldn't have to sit in the truck too long.

When the cab dropped us off, there was no sign of the police SUV. We got inside to wait and Jilly raised her eyebrows. I opened my jacket and pulled back the towel, expecting shock... dismay... *something*.

"What exactly is that?" she said. "Bolt cutters?"

"Sort of." The 18-inch-long contraption looked like pliers, with handles at one end and rounded pinchers at the other. "It's a castrator, also known as an emasculator."

"Okay. But why did you need to steal this contraption from Tess Blade?"

"I didn't steal it, exactly. I reclaimed it for Senna. Her castrator went missing at Runaway Farm the day she snipped Archie. But when she was lecturing Tess about humane castration on her last visit, I got a funny feeling. I couldn't put my finger on it till we saw the truck today. Then I put two and two together and realized Tess stole the castrator when she was hanging around after Wilf's murder. She was inside the barn that morning, so she had access."

Jilly squinted, trying to keep up. "Why would she want the castrator?"

"Well, either she didn't want to spend County dollars to buy her own, or..."

"Or *what*?"

"Or, if I'm correct, this is the murder weapon. I wouldn't take too close a look if I were you. Senna says it's a bloodless procedure, but this castrator isn't entirely clean, if you catch my drift."

"Are you saying Tess Blade used this thing to kill Wilf? Why would she do that?"

"I've speculated that Piers Frankel may have paid someone off to do the deed. And they did stop to chat when their vehicles passed in my lane, right?" I shook my head and signed. "For the moment, all I know is that Senna told me she left her castrator behind, and Tess reacted when Senna mentioned it."

"And you put this together when we saw the truck here today?"

"Actually, Keats put it together," I said. "He wanted me to search that truck."

She shook her head uncertainly. "I was here, remember. I didn't hear him say that."

"I know." I patted her arm with a very dirty hand. "He was agitated when he saw the truck so I knew he wanted me to do *something*. I don't know how Keats knows what he knows. He was trapped in the stall during the murder, so he must have some idea about what happened and possibly who did it. Look at him now." We turned to see him positively grinning in the back seat of the pickup. "He's jubilant. If this thing isn't the murder weapon, I'd be very surprised."

She sighed and then nodded. "Me, too. I don't know how Keats does it, but I trust him." She closed her eyes for a second. "I just wish I didn't have to hear you explain all this to Kellan."

I closed my eyes, too. "It's so hard with skeptics like him. But I'll do the best I can. Justice must be served."

"Poor Wilf," she said, opening the door as the police SUV pulled up behind us. "A man like him would hate the optics of being taken out with a castrator."

"No man would ever want to go that way," I said. "Guaranteed."

CHAPTER TWENTY-ONE

D orset Hills had been nothing more than a bigger, equally boring version of Clover Grove when I was growing up. Still, it was the destination of choice for every teen upon getting a driver's license, because it had a couple of diners where we could congregate out of direct view of our parents. That's about all the town had going for it then, but it was more than enough. Dorset Hills' teens headed over to Clover Grove, or nearby Brenton, to do the same thing. Things had certainly changed since I'd left hill country for college.

Today, the sun shone over the more successful town—now a small city—as I piloted the big white rental van around the outskirts. Dorset Hills had left Clover Grove in the dust because of its unique marketing claim of being the "best place on earth for dogs and dog-lovers." The buzz around Dog Town annoyed me so much that I'd never bothered to check it out on my rare visits home. Growing desperate for distractions for my guests, however, I decided to see what the fuss was about.

Our first stop was the diner once known as Hills Hamburgers. It had been popular because of its extensive variety of toppings and spectacular fries. Kellan Harper and I had our first date there. And our second, third and probably our tenth. We didn't call them dates, of course. He was my brother's pal and hence, we could only be friends.

So, on Friday nights, when Asher was playing one of the many sports at which he excelled, Kellan and I would be "friends" over a hamburger at Hills. I took mine plain, with a side of ketchup, and Kellan got the Hills' Hill, featuring two patties and a massive pile of toppings. The thought of his grin as he tried to wrap his mouth around that mountain made my heart do a crazy new move as I pulled into the parking lot. It was like a kung fu kick in my chest, meant to protect me from romantic incursions. This was no time to let my guard down.

I was both disappointed and grateful to see that the diner's current incarnation in no way resembled Hills Hamburgers. Instead, it was a prime example of a Dorset Hills makeover. Now it was called the Bone Appetit Bistro. The signage featured a couple of dog silhouettes, and a chalkboard outside promised the Doggone Best Burger in Town. Completely cheesy, but people obviously fell hard for this stuff.

"Okay, troops," I said, parking the van. "We're going to split into three groups today and meet back here in three hours." Unbuckling my seatbelt, I turned to Jilly, who was riding shotgun with Keats in her lap. "Jilly, you've got Nellie, Kate and Macy. I'll take Keri and Paulette, and Ben and Neal will go with Asher, who's meeting us here shortly."

"I want to be with Asher," Nellie said.

"What's so great about Asher?" Ben asked.

Nellie smiled and ran her hands over hair that stayed remarkably sleek regardless of weather. "Every girl wants a hero, right ladies?"

Kate and Macy chimed in with more enthusiasm than expected. They'd come out of their shells quite a bit in the past few days. Jilly's coaching was paying off.

"Heroes come in different shapes and sizes," I said, giving Ben a smile. "We've all got the capacity. One day, one good decision and—"

"Ivy?" Nellie said, with a smile that revealed lovely teeth I didn't see often enough. "We don't get paid to listen to your pep talks anymore. In fact, we pay you to show us a good time."

Paulette started to defend me but I shook my head. "Nellie's right. Sometimes I forget my new role. So, we're going to have fun today. But no one's switching teams."

Asher had insisted on taking the men, probably because they were still near the top of the list of suspects. As a cop, my brother was better equipped to supervise and he might even manage to bromance some clues out of them.

Kellan had sent the castrator to the lab and was meeting with Tess Blade in the meantime. He wasn't sold on her involvement, that much was clear. Or maybe he just wouldn't show it because he was annoyed about my exploits in the Animal Services truck. He'd almost vetoed the Dog Town excursion because of that, but at the last moment, he sent Asher to chaperone.

"We should get a say in the teams," Macy said. "We're not at Flordale anymore."

"No arguing, or we have to go home," I said. "You can stick with the plan or spend the day learning the fine art of manure management."

The communal groan almost shook the van. They'd had enough of the quaint farm experience, even with the exciting condiment of a murder investigation.

"This is going to rock," Jilly said. "You'll see."

She managed to pull a stack of paper out of her big bag despite Keats being firmly planted on it. He preferred perching on Jilly to co-pilot the van over being relegated to the back seats with the Flordale staff he hadn't grown to like. Luckily, the van offered a much smoother ride than my truck and driving it boosted my confidence. Kellan was probably right about getting a more cooperative vehicle.

"We're doing a treasure hunt," I said. "It's going to be epic."

"Are you kidding?" Nellie said. "We're not five years old. I want to shop."

"I want to play mini-golf," Ben said. "There's a course where you fire the balls into dogs' mouths and they come out the derriere. Sounds hilarious."

"Pass," Neal said. "But there's a vintage vinyl record store I want to see, and a good comic book store."

"Just let us go our own ways for once," Macy said.

I straightened in the driver's seat. "I hate to say this, guys, but it's not a democracy. Chief Harper agreed to the day trip only if we followed his orders." I took one of Jilly's print-outs and handed the rest to Nellie, who was sitting in the middle seat behind me. "This is a map of all of the bronze dog statues in Dorset Hills. The team that comes back with the most photos taken with these statues gets a very cool prize."

"A ticket out of here is the only prize I want," Nellie said.

"Maybe you'll settle for a spa visit," I said. "Manis and pedis are on offer for the winning ladies. If the gents win, they get dinner at the new Smoking Dog cigar club." Rolling my eyes, I added, "I don't have to agree with the premise to know it's a sweet prize."

There was a brief silence and then Nellie reached across Paulette, elbowing the older woman's chin as she opened the van's door. "Hit it, girls. I see two dog statues right now."

She clambered over Paulette, jumped out and started running toward a pair of eight-foot bronze Italian mastiffs. I would have said nothing could make Nellie run, but she was as efficient as a Hollywood cop in heels. For some, a manicure was powerful motivation.

Ben pushed the door open the rest of the way so he could unfold himself from the last row of seats. "Where's Asher? I like the sound of this men's club."

"Pass," Neal said again. "I'll play along, but if our team wins, I get to visit the vintage vinyl store."

I hopped out, too. "Talk to Asher," I said, as my brother pulled up in his truck. "I leave you in his capable hands."

Asher flashed a grin at Jilly as he joined us and accepted his treasure map. "We've got the advantage, men," he said. "I know my way around Dog Town."

Kate and Macy lingered to stare at him, heads tilted like birds, until Nellie's voice drifted back. "Ladies. I need this prize and I can't do it alone. There are like thirty of these stupid statues."

"Fifty or more," I said, staring at the map myself. "What's become of Dorset Hills?"

"It's a bit tacky but I like it," Asher said. He glanced at the refurbished diner. "Remember when you and Kellan used to sneak over here on Friday nights?"

I looked at him quickly. "You knew about that?"

"Of course. I used to sneak over with Mia Douglas after my games. If you two were still here, we'd go someplace else."

"Mia Douglas? She was one of my best friends, Asher. You promised—"

"And you promised. The only reason I didn't call you on it is because I trusted Kellan." He gave me the classic Asher grin. "Good thing, since he ended up my boss."

"Okay, you two," Jilly said. "Skip the sibling bickering or forfeit the spa day to my team."

There was a chorus of protests behind us, male and female.

"Challenged accepted," I said. "Paulette and Keri, we are going to kick their butts."

I knew that was a long shot. Paulette and Keri would be stressed out even trying to compete with the others. That was fine with me. I knew this trip had probably been hardest on them and they deserved a pleasant morning to recuperate.

"What a quaint town," Paulette said, as we strolled down the main drag of Dorset Hills. "Absolutely precious."

My eyes were practically rolling back in their sockets at how hard the City was pushing the "Dog Town" theme. But Keats was enjoying the adventure with tail up and eyes bright. That tended to change my perspective on anything. With him around, I hardly had a cynical thought to call my own anymore.

Besides, it was nice to see a smile on Paulette's face as we posed with the eight-foot St. Bernard bronze outside the hospital, the Dalmatian outside the fire station, and then the wolfhounds flanking the front doors of the art gallery.

When Keri went to take a closer look at City Hall, I perched beside Paulette at the base of the German shepherd statue in Bellington Square. "I'm glad you're enjoying this, Paulette," I said. "It's been such a rough week."

"The worst week of my life," she said. "My feelings about Wilf were so conflicted. He had a kind side, you know. When he first arrived at Flordale, he bought me lunch all the time and gave me a raise after just a few months. Not everyone treats admin staff so well."

"Definitely not at our company," I said. "*Your* company, I mean. I'm glad you saw another side of Wilf. Nothing's black and white, is it?"

She shook her head. "He let the stress eat him alive. Piers Frankel bullied him, and he bullied your team. It rolls downhill. I wanted to tell Piers so when he came to see us at the farm, but I lost my nerve."

"No wonder. Piers Frankel is an intimidating man."

She looked at her fingernails and then clenched her fist. "It's hard to believe anyone on our team is responsible, but who else would it be? What if we never find out, and need to go back to work not knowing? I couldn't handle the stress of thinking it might happen again."

I tipped my head back, staring at the open mouth of the bronze dog with its huge teeth like scythes. "Chief Harper won't let that happen, Paulette. I feel like we're getting closer to solving this murder."

I really did feel that way, although there wasn't much to go on. The same thing had happened when we were trying to figure out how Lloyd Boyce, the dogcatcher, had died. It seemed like the truth was fluttering like a black crow around the periphery of my mind but I couldn't get a good look at it. This time I was trying not to leap around grabbing at it, and aside from my crazy ride in Tess Blade's truck, I thought I was showing admirable restraint. My hope was that by staying still, that circling crow might land and reveal itself.

Paulette's fists were still clenched when she asked, "Who do *you* think it is, Ivy? I mean, if you had to guess."

"Chief Harper has ordered me not to guess." Studying her anxious face, I added, "If it helps, I think there might be suspects beyond our team."

"Like Avis' husband?" Paulette asked.

My eyes widened before my poker face could land. "So you did know who it was."

"I'm sorry I didn't tell you earlier, but now I'm done with keeping secrets. I also know Piers was looking for an excuse to fire Wilf. Their performance management meetings stepped up after Wilf drove you out."

"Why didn't he just package Wilf out?" I asked. "It would have been better for the company and for staff morale."

She sighed. "I think Avis was pushing back and she's valuable to Piers. Plus, Wilf said he had leverage. I guess he had something on everyone... except you."

"Until I played the 'crazy' card by rescuing Keats," I said, stroking the dog's head. "I can't imagine Piers was so desperate to get rid of Wilf that he'd..." My voice trailed off. I couldn't speculate about that in front of Wilf's only defender.

"Hire a hitman?" she asked, with a frankness that shocked me even more. "It crossed my mind, but that really would destroy the company if it ever got out. So I doubt Piers went that far." Looking up at the bronze shepherd, she shrugged. "Maybe he influenced someone to get Wilf into a situation where he could harm himself. Did you notice how Neal kept filling Wilf's glass that first night? Everyone knew he couldn't hold his liquor."

"I didn't notice," I admitted. "I was too busy being mortified by my mother."

Paulette managed a shaky laugh. "The police chief hasn't ordered *me* not to guess, so I say it's Neal. Ben's more capable, obviously, but Neal had more cause."

"Wilf hired Neal, though," I said. "What changed?"

"All I know is that he was meeting with Neal a lot. Wilf's face was always red afterward, and Neal looked like... I don't know. What does a weasel look like?"

I laughed. "I'm not quite sure."

Paulette unclenched her fist to wave as Keri rejoined us.

I got to my feet and beckoned. "Come on, ladies. We only have five dogs checked off so far and Nellie was set on winning."

"Let her," Keri said. "Who cares about manicures? I'd rather just enjoy the sunshine and these views. I love Dorset Hills."

"Me too," Paulette echoed.

They didn't notice my failure to chime in. Dorset Hills had a superficial charm, but it didn't feel authentic to me. With the way things were going, however, Dog Town might eventually subsume Clover Grove. I'd have to advocate hard for a big bronze border collie at Runaway Farm.

As the other two chatted, I pulled my buzzing phone out of my pocket.

"Red alert," Asher texted. "Neal is MIA."

My throat tightened as I thought about Kellan's reaction to losing one of the guests. Then it loosened when I realized Asher, the cop, had been the one to lose Neal. Luck was on my side for once.

We converged quickly at the Bone Appetit Bistro again. There was an empty squad car beside the van. The officers had presumably gone on foot to search for Neal.

Everyone paced back and forth in the parking lot in relative silence for close to an hour. I sensed I wasn't the only one worried that Wilf's killer may have struck again.

Finally Asher's text came: "Got him. Vinyl store. Automatic default on the game."

"Manis and pedis for all," I said. "On the house. Ben, I'll take you to the Dapper Dog Barber Shop for a shave and a hair cut as your prize for not running away."

He held up his treasure map. "Won it fair and square. We got sixteen dogs and a good workout before Neal gave us the slip."

"What happened?"

"An old lady fell and knocked herself out. Asher and I were busy helping her when Neal took off."

"That's terrible," Paulette said, oozing disapproval. "He got everyone worried for nothing."

"Let's salvage what we can from this day," Nellie said. "I need a nail intervention, ASAP."

I watched Keats circle around them, bringing the herd to the van. His ears and tail were limp and listless. Normally I could interpret so much about individual "sheep" from his body language. The problem here was that he didn't like *any* of them. Not even Paulette or Keri, surprisingly. I didn't for a moment believe they'd banded together as a herd to pull off the murder, when they couldn't agree on the simplest things. They'd have turned on each other by now. Maybe to Keats they just reeked of our old life, which we'd both desperately wanted to escape.

"Into the van," I called. "Your reward awaits."

Keats dove in for a little nip at Nellie and she tried to kick him.

"Look, dog, I won't hesitate to break a nail on you since I'm getting acrylics."

He took another little lunge at her heels until she slammed the door of the van in his face.

His tail rose and fanned as he followed me around to the driver's side. "Proud of yourself?" I asked.

When I opened the door, he took a leap and landed in Jilly's lap. She gave a startled squawk but her bag shielded her from his claws. He found his footing on the leather and then put his paws on the dash, sweeping her face with the white plume of his tail.

"Honestly, Ivy," she said. "I don't mind playing second fiddle, but there are limits."

"Keats, don't push your luck," I said, pointing to the footwell. "I adore you, but without Jilly, we don't eat."

CHAPTER TWENTY-TWO

I didn't need to lecture Neal because Kellan had done a thorough job of it. The chief collected Neal in Dorset Hills, gave him some quality time at the police station, and then drove him back to Runaway Farm. By that point, the rest of us were home, and most considerably better groomed. Since I'd only escorted Ben to the barber shop, I looked the same as usual when Kellan asked me to "take a walk."

Following him out to the pastures, I thought about how that request used to make my heart race. I'd been conditioned, just like my dog. Today, my heart still raced, but now the excitement was mixed with dread. Was I going to get another sermon? Had I messed up some crucial aspect of his investigation? Was I going to be trapped with these people forever?

Keats circled Kellan again and again, trying to keep him away from both the livestock and me.

"Really, Keats?" Kellan said, stepping lightly around the dog yet again. "Is this harassment necessary?"

"Leave it, Keats," I said, although I enjoyed watching the show. Kellan was surprisingly graceful for a tall, muscular man. I wondered if he was a good dancer. The only time we'd ever tried it was at our senior prom, and that night we were both stilted and awkward. Just like we were now, actually.

Keats, on the other hand, wasn't awkward at all. He blatantly flouted my command and continued his game. I knew it *was* a game because of his pricked-up ears, lolling tongue and waving tail. This was apparently even better than herding ducks, his number one favorite hobby.

Kellan tried a new tactic and stood still. "Why me?" he asked. "How do I merit this special treatment?"

"Oh, he herds everyone now," I said. "He's maturing and exploring his natural gifts. Obviously we have a little work to do on his self-control."

Keats tried to herd almost everyone, that much was true. The difference with Kellan was the spirit behind it. There was a mischievous persistence in the dog's moves that probably stemmed from the feelings he picked up from me. Obviously I couldn't say anything of the sort to Kellan. Instead, I let him fight his own battles with my quirky dog.

Keats started taking lunges at Kellan's cuffs to get him moving again. Herding was no fun unless you were going places. When that didn't work, he lifted his muzzle to see if he could mesmerize the police chief with his mismatched eyes.

Kellan wasn't unnerved by his hypnotic stare at all. In fact, he laughed. "Go work your sheepdog mojo on someone else."

There was no way Keats was leaving me alone with Kellan. Instead, he gathered himself to pounce.

"That's enough, Keats," I said. "I mean it."

Keats went back to lunging at Kellan's feet, eyeing me defiantly. I could only assume he wanted to move things along between us and dispel the tension. If so, he had his work cut out for him, because Kellan and I were two stubborn, flighty sheep.

Eyes still on the dog, Kellan said, "Keats, you should know by now that I'm on Ivy's side. Even if Ivy herself doesn't believe it."

"Oh, I believe it," I said. I did know he had my best interests at heart... at least in his official capacity. It was his personal capacity I doubted. Seeing him with that woman at the harvest fair had rattled me, despite what he'd said later. Maybe I'd been wrong about the "moments" we'd shared. A few sparks shooting up my arm when we brushed against each other. A look here and there that shimmered with emotion. A tone of voice that sounded too intimate for everyone else. Was it all wishful thinking on my part? Maybe our long-dead romance clung to our interactions like the bouquet of the barn—familiar and oddly comforting, yet slightly ripe from decomposition.

"If you believed I had your back, you wouldn't be hitching rides in the Animal Services truck," he said, hopping twice to evade Keats' teeth. "You'd have called me to handle it."

"That was a spur of the moment thing. A hunch. I acted on impulse and I'm sorry."

Keats managed to get Kellan moving again and the fancy footwork continued until they reached the alpaca pasture.

"I believe in hunches," Kellan said. "Intuition is just your subconscious making connections in the background." Crossing his arms over the top rung of the fence, he effectively cut Keats off from circling. "Where we differ is what we do about those hunches. You get a sudden idea and then take action immediately. Where's the beat in between where you stop and think, "Oooh... great idea. How about I call the police so they can do their job?"

I smiled at his delivery. His voice was high and lilting, like a teenage girl's.

"You're right about that missing step," I said, staring out at the alpaca and the two llamas, who'd retreated to a corner. Unlike most of the animals, they hadn't embraced Keats at all. The sheep and goats seemed to be grateful for his leadership, and the cows tolerated him. The camelids had each other and their two cranky donkeys. They didn't want another boss—particularly a young dog who liked to flaunt his moves. "I worry about sounding like an idiot with some of the odd notions that cross my mind. Plus a lot of my hunches don't pan out and I hate to trouble you when you've got so much to do."

"A lot of my hunches don't pan out, either." He turned to look at me. "Let me decide if yours are crazy or not. Only I can see the big picture, the web of interconnections. Only I can decide whether and when to pursue a lead. Doing things in the right order can be crucial, Ivy."

"I know. I've watched a few TV police procedurals in my time." I directed an imaginary remote control at him and flexed my thumb. "Normally, I want to fast-forward. I don't see the point of dragging out the suspense when you can just get on with it."

Now he turned right around. "Ah-ha. I see. You're mixing up real life with TV. A very common problem that can get people killed. Guns are real, too, by the way."

"Very funny, Chief Comedian. Add another chapter to your crime scene etiquette book. This could become a whole series."

Keats renewed his assault on Kellan's uniformed ankles, darting in and out. "Stop that, you cur."

"He doesn't like your preachy tone, I'll bet. Keats takes his job of protecting me—and the farm—very seriously. He's on duty around the clock."

"We've talked about getting a proper security system—one that doesn't treat the chief of police like a chew toy."

"Keats, enough," I said, more forcefully this time. "He never cared for chew toys, you know. This isn't a typical dog, Kellan."

"Tell me about it." He climbed up on the fence to evade Keats, who had fallen back but was still eying Kellan's cuffs like wayward lambs.

After a pause, I said, "One reason I don't share all my hunches is that some come from Keats." I studied the llamas to avoid meeting his eyes. "Take Tess Blade, for example. I assume Keats knew she grabbed the castrator after the murder and he definitely wanted me to check out her truck."

I thought he'd dismiss this with a snort, but instead he shrugged. "I know he has talent, but what I said earlier still applies. If Keats gets a notion, you still need to let me follow through. Jolting around in the back of a truck with a feral dog is not the way to handle it."

"That dog wasn't feral at all. I called about her this morning and she's been claimed by her owners."

"Evading the point. You could have been injured."

"True." I sighed. "I didn't expect so much stuff rattling around back there."

"And you could have riled up the County even more about your farm. I had some explaining to do about how that device came into my possession, without implicating you."

I nodded. "Thank you for that."

"As for the bogus call about the rabid raccoon... All of Main Street was in a panic, and no wonder. I could charge you with public mischief."

I felt the heat creeping up from my chest and over my collar. "Oh. I didn't think about that."

"Right. Did you think about how I could charge Jilly with public mischief for making that call? Or Teri? How would you like that?"

"Obviously I wouldn't like that at all, Kellan. So I take your point and you can stand down." I looked up at him. "Or climb down, in this case. Then maybe you'll confirm for me whether Keats and I were right about the murder weapon."

He hopped off the fence. "I hate to give you the slightest encouragement, but the device—"

"The castrator. Or emasculator, if you prefer." I grinned at him.

"Do you want to hear this, Ivy?"

"Definitely."

"There was DNA evidence from Wilf Darby."

Keats' tail rose and the white plume lashed in seeming triumph.

"I knew it!" I beamed at the dog. "You're brilliant."

Keats mumbled something to me that sounded both proud and quizzical.

"Sometimes it seems like he understands human conversation," Kellan said.

"I know, right? And I've noticed you chat to him directly now. Didn't you tell me you'd surrender your badge the day that happened?"

He turned and started walking back to his car. "True. I'd better get right on that."

"Not before telling me if there were prints on the cutter," I said, rushing after him.

"Nope. Whoever used it was careful."

"Well, what did Tess Blade say about stealing that thing?"

"She said she picked it up behind the barn and didn't think twice about 'borrowing' it. She wanted to try it out and educate the farmers about bloodless..."

"Castration," I offered, smothering a grin.

"Well, it sounded legit," he continued, trying to stay ahead of me. "She truly seems to care about animal welfare."

"A castrator costs about twenty bucks. Why did she have to steal it from the crime scene and hide it under towels in her truck?"

"Apparently she acted on impulse and only realized after the fact how it looked. That's why she hid it."

"You actually bought that story?"

"I did, as farfetched as it sounds." He turned and met my eyes. "Her attitude is mostly a front."

"You mean her ego. I hope you're still checking into her conversation with Piers Frankel."

"She has an alibi," he said. "And yes, I met with Piers." He blew out a disgusted snort. "Talk about ego. There's no question he wanted Wilf gone but a man of his stature likely wouldn't hire someone like Tess Blade to do his dirty work. There were more expedient ways, and Wilf was about to get an offer he couldn't have refused. Even Avis supported the move."

"What kind of offer?"

"A very large payout, from what I understand. And a face-saving move to another firm where someone owes Piers big."

I stopped walking, too disappointed to move. "So, we're no further ahead, then."

"Sure we are," he said, turning. "We have a murder weapon. We've ruled people out. That's how this usually goes."

I groaned. "But it's so slow."

"Fortune favors the diligent detective," he said, smiling as Keats frolicked around him, tail still swishing. "Don't act so happy to see me go, buddy. It hurts my feelings."

I followed Kellan the last few yards. "What about Neal? What was he doing when he gave us the slip?"

"You mean Keats doesn't know?" he said, teasingly.

"Only because he wasn't with them. Neal never gives Keats the slip."

"And I'm not thrilled he pulled the wool over Asher's eyes, trust me." Kellan shook his head. "Your brother will be hearing about this for a while."

"Was Neal in the vinyl store the whole time?" I asked.

"Nope. My officer got there before Neal did. So that means we can't account for his whereabouts for about an hour. He said he was taking in the sights, but there's no proof."

"Interesting," I said.

"Interesting indeed," he said. "I'm checking security feeds from the area and I've got a few leads to check out." He turned as he reached the police SUV. "Now it's time for you to check out of this investigation, okay? Keep your guests here. Keep your guests busy. Keep yourself from talking about anything related to the case. Got it?"

"How do I keep myself from going insane?" I asked. "I quit Flordale for a reason."

He got into the car, turned the key in the ignition and rolled down the window. "Vipers. I remember. But you let them into your house and you're stuck with them until further notice."

As he backed the car around, I called, "Keats will get to the bottom of this. I bet you a hamburger with all the toppings."

He hit the brakes and a smile lit up his face. "That's a bet you'd lose, Ivy. But then *I'd* lose because I can't handle that kind of thing now. I'm not a kid anymore."

I wasn't sure if he meant the burger or our old romance, but the smile vanished as fast as it came. He raised one hand as he turned the wheel hard with the other and then sped off, blowing a cloud of dust in my direction.

Keats shoved his head under my left hand as I covered my mouth and nose with my free arm to keep from choking on dust.

"Don't worry, buddy," I said, heading for the house. "One day he's going to admit that he needs you." I sighed and then added, "But he doesn't need me. Unfortunately, I've become bad for his digestion."

CHAPTER TWENTY-THREE

I'd expected Keats to help me flush out the truth about Neal's joyride in Dorset Hills, but the answer came not from a dog, but a dog rescuer.

Before I even got up the front stairs, my phone rang. It was almost as if someone knew I was still alone. "Runaway Farm. Ivy Galloway speaking."

"Hey, Ivy," a woman said. "You don't know me, but you will." The voice was assertive, yet oddly calming. I could tell she was used to issuing commands and having them obeyed. "My name is Cori Hogan and I'm a dog trainer in Dorset Hills."

"Cori! We may not have met but I know you by reputation." My voice spiked, giving away my nerves. "You're famous around these parts."

"Notorious, you mean. I won't say I don't like that." She laughed. "We've been meaning to throw down the welcome mat for you, like Hannah asked. But we want to do it properly and most of us are out of town dealing with a... situation."

"A rescue situation?" I walked back down the front stairs and headed for the barn. "I watched the show—The Princess and the Pig—and I've heard the stories."

"Myth and legend," she said. "Mostly. But yeah, we keep busy. We're on a mission out of state right now."

"It's just as well you haven't come," I said. "The farm is crawling with cops all the time anyway. Including my brother."

"I've heard," Cori said. "I was pretty impressed with your work on the dogcatcher case."

"Yeah?" I looked up at the rafters and smiled, as if gold stars might rain down on me. "That means a lot coming from you."

"I know," she said. She sounded quite serious, but then she laughed. "Look, I've had my share of hair-raising rescues, but I've never solved a murder. You've got me beat, and that takes some doing. Plus, I heard from Charlie you're doing well with the animals. Hannah's happy she left them in your hands. It made a tough situation easier."

My smile faded and tears filled my eyes. "What's happened here is awful and I worried she might regret her choice. It feels like death is following me." I turned to make sure no one *was* following me. All I saw was Keats, staring at the phone with his blue eye glowing and his tail fanning fast and furious.

"Say hi to that clever dog," Cori said. "He's looking at me right now, isn't he?"

"How did you—?"

"I know things," Cori said. "I know dogs like Keats, because I have a border collie, too. It's like they have an extra gear over the average dog. Not everyone can handle that, but you can."

I touched the dog's head. "I'm the one getting handled."

"Exactly. And you roll with it, like you should." She cleared her throat. "I assume you're in the barn now, and taking appropriate precautions?"

"Yeah. We're good." Did she have a camera on the place?

"Then I have some information for you, but I'm going to need you to keep your source confidential, okay? I'm sending it from an anonymous account, although I bet your cop boyfriend will figure it out. He's apparently not stupid."

"He's not my boyfriend. But yes, the chief is quite smart."

"One truth, one lie," she said. "Don't waste my time on the lies. I'm as smart as a border collie, which is saying something."

I was saved from replying by the ping of my phone. "Got it," I said, putting the phone on speaker so that I could open the video and play it. "Oh my god, it's Neal."

"Quiet," Cori said. "The barnboards have ears."

Keats jumped on me too, signaling agreement with his new friend.

"What's he doing?" I whispered.

"Running," Cori said. "Away from the chow chow bronze statue on the outskirts of Dog Town. It's the secret meeting spot for our rescue group and we have it rigged. When your guy sat on the base of the statue, it triggered an alarm and our remote camera. So he bolted."

"What was he doing out there alone?"

"He wasn't alone. Keep watching."

I moved slowly through the barn to the far side as I watched the small screen. Finally I gasped even louder. "It's Piers Frankel. The president of Flordale, my old company. What were they doing?"

There was a sigh at the other end. "Talking. I only wish we'd rolled sound. You can be sure we'll update our setup. In the meantime, I can tell you they didn't chat long before the alarm sent them running like the chow had come to life. The foliage is thin enough to see them drive off in a black Porsche. Watching them clamber over each other to get into that dinky car was the best laugh I've had in a while. The weaselly guy actually tried to drive and the old guy slapped him away."

I clicked stop on the video. "I'll save the laugh for later. I'm going to need it."

"Yeah," Cori said. "I got this to you as fast as I could because we're as anxious as you are to make sure that farm and the animals are safe. Keep me posted, okay? And we'll be out as soon as we can."

"Thank you," I said. "It's really such a thrill—"

"Ivy? I hate suck-ups," Cori said. "You need to know that." Keats' tail waved harder to let me know she was joking. "Tell the dog I'm not joking," she added, laughing as she hung up.

I turned and scanned the barn with new eyes. It felt like I'd been formally initiated into a fabulous secret club where my admitted idiosyncrasies might not only be accepted but valued.

Suddenly the place felt a lot more like home.

"WHERE HAVE YOU BEEN?" Jilly asked, when I finally went inside. "Kellan left ages ago."

"I know, but then I had to send him more information and explain how I got it." I pulled her into the kitchen and whispered the story. "He's coming out later to talk to Neal again. We need to do something to keep these people busy, Jilly. Nerves are fraying, mine included."

She nodded. "Keats is the only one enjoying this party." Holding up a finger, she said, "Party! Right? Let's do a theme party for dinner. I'll see what I have in the pantry and get people to vote on the theme."

"What are you two scheming about?"

Jilly and I both jumped as Neal joined us. I felt Keats move into position directly on my feet. His hackles had lifted and his tail drifted down. His ears were still upright and forward, however, so while Neal was getting a failing grade, he hadn't been relegated to the scrap heap quite yet. If Neal had killed Wilf, Keats wasn't fully convinced yet.

"A theme party," Jilly said, barely missing a beat. "Black tie, maybe. Or beach. Or zombie apocalypse, complete with makeup." Her shoulders straightened and she tossed her curls. "This is going to be amazing."

Neal groaned. "I'm not into theme parties, only theme parks."

As Jilly started rummaging in cupboards I slid onto a stool at the counter and patted the one beside me. "I know you used your vacations to visit parks around the world. What's your favorite?"

His face brightened and it was quite possibly the first time I'd seen him with a truly genuine smile since he arrived. "Six Flags in Jackson, New Jersey. Tallest roller coaster in the world. It's called Kingda Ka." He pulled out his phone. "Want to see pics?"

"Sure." Keats had managed to slide under the footrest of the stool and perched between my feet. I knew this meant he was uncomfortable. In fact, he'd done pretty much the same thing when I encountered the dogcatcher's murderer. Still, I wasn't nervous because Jilly was poking around in the pantry nearby and Kellan would be along later. I leaned over Neal's phone and gasped, "Oh my god, Neal. What is wrong with you?"

He cackled like a madman during the zombie apocalypse. "Tricked you."

The video he'd cued up was taken during the plummet from what seemed like mountainous heights. He knew better than anyone how I felt about rides. Even seeing it in a small frame made my stomach heave. Pushing the phone away, I said, "Moving on."

He regaled me with his greatest roller coaster hits in excruciating detail, and I pretended to listen while watching Jilly weigh her party options. Finally she went into the family room, presumably to consult the guests on their preferred theme.

"I'd show you my photo albums, but they're on my laptop," he said.

"Guaranteed to make me barf," I said. "No thanks. It's enough to hear about them."

That apparently inspired him to persist, because he jumped off the stool. "Seriously, you're going to love this. I have a social media site with my ratings and recommendations." His smile became almost bashful. "I've got a bit of a reputation for expertise in this area."

The former HR exec in me silently whispered, *Keep him talking. People who talk too much reveal too much.*

"Well, okay. I do like hearing from experts about anything. But I can't handle more than two roller coaster videos, so pick your finest."

Neal didn't wait for me to change my mind and hurried upstairs.

His phone was still on the counter, and when I leaned over to check out his photo gallery, I saw something interesting.

Very interesting.

"Keats, follow Neal," I said. "Keep him up there as long as you can."

I got off my stool as the dog darted away. Grabbing Neal's phone, I slipped into the pantry, a small room stocked with everything Jilly might need for any spur-of-the-moment party.

Shutting the door, I leaned against it. I checked the date on the video I'd seen and then pressed play.

Neal's voice rang out, and my heart pounded until I realized it was coming from the phone in my hand. Fumbling for the volume controls, I turned it down and held the phone closer to my face so I could hear without being overheard.

My heart didn't slow down for long though, as I realized I was watching Wilf Darby's last night unfold on the phone. I could tell Neal had been standing just outside the barn door and filming as Ben struggled with Wilf near the cow pen. Ben was wearing a hoodie and track pants, while Wilf's pajamas and robe looked much the worse for wear.

"I put you to bed," Ben said, grappling with Wilf, who was

indeed acting like a slippery hippo. He pretended to be boneless and slid out of Ben's grasp to land on the floor. "You're still drunk, Wilf. You can't drive to town like this."

"I've got a date," Wilf slurred. "She's expecting me."

"Too bad. You've smucked Ivy's truck and you're not going anywhere." Ben tried to haul Wilf off the floor and failed. "She's not going to be happy."

"Good. She left me. She left us. They always do, Ben. You're going to find that out for yourself soon."

"What are you talking about?" Ben said. "Never mind. I don't want to know."

Still on the ground, Wilf stared up at Ben. "I know about your secret affair. I never thought you had it in you."

"What?" Ben looked perplexed. "There's no secret affair. The only person in the department having an affair is you."

Rolling onto his hands and knees, Wilf tried to push himself up and fell over again. "Not true, not true," he said, laughing. "I've got the goods on ya. A digital file with your name on it. Hangman's coming for me, big buddy, and I'll take you down too."

"Wilf, all I care about is getting you back up to your room so you don't hurt yourself or the animals."

"I came to this farm to milk a cow and I'm not leaving before I do it," Wilf said.

Ben looked at the camera. "Could you get over here and help, Neal? This is a five-man operation but two will have to do."

"I'll fire you both while I still can," Wilf said. "You for using company equipment to exchange love notes, and him for double-dealing." He wagged a finger at Neal. "I don't care who you've got on your side. As soon as I get Ivy back on board, you're both gone. I think she hired losers to make herself look good."

"*You* hired me," Neal said. The camera shook a little, either because he was furious or amused.

Wilf swore again. "Just get out of here, both of you. I need time alone."

"Ain't gonna happen," Ben said. "You're going to hurt or get hurt. Now get up or I'll drag you back to the house by your feet. Don't think I can't, Wilf."

"Don't think I can't kick your pretty face while you try," Wilf said.

"Neal, can you film Wilf getting dragged by his feet?" Ben said. "We can share it with his lady. Get a shot of the dinged Corvette on the way by. She'll be super impressed with that, too."

Ben and Wilf stared at each other for a moment and then Wilf started to scramble to his feet. Grabbing his boss by the scruff, Ben swung him around to face the door.

That's when I noticed Keats milling around their feet. He was darting in and out, just as he had with Kellan earlier. Only this time it wasn't a game. His ears were back and he meant business. My heart raced faster, forgetting that I already knew my boy was alright.

"Bug off, dog," Wilf said. "I'll kick you to high heaven."

It was an idle threat since Wilf couldn't coordinate his feet to walk, let alone land a kick.

Ben gave up on Wilf's ability to propel himself and half carried his boss toward the barn door. Meanwhile Neal was backing away, leaving Wilf and Ben framed against the light in the doorway.

"There you have it, Piers," Neal whispered into the phone. "The whole department's a train wreck. I'm not going anywhere without the biggest buyout Flordale's ever seen."

The video finished and I quickly swiped to the home screen and slipped out of the pantry. In real-time, Neal was bellowing my name from upstairs.

"Call off your stupid dog, Ivy, or I'll knock him down the stairs."

"Keats," I called. "Come here."

The dog was down in a flash, and I was back on the stool, with the phone in place, before Neal arrived, flushed, with his laptop under his arm.

"If he nips me again, so help me, I'll..." He met my eyes and backed down. "That dog has a death wish."

"Says the man who travels the world riding roller coasters," I said. "Now, bring on your worst."

CHAPTER TWENTY-FOUR

One thing I never really wanted to see was my colleagues in swimwear—especially in my living room in October. Nevertheless, I'd proposed a beach party that evening, basically overruling Jilly's decision to go with the black tie theme. The men looked relieved and Nellie was actually excited when I told them about the change of plans. She'd packed a bikini after hearing there was a sauna on the farm, when in reality, the closest body of water was the old well that had played a starring role in the dogcatcher's murder investigation. Everyone except Nellie needed help in the costume department.

"A beach party? Why?" Jilly asked, when I joined her in the kitchen where she was already assembling classy canapes.

"Just trust me," I said. "It'll be casual and fun. Think burgers and salads. We'll put on the Beach Boys and dance later." I started humming the song, "Wouldn't It Be Nice."

"Ivy, are you on something?" She started putting frozen shrimp and puff pastry back in the freezer. "I am not wearing a bikini inside in October."

"I'm not wearing a bikini ever." I adjusted the shoulder straps on my overalls. "A farmer in a bikini could never be taken seriously.

And you can't accuse me of being stoned every time I come up with a good idea. The Flordale people haven't turned me to drugs. Yet."

"Then what's going on?" she asked. "Is this something Kellan would want to know about?"

"I regret that he wouldn't care at all about my swimwear choices," I said.

"Oh, that's not true," she said. "He's human, and he's male. I'm sure he'd quite enjoy seeing you flip burgers on the back deck in scraps of fabric."

"First... never going to happen. And second... you don't want me charring the food. So I'll take care of picking up a festive cake and some sparklers, when I grab the costumes."

Jilly glanced at the big clock on the wall. "The stores close in an hour. Where are you going to find costumes now?"

"I happen to know someone with built-in closets full of crazy get-ups."

"Just tell me you'll make it back for dinner," she said. "Otherwise, I swear I'll hitch a ride back to Boston with the Flordale crew... never to step foot on Runaway Farm again."

"Jilly, I want us to grow old here together. Picture it: two quirky old ladies with so many animals they don't know what to do." I smirked as I gathered my coat, purse and car keys. Keats had been waiting by the door for nearly 15 minutes—before my plan was even fully formed. "I won't jeopardize that dream, I promise."

"Aim a little higher," she said, snapping a dish towel at me. "But I promise we'll still talk every day."

"A BEACH PARTY? Surely you can come up with a better idea than that, Ivy," Mom said, ushering Keats and me into her small second bedroom that was lined on three sides with closets. She didn't qualify as a hoarder, per se, because the place was neat and carefully organized. But she did have way too much stuff and an emotional attachment to some of it that defied logic. Normal people didn't treat a 10-year-old secondhand dress like a treasured pet. Mom remembered exactly where she found it, what she paid, how she altered it and every event at which the dress had appeared. She kept notes to make sure she didn't wear the same outfit twice with the same people. I'd heard royal families did the same thing.

"A beach party is exactly what we need to lift everyone's spirits," I said. "Lighthearted summertime fun. I got sparklers and sangria and we can light a bonfire later."

"You'll need a fire if you're going to be socializing in bathing suits." She pursed her lips. "Ivy, I don't think this is entirely professional. How are these people going to take you seriously in meetings when they can imagine you practically naked?" She gave me a critical onceover. "Although I daresay it would be an improvement over what you're wearing."

Mom was in a silvery knit dress and heels with a full face of makeup. No doubt she was on her way out with a gentleman, but I wasn't going to ask.

"If you're still laboring under the delusion that I'm going back to work for Flordale, I repeat that it will never happen." I bent over the drawer she opened and started pulling things out. "I plan to get carried off the farm in a pine box, with all the livestock yelling goodbye." I looked up at her. "Why on earth do you have men's swim trunks in here?"

I wasn't actually surprised. In fact, I'd counted on it.

She gave me a coy smile. "Wayne down the road has a hot tub. That's all I need to say."

"It most certainly is." One pair had a zebra print and the other leopard. I could hardly wait to see Ben and Neal prance around in those—especially since they were too big for Neal and too small for Ben.

I selected a sarong, and some bathing suits and shorts for the other women.

"Take sundresses," Mom said, pulling out a few hangers. "Much more appropriate for a work function."

"I need people showing flesh," I said, trying to block the image out of my mind.

"I disagree," she said. "It's better not to mix business with pleasure. For all my liberal attitudes, that's something I never did." She carefully spread the sundresses on the bed so they wouldn't wrinkle. "You can imagine it was a challenge given how often I changed jobs."

"I bet you sometimes changed jobs so that you could date a colleague," I said, starting to stuff items into my bag.

She offered another coy smile that vanished fast as I manhandled her treasures. "Be careful with my things, please."

"If your things aren't pristine when they come back, I'll drive you anywhere you like to replenish," I said.

"I'm not getting into that truck. It's covered in dog hair." She looked down at Keats and he fanned his white plume. No matter how she felt about him, he quite liked her. "Don't try to flirt with me, mister. You've stolen my sweet baby girl and replaced her with this crazy farmer."

"Love you too, Mom," I said, heading for the door.

"What will Kellan say about all this?" she asked. "He won't want you cutting a rug with that gorgeous giant. Although I'm sure the little weasel doesn't stand a chance with you. We Galloway women have standards."

I paused at the door. "You don't approve of Kellan anyway."

"Of course I do." She shook her head as if I were dense. "But I can't just hand my best daughter over on a silver platter. He needs to earn you first. So far, he hasn't made nearly enough effort."

"That's because he isn't interested anymore." I leaned over to kiss her cheek and almost choked on perfume. "Water under the bridge."

"Oh, Ivy." She rested elegant fingers on still-slim hips. "I may not understand corporate politics, but I have an advanced degree in men. So you can trust me when I say that our chief of police is merely biding his time before making his move. Like me, he's probably concerned you're crazy." She held the door open as I tried to close it. "But here's a secret, sweetheart: men like a hint of crazy. It keeps them guessing."

"Keep it up and I might vomit in your hallway, Mom."

There was something oddly reassuring about the disgusted look she gave me through the crack in the door. Maybe I needed to see that everything was normal in one sector of my life when it was so abnormal everywhere else.

"Don't you dare, Ivy Galloway. I expect my things to come back dry cleaned, pressed and without a single dog hair." She peered down at Keats. "Do you hear me, handsome?"

"Handsome?" I said, grinning. "Careful, buddy. A place must have opened up on her rotation."

I didn't get to slam the door because Mom pushed it shut on me first.

CHAPTER TWENTY-FIVE

My hamburger sat on my plate virtually untouched because I was too disappointed to eat. I had been so sure that the beach party would reveal everything and end the investigation into Wilf's murder. But it had only revealed everything I *didn't* want to see and nothing that I *did*.

As suspected, the swim trunks I'd borrowed were too small for Ben. He exploited that for laughs by preening and prancing around the living room and out onto the deck, doing bodybuilder poses. It worked to lighten the mood and all the women played along.

Neal had the opposite problem with the swim trunks slipping down despite his efforts to cinch them till they puckered. When he bent over the buffet table, he flashed plumber's butt. That caused Kate and Macy to giggle, a rare and disturbing sound for the Raptors. But they really had changed, even visibly, since their arrival. Tonight, Macy wore a high-cut strapless one-piece with a peephole and strolled around the house barefoot. She looked completely comfortable, even without her twin glued to her side. Kate was more sedate in a sporty tankini covered with a down vest and shorts. There was no denying that the two women were becoming independent units.

Nellie was certainly comfortable in her black bikini and heels. She wore my mom's colorful sarong around her waist and her white spa gloves to protect her fresh manicure.

Jilly and I had followed Mom's advice and put on sundresses over our bathing suits. When people chided us for not fully embracing the theme, I pointed out that we had to stand outside tending to the barbeque and the bonfire.

"What's wrong?" Jilly asked, arranging chocolate, graham crackers and marshmallows on a tray so that people could make s'mores. "You barely touched your dinner. I thought this was exactly what you wanted."

"It is, but it didn't reveal what I'd hoped," I said. "I thought I had the answer."

She gave me a warning look as Neal came into the kitchen. "Hey, Neal," she said. "Could you help me carry this stuff out?"

As he stood at the kitchen counter, I dropped a serviette and bent over to pick it up. That gave me a chance to confirm what I already knew: Neal's calves were just normal hairy man legs. After watching the video on his phone, I was confident I'd see healing fang marks. Keats had clearly been beside himself in the barn that night with strangers threatening his livestock. The men had hopped around as if they felt teeth, yet Ben's legs were also free from wounds.

My hopes of presenting Kellan with the evidence when he stopped by later were dashed. He'd have to find a way to examine the legs of Piers Frankel, Avis Arron and Tess Blade himself. Maybe they could have a beach party, too.

"I'm heading out to put the critters to bed," I said, slipping my arms into my down jacket and grabbing the bucket of kitchen scraps Jilly collected every night for Wilma. I pulled on a woolen toque, as well. "Save me some s'mores."

"You bet," Ben said, coming into the kitchen. "And then you promised sparklers and dancing."

"I'll deliver. It's a clear night and they'll hear our party over in Dorset Hills."

Slipping outside with Keats, I walked around the house swinging the bucket. My breath came out in steamy white plumes. It wouldn't be long till the first flurries flew.

"Well, that was a bust, buddy," I said. "I thought I'd figured it out. I thought *you'd* figured it out." I looked down at him and his blue eye glittered eerily in the wide circle of the porch light. "I'm sure you have, and I've let you down in not piecing things together."

He mumbled a response that sounded like a pep talk. "I know the game's not over yet, but I'm tired of this. I want these people to go home so we can take a break and start fresh."

It didn't occur to me till I was nearly at the barn that my feet were cold. I was still wearing flipflops, which was a stupid oversight. One hoofed misstep and I'd be out of commission.

"Well, we're here now," I said. "I'll just be extra careful. No more musing about murder till we're done, okay?"

Keats gave a mumble of agreement, although I sensed he wanted to talk more about it. Maybe we were close to a breakthrough. But breakthroughs don't come to farmers in flipflops.

Soon we got into the flow of our usual routine. I opened the pens and Keats brought in the sheep, then the goats, then the cows and finally the pig. The alpaca, llamas and donkeys stayed out all night, and had already grown dense woolly coats for the winter.

Once every creature was in its place, I began distributing the evening meal. As I worked, I called Kellan to tell him about my good idea gone bust. He listened patiently for a change—probably because a beach party didn't qualify as a risky move, other than professionally. Eventually he put me on hold, so I pressed the speaker button and set the phone on a ledge near the cow stall. Using both hands to dish out the grub would be faster and my toes were numb.

When we'd spoken earlier, Kellan hadn't asked as many questions as I'd feared about Cori Hogan's video and I wondered if the Clover Grove police department had agreed to turn a blind eye to the vigilante rescuers who networked through the region. I hoped he'd followed up with Piers Frankel about the clandestine meeting at the bronze chow chow, but I'd have to wait to ask.

I'd also told him about the video on Neal's phone, which I'd been too nervous to forward directly. Kellan said it had proved nothing except that Neal and Ben were both motivated to want Wilf out of the picture—but probably not motivated enough to come back out later in the night to kill him. Ben had been putting up with abuse like that for a long time, so it was nothing new. Neal had all the evidence he needed to get a buyout from Flordale without taking more drastic measures.

"Everyone wanted Wilf out of Flordale except Avis," I said. "But no one wanted him gone from the planet. Keats, I've racked my brains long enough. Can't you just give me the answer?" I shook the last of the apple peels into the trough and enjoyed Wilma's delighted snorts. Of all the animals, she was the least predictable— the porcine wild card. But when she had a full trough, she was adorable.

Now finished with his work, Keats jumped up on the hay bales in the corner. Charlie had restocked that morning, piling them up to the rafters with a backhoe. It wasn't the first time Keats had used them to practice his mountain goat moves while he waited for me, but tonight he went higher than he ever had before.

Staring up at him, I beckoned. "Keats, no. That's not safe."

Instead of obeying, he hopped up another level and grumbled something at me.

"Don't you dare go any further. Get down here at once."

A grumble floated down from above but he picked his way back.

"Honestly. As if I don't have enough to worry about."

I collected some feed for Wilma in the bucket and topped her up.

"You know what's weird, buddy?" I went on. "Wilf accused Ben of having an affair, but I've never heard a single rumor. Maybe he'd have done something drastic to keep a secret like that from coming to light. People do crazy things for love. But I guess you'd have chomped his leg in the scuffle, no matter how big he is."

The sound of heavy footsteps made me turn. Ben was standing in the doorway. My mom's sarong was now tied around his swim trunks.

I was quite sure he hadn't heard me muttering to Keats, so I smiled. "You look like Tarzan," I said.

"If Tarzan were a drag queen," he answered, laughing.

I tapped the pail once more over Wilma's trough to drop a lettuce leaf. "What's up, Ben? You promised you'd tend the fire while I was gone. We're going to need it."

"Just wanted a word with you," he said, walking across the barn. "It's almost impossible to get any privacy."

"Tell me about it," I said. "Everything okay? This must be the worst week of your life."

It wasn't the worst week of *my* life, which was saying something.

"Wilf's passing was terrible, obviously," he said. "Otherwise it's been... fun."

"Fun? Well, I'm surprised to hear you say that. And pleased." Maybe the inn wouldn't sink into oblivion after all. If Jilly and I could pull off a good time after a murderous start, we had something going for us. "So, what did you want to talk about?"

He came closer and I was suddenly aware anew of just how big he was. Keats must have found it unnerving, too, because his ruff rose and he crouched until his belly nearly touched the dusty floor. There was a whine probably only I could hear, because I was used to listening for it.

"Let's go up to the house and talk," I said. "My feet are freezing."

"It'll only take a minute, I promise," he said. "I figure you may have heard rumors about this and wanted to tell you myself. I hope you won't be shocked or upset."

Goosebumps rose on my skin and it wasn't just from the cold. Was he about to confess to the murder? "Ben, I'm harder to shock than you might imagine. But I'd always choose to be shocked beside a roaring fire, wouldn't you?"

"No," he said. "I'd rather be alone in a cold barn with you any day of the week."

I blinked a few times, taking that in, and then dug deep for my poker face. Was Ben saying what I thought he was saying? "Well. That's very kind of you, Ben."

"You are shocked," he said, taking a step closer.

"Surprised, for sure." I took a step backward. "Very surprised."

"I thought it was totally obvious." He came closer—so close I had to look up at him. "I know you don't think of me in that way, but I was hoping you'd agree to get to know me a little better."

"I know you pretty well by now, Ben. We travelled together dozens of times. That creates either friends or enemies, and happily we're the former."

"It's more than that for me." He tried to ease a bit closer but I wedged the slop bucket between us. "It has been for two years. That's why I never left Flordale, even with Wilf treating me like garbage. I kept hoping if I hung around long enough you'd realize you had feelings, too."

Keats had been circling me, brushing one side and then the other. Now he settled on my feet. I could barely feel his fur because my feet were so numb from cold.

"I—I don't know what to say. Flordale wasn't a place to have feelings, Ben."

"True." His laugh had a bitter edge. "On his last night alive, Wilf accused me of having an affair with you. He said Neal had evidence to prove it."

"Well, that evidence was obviously fabricated," I said. "Neal's an IT guy. He could hack into your account easily enough. Were you afraid Wilf would fire you... for real this time?"

My heart beat faster, till I was sure it would rattle the pail.

He shook his head. "I'd have welcomed it. All I wanted was to be packaged out and use the money to start over. I figured Jilly could find me a new position as soon as I could shake off the Flordale shackles. But now that I *wanted* to be let go, Wilf changed his tune. He was already in trouble from senior management over you and couldn't afford to lose anyone else."

I wondered if being thwarted like that was enough to kill for. "You were caught between a rock and a hard place."

"I was going to have to leave empty-handed, and I was working up to it." He gave me a sad smile. "But how could I sweep you off your feet if I was broke and jobless?"

"Well, let's not talk about sweeping tonight," I said. "This is all so unexpected, but I promise to think hard about what you've said."

Looking down at Keats, I saw the sarong had slipped over Ben's swim trunks and landed in a colorful puddle at his feet. The image triggered something in my mind and I looked quickly to the haybales where Keats had been climbing earlier. There was something hanging from the rafters... dirty white fabric.

Finally, the pieces came together.

Ben was a handsome man. A smart, kind and funny man. A gentleman in every sense of the word. He was the type of man who could really turn a girl's head if she hadn't already given her heart away, like I had.

No, Ben hadn't killed Wilf. Maybe he had a crush on me, but he was probably just grasping for kindness in a toxic environment. If his feelings had been strong enough to kill for, I'd have known long ago. Even if I hadn't noticed it, Jilly would have. I had a good support system, even before Keats. Many didn't, and with all the stress at Flordale, someone with a bad case of feelings might very well go crazy, given the opportunity... and a castrator.

"We need to go, Ben," I said. "Now."

My intuition was firing off all kinds of alarms and my canine security system had also gone to red alert. At my feet, Keats had puffed to nearly twice his normal size. His tail stood out straight like a fuzzy bottle-brush. Someone was coming.

"Just tell me," Ben said. "Do I stand a chance with you?"

Keats answered first with a low growl that reverberated through the barn. I'd never heard a sound like that come out of him before.

"No. There's no chance. No chance at all."

That was absolutely true. Only the words didn't come from me. They came from someone standing in the shadows just outside the doorway.

She was wearing a bikini and stilettos. And white spa gloves.

CHAPTER TWENTY-SIX

"Nellie, what are you doing down here without a coat?" I said. "You'll catch your death, and I won't have that on my conscience."

I shrugged off my own jacket and walked toward her. "Don't," she said, holding up her gloved hand. "Don't come near me."

"Why?" I said. "Have I done something wrong?"

She cocked her head to one side, dark hair shining under the fluorescent lights. "Done something wrong? You never did anything right where I was concerned. You wouldn't hire me, so Wilf went around your back and brought me on board. You called me on the carpet for half a dozen stupid things. Like wearing too much perfume or a tube top on casual Friday." She swept her hand over her nearly naked body. "I can pull it off, obviously."

"Too well," I said, gently. "None of the men could concentrate."

"He could." She flicked her fingers at Ben. "Because he only noticed you. You in your sensible suits and your sensible loafers with your sensible air-dried hair."

Oh, poor Nellie. She'd stripped down to a bikini and tossed a sarong to win Ben's heart and he was handing it to me in my sensible down jacket and toque.

"Nellie, there's no reason to worry," I said. "Nothing's going on between Ben and me. Never was."

"That's not what Neal said. He showed me emails between you two. Personal stuff." Her eyelids fluttered. "*Really* personal stuff. I didn't want to believe it... until now."

"Well, stop believing it again," I said. "Because honestly, do you think sensible Ivy in her sensible shoes would exchange 'really personal' emails on company equipment? Especially after I called you in about using company equipment for online shopping?"

She shrugged bare shoulders. "You always singled me out and bullied me. Just like Wilf bullied Ben all the time. It hurt so much to watch Ben being browbeaten, and you let it happen, Ivy. You never intervened when you could have."

Ben had turned to face her but he was apparently too shocked to speak. Obviously the pieces were coming together for him, too.

"I intervened a lot," I said. "Behind closed doors. Wilf was a steamroller, unfortunately." I pulled off my toque and wrung it between my hands. "That said, I realize now I should have done more."

"Yeah, you should have. You *broke* Ben. He hasn't been the same since you left, and that just made the bullying escalate. You only thought about yourself."

"I did, it's true," I said. "I'm sorry, Nellie. When I got out, I just kept running."

"Nellie," Ben said at last. "It's okay. I'm not broken and Ivy couldn't have done anything more. The system was corrupt right up to Piers Frankel. That's all changed now and we'll be fine."

But Ben didn't say the only words she wanted to hear. That sensible Ivy had been a mistake. That she, Nellie, was actually the girl of his dreams. I studied her face carefully, and then glanced down at Keats. He was coiled and ready to leap into action if needed.

"Ben, don't you see what she is?" Nellie said. She was giving him one last chance.

"See what?" he asked. "It's Ivy. Just Ivy. And she's right, nothing is going on or ever was. Obviously we were framed."

"Wilf was going to fire you for it. He wanted to make an example of you." She came toward us, stilettos clicking on the barnboards. "He said you'd never work in HR again."

"That's okay. I'm good. It's all good."

"It's all good *because of me*." She stared up at him. "Not Ivy. Me."

Ben didn't have a clue what he was dealing with. He was just a confused man standing between a woman who didn't want him and one who'd kill for him.

Had *already* killed for him.

I was quite sure if she turned around right now, I'd see fang marks in the calves of her shapely legs. Keats was waiting to leave a few more. Wilma gave a menacing squeal from her pen, prompting Florence to let out a shrill neigh. The sheep and the goats picked up on the tension and started bleating a startled conversation among themselves. All the creatures around us were stirring and hay particles floated up like fog. Finally, Heidi and Clara hung their heads over their stall and unleashed a deafening bellow in tandem that practically blew me over. Little Archie added some bawling as punctuation.

Nellie didn't notice any of that because her entire world had narrowed to one gentle giant of a man.

"What do you mean, Nellie?" Ben asked, still not comprehending. He was such a decent guy that he probably couldn't process it. "Did you talk to Wilf?"

She clicked around him in a semicircle and he turned to watch her. Meanwhile I checked out the array of half-healed punctures all the way up her legs. Keats had even landed a sharp nip on her exposed butt cheek.

"Yes, I talked to Wilf," she said. "I followed you and Neal out the first time that night and I heard everything. He said he knew about your affair. He was going to hire Ivy back and fire you."

"He didn't mean it. He never followed through."

"He humiliated you. I just couldn't take it anymore. You deserved better."

Ben nodded. "I know I did. We all did."

"That was really brave of you, Nellie," I said at last. "To come out later and defend Ben to Wilf. Heroic, even."

Her head turned so fast sleek hair covered her face. "I don't just abandon people like you do, Ivy. So yeah, I came back out when I heard Wilf staggering around again. I only wanted to tell him Ben's side of the story: that you had mesmerized him and things would change once he realized you'd dumped all of us for good. But Wilf... he was just so stupid and mean. He went into the cow stall and kept blathering, saying horrible things about Ben and me. I was so mad it was all I could do not to kill your dog, too. He was biting me, and he wouldn't take the wieners I'd found in the freezer. I used the rake to shove him into the stall, and then I found that tool in the corner."

"The castrator," I said.

"Whatever." She shrugged. "When I turned around Wilf was trying to unlatch the pen and come at me. He was still mouthing off and mouthing off. He never shut up until I finally stopped him. For good. Then I dropped the tool behind the barn intending to hide it in the morning. That's the only reason I came with you to see that disgusting henhouse. But Keri was all over me, like usual, micromanaging even egg collection." Her lips pressed into a thin line before she added, "I never could catch a break with you people. I honestly think Wilf's last word was 'Ivy.' Just to drive me nuts."

Her eyes were glazed now with an expression I'd seen before in this very barn. "Let's all go up to the house, have some hot cocoa and talk some more," I said, knowing it was no use. The crazy train had left the station.

"Oh, you're done talking, Ivy," she said. "I'm tired of hearing your sensible voice saying sensible things."

Turning quickly, she grabbed the pig poker and swung it in an arc. I saw it coming, as if in slow motion, but I couldn't move. Keats had darted toward Nellie, but he turned back and flung himself at me. The black-and-white missile hit me in the chest and I fell backward. The poker kept going, swinging up till it struck Ben's temple. He went down with a thud, ending up with his head on my shins.

"No, no, no!" Nellie ran the last few steps and dropped to her knees beside me. She grabbed Ben's head and cradled him, crooning. "You're okay. Please be okay."

I saw Ben's eyes flutter and said, "He'll be okay, Nellie. But you need to get help."

Her furious eyes landed on me. "Don't you dare tell me what to do. And get away from him right now."

I pushed myself backward, out from under Ben, and scuttled like a crab halfway to the door.

"Far enough," she said. "You don't think I'm letting you leave, do you?"

"Nellie, don't do this." Ben's voice was nothing more than a croak. "I—I love that you were trying to look out for me. Thank you. But stop. Please..."

His voice trailed off and his eyes closed.

"Nellie, he needs an ambulance. Now."

Slipping out from under Ben, she reached for the fallen sarong and bunched it up to cushion his head. Then she scrambled to her feet and clicked toward me deliberately. I had to give her credit, she knew how to work those shoes. Even in a bikini, she was fearsome.

But this time, she was unarmed and I gave Keats the signal. He lunged for her face and she flailed, squealing like a schoolgirl, not a murderer.

Keats dropped to the floor and she reversed until she was stuck between the heads of Heidi and Clara. A cow sandwich. They let out another bellow and this time when Keats jumped, he nailed his target: Nellie's right ear. She couldn't turn because of the cows but she slapped at Keats and her terrible screech set off a barnyard cacophony, the likes of which I'd never heard. I bent over and grabbed the pig poker.

"Leave it," I shouted, and Keats dropped to the floor.

Nellie cupped her ear, still screaming, and I shook the poker at her. "If you get anywhere near Ben or my dog, Nellie Cassios, I swear I will bury you in manure and you'll be grateful when it finally detonates and blows your bikini back to Boston."

There had never been a more welcome sound than sirens, followed by the thump of boots. Kellan, Asher and two other officers pulled Nellie away from the cows. She tried the slick hippo ploy but they just carried her, kicking, right out of the barn.

"Are you okay?" Kellan asked, taking the pig poker away from me. "Did she hurt you?"

I shook my head. "Just shook up. She totally lost it, Kellan."

"I know. I heard everything," he said. "The phone, remember? Where is it?"

I pointed to it on a ledge above the cowstall. Then I pointed up, to the white spa glove hanging from the rafters. "She wore that when—"

"Okay. We'll talk a bit later, Ivy."

The ambulance arrived and within just a few moments, the paramedics whisked Ben away. He was awake by the time they left. I stared after him sadly.

"Ivy? Ivy!" Kellan's voice was urgent. "Right now you need to go up to the house and rest. But first, can you please tell your dog to let go of my pant cuff so I can do my job?"

Keats was darting in for little nips and I couldn't help laughing. It was more like hysterical cackling, but I was powerless to stop it, or stop Keats from assaulting the chief's uniformed leg.

Jilly ran into the barn, panting. She spun around, wide eyes taking everything in. But then she shook it off and calmed right down. "Keats, leave it," she said, assuming command. "Right now. You have work to do. Take Ivy to the house. In fact, take all the guests to the house. *Stat*."

Keats slunk away from Kellan and circled around to herd me toward the barn door, where the others had gathered.

"Don't tell me that dog understands you, too?" Kellan asked Jilly.

"Of course he does. And he knows exactly what you're doing, too, Kellan Harper. Or *not* doing. So you'd better step it up."

"I don't know what—" He looked down at Jilly's fierce face and stopped talking.

"I'd just give up if I were you, Chief," Asher said, grinning as he came back in.

By that time, I'd given up, too, and I gratefully let my dog herd me and the remaining guests up onto the porch. I sent them inside, turned out the porch light and collapsed on the swing with Keats in my lap. He never had much patience for hugging, but tonight, for a short moment, he rolled on his back and let me rock him like a baby. Then he sat up and looked around, as if to make sure no one saw us.

"You're good, buddy," I said, tears falling on his dusty coat. "So good."

CHAPTER TWENTY-SEVEN

It was nearly midnight by the time the remaining Flordale guests joined Jilly and me outside at the bonfire. I'd found a couple of puffy old snowmobile suits in the shed and Jilly and I put them on. It was the only way I could shake the deep chill that racked me.

Our guests had already changed into warmer clothes as they packed up to leave first thing in the morning. Ben was spending the night in the hospital but the doctor had said he'd recover fully from the concussion Nellie had caused.

I wondered if the injury would give him a new lease on life. There was no doubt he'd see the world quite differently tomorrow. Looking around the large yard behind the inn, that didn't offer much yet but a firepit with a rather magnificent fire, I smiled. I could only hope Ben's conk on the head brought as much good for him as mine had for me.

"Make me a s'more, Neal," Kate said. "I don't want to burn my fingers."

He hopped up, toasted a marshmallow, assembled the sticky treat and presented it to her with a flourish. Jilly and I exchanged looks. Was a new romance blooming after crime? It seemed an unlikely match, but as Mom said, there was a lid for every pot.

Jilly tried to get out of her lawn chair but got stuck because of the bulky snowmobile suit. Keri and Paulette jumped up to take her arms and pull. Once Jilly was mobile, she carried a thermos around our small circle and filled everyone's mugs. Keri followed, topping the creamy, steamy brew with a dash of coffee liqueur.

I worried they'd press me for details about what happened in the barn, but Kellan's warnings had the desired effect. It was a relief because I wasn't ready to relive that yet. All I wanted to do was stare at the fire and let the shock gradually recede. A couple of slices of Mandy's zesty Lemon Dazzle cake had gone a long way to revive me.

Keri finally spoke up. "I'm sorry we got your inn off to such a rocky start, Ivy. I really wish I'd never asked to bring the Flordale circus down here."

"It's not your fault," I said. "That place was a powder keg waiting to blow. I guarantee you that Piers and Avis are having a very serious discussion about the future of the company right now. Everything is going to change for the better."

"And if it doesn't," Jilly said, "you can count on my staff in Boston to find you a soft landing elsewhere."

I looked around the circle. "Nellie said I abandoned you guys, and that hit home. I'm sorry."

Keri squeezed my hand in its waterproof mitten. "You protected us for years. It wasn't sustainable anymore, and no one blames you for going. In fact, you've inspired all of us to stand up for ourselves."

I sighed in relief. I'd never wanted my gain to be their loss. Now, out from under terrible leadership, they could find the sunshine and grow.

"My sister's in a book club that would love it here," Paulette said, trying to change the subject. "I'm going to recommend Runaway Inn for their next getaway."

Macy spoke for the first time in hours. "My dad runs an

oenophile society. They do vacations like this twice a year. So I'll give him your card."

"Remind me to get cards made," I told Jilly.

"We'll all recommend you far and wide," Keri said. "You two are wonderful hosts."

Neal cleared his throat. "Honestly, if I never hear about this place again, it'll be too soon." There was a clamor of protest and he added. "Kidding... *Not.*"

"It's okay, Neal," I said. "You can find thrills and chills some-place else. I, for one, will never ride a roller coaster again."

"Good call," Jilly said, grinning at me.

Waving my mug at Keri, I said, "Hit me."

"You'd better take it easy," Jilly said. "After the shock you had, it'll go straight to your head."

"Well then, let's dance," I said, getting up. "I promised the Beach Boys."

When Kellan and Asher came around the house an hour later, everyone else had gone inside but Jilly and I were shaking it hard in our snowmobile suits to "Surfin' USA." Dancing had proven just the thing to get the blood flowing and I was finally warm.

"Ladies," Kellan said. "We've had a noise complaint from Edna Evans."

I turned to face her house, knowing she was watching right now with her night vision goggles. "Edna!" I yelled, beckoning with a wide sweep of my arm. "Come join us. Dancing is good for your soul."

"She doesn't have one, sis," Asher said. "Do you remember her dragging me down the hall by my feet to get a vaccination? A horror movie come to life."

"She said Kellan was stoic," I told him. "He endured. That's why he's chief now, Edna says."

"Are you drunk, Ivy?" Kellan asked, grinning.

I shook my head. "Just happy. Relieved and happy."

"And tipsy," Jilly added. "This calls for more dancing."

Asher held out his hand to Jilly, and Kellan said, "We're on duty, Officer."

Keats came out of the shadows and gave Kellan a little nip in the ankle that made the chief jump and yelp.

I couldn't help laughing and everyone joined in. "I hope Edna caught that," I said. "Not so stoic now, are you, Chief?"

Kellan surprised me by taking a little lunge in my direction. "If you're going to mock the chief of police, you'd better be able to outrun him," he said.

I gave it my best but the bulky snowmobile suit made short work of his pursuit. Catching me, he spun me right around, just as the strains of "Wouldn't It Be Nice" drifted over the yard, the farm and perhaps even down the range of hills.

He held out his hand and we started to dance. It was like prom all over, except for my snowmobile suit and his uniform. Plus 15 years and a couple of murders.

"Can I ask you something?" he said.

"Sure." My heart kicked up with its baby goat dance.

He gave my waist a gentle squeeze. "Have you put on weight?"

"Kellan," Jilly called. "I heard that."

"Pay attention to your own partner," he called back, before dipping me dramatically.

I hung there for a moment, staring up at the stars, and then a warm tongue licked my face all over.

"Nice," I said. "Dog breath."

Kellan pulled me upright, shaking his head.

I grinned up at him. "How about a kiss? My face is freshly washed."

"Maybe I'll wait," he said, grinning back. "I'm not nearly as stoic as Edna Evans thinks."

Lifting me off my feet, he swung me around and around while Keats kept pace below, his tail lashing.

I laughed and then sighed as Kellan set me down. Long ago, I'd "runaway far" from Clover Grove, only to get desperately lost in the big city. Every day for the rest of my life, I'd be grateful that this very clever—and very bossy—sheepdog had found me and herded me right back where I belonged.

Sign up for my mailing list at **ellenriggs.com/opt-in** to find out more about this series and my work. My newsletter is full of funny stories and photos of my adorable dogs. Don't miss out!

RUNAWAY FARM & INN RECIPES

Rockin' Moroccan Chickpea Stew

(Serves 8)

This recipe is like a warm hug in a pot. Flavorful, earthy, and hearty. It can be enjoyed on its own or served with short-grain brown rice or couscous.

Ingredients:

- 2 tbsp olive oil
- 1 large onion, diced
- 4 cloves garlic, minced
- 1 tsp smoked paprika
- 1 tsp ground cumin
- ½ tsp ground coriander
- ½ tsp turmeric
- ½ tsp ground ginger
- ¼ tsp ground cinnamon
- ½ tsp ground black pepper
- 2 pinches cayenne pepper
- 1 (28-oz) can diced tomatoes (about 2 cups)
- 4 cups vegetable broth or water
- 1 tsp salt
- 1 large sweet potato, peeled and cubed
- 1½ cups chickpeas, cooked or canned
- 1 cup brown lentils
- 3 cups spinach
- Juice from 1 lemon
- Roasted slivered almonds (for serving)

Directions

1. In a large pot, heat olive oil. Sauté the onion until translucent. Add garlic and sauté for an additional minute. Add paprika, cumin, coriander, turmeric, ginger, cinnamon, black pepper, and cayenne pepper and stir until well combined.

2. Add the tomatoes, vegetable broth or water, and salt. Bring to a boil, and add sweet potatoes, chickpeas, and lentils. Cover and simmer for 30 to 35 minutes until the sweet potatoes and lentils are tender.

3. Turn off heat and stir in spinach until wilted. Stir in lemon juice. Sprinkle with roasted slivered almonds.

Shared with permission from Heather Lawless, author of *The Chickpea Revolution Cookbook: 85 Plant-Based Recipes for a Healthier Planet and a Healthier You.*

More Books by Ellen Riggs

Bought-the-Farm Cozy Mystery Series

- A Dog with Two Tales (*prequel*)
- Dogcatcher in the Rye
- Dark Side of the Moo
- A Streak of Bad Cluck
- Till the Cat Lady Sings
- Alpaca Lies
- Twas the Bite Before Christmas
- Swine and Punishment
- The Cat and the Riddle
- Don't Rock the Goat
- Swan with the Wind
- How to Get a Neigh with Murder
- Tweet Revenge
- For Love Or Bunny
- Between a Squawk and a Hard Place
- Double Dog Dare
- Deerly Departed
- Think Outside the FoxMouse of Ill Repute
- Bee All and End All

- Sheep with One Eye Open
- Roo the Day

Bought-the-Farm Mysteries - Boxed Sets

- Bought the Farm Mysteries - Books 1-3
- Bought the Farm Mysteries - Books 4-6
- Bought the Farm Mysteries - Books 7-9
- Bought the Farm Mysteries - Books 1-10

Mystic Mutt Mysteries Paranormal Cozy

- I Want You to Haunt Me
- You Can't Always Get What You Haunt
- Any Way You Haunt It
- I Only Haunt to be with You
- All I Haunt Is You (Novella)
- Do You Haunt to Know a Secret?
- All I Haunt for Christmas

Books by Ellen Riggs and Sandy Rideout

Dog Town Series

- Ready or Not in Dog Town (The Beginning)
- Bitter and Sweet in Dog Town (Labor Day)
- A Match Made in Dog Town (Thanksgiving)
- Lost and Found in Dog Town (Christmas)
- Calm and Bright in Dog Town (Christmas)
- Tried and True in Dog Town (New Year's)
- Yours and Mine in Dog Town (Valentine's Day)
- Nine Lives in Dog Town (Easter)

- Great and Small in Dog Town (Memorial Day)
- Bold and Blue in Dog Town (Independence Day)
- Better or Worse in Dog Town (Labor Day)

Dog Town Boxed Sets

- Mischief in Dog Town - Books 1-3
- Mischief in Dog Town - Books 4-7
- Mischief in Dog Town - Books 8-10
- Mischief in Dog Town - The Complete Series